THE SEARCHER

T. J. ALEXANDER

JOFFE BOOKS

Revised edition 2019
Joffe Books, London
www.joffebooks.com

First published in Great Britain 2018

We hate typos too but sometimes they slip through.
Please send any errors you find to
corrections@joffebooks.com

We'll get them fixed ASAP. We're very grateful to eagle-eyed readers who take the time to contact us.

ISBN: 978-1-78931-154-9

PART ONE

LOST

THE CHILD'S STORY

October 1814

IN THE BEGINNING, EACH sensation is cosmic, vast, all-encompassing. The warm sweet smell of milk from a leaking breast. The soft darkness within embracing arms, thrumming with a regular beat that seems like the beat of the world itself. Sounds still lack shape or name. Humming, wailing, clanking, clopping: without a net of words in which to catch these sensations, they all flow past, endlessly flowing into wind and sky and the ceaseless circling of light and darkness.

If she had possessed words with which to catch her feelings, she might, later on, have remembered what it felt like to lie in the crook of her mother's right arm, her toes occasionally tangling with the wriggling thing which lay in her mother's left arm. She might have remembered the swaying sensation of being carried along in her mother's embrace, on the day that changed her life and the lives of everyone around her. The motion was soothing, and she snuggled into the darkness, hearing the drone of voices above her head.

Then, abruptly, the warm dark was ripped open by a gust of chill wind. Light and a chaos of shapes and sounds assailed her eyes and ears. The cloak which had covered her whipped back and was swept away by the wind. Panic rose through her throat towards the gaping circle of her mouth. But at that moment some tickling speck of dust entered her throat, and the sound that came out was not the impending scream of terror, but just a small sneeze.

Now new arms reached out to her, and she was again enfolded and wrapped in an embrace which smelled completely unfamiliar: sharp and un-milky. She whimpered a little, but the regular rocking movement began again, and warmth flowed through her body, and she saw nothing but the drowsy red darkness behind her own eyelids.

It was a change in the rocking movement that woke her: a sudden speed. No longer rocking, but jolting, jerking. She opened her mouth, and now the screams came freely. And from somewhere behind, she heard an echoing scream, growing fainter and fainter as the beat of feet accelerated.

In those moments, the sensations were everything: her entire world. But she had no words to hold them. And so they flowed and floated away, leaving not a single trace of memory. They were caught up by the wind, and mixed into the dust and sand and scraps of straw, and amidst the detritus of wood shavings and chicken feathers, they blew away, high into the grimy autumn sky that hung over the Commercial Road, and then out over the great river beyond.

ADAH'S STORY

January 1822
The Stranger

The little girl lies on a small truckle bed in the watch-room of the Norton Folgate courthouse. She lies perfectly still on her back, hands folded across her chest. Strands of damp brown hair adhere to her forehead. The room is so dark that Adah Flint can barely see the child's face.

'Open the shutters, please,' she says to Jonah Hall, who is standing impassively at the opposite end of the room, arms crossed above his expanding paunch.

Even when the wooden shutters creak open, the light that falls through the glass is weak and dusty. Adah notices the shadows of cobweb in a corner of the window. The room looks more untidy than usual – the big table along one wall littered with lamps and candle-holders, quills and ink stands, and piled high with books of all sizes for recording the long litany of local crimes. The ropes for restraining uncooperative offenders are not neatly coiled as they should be, but sprawl in untidy heaps under the table. Adah remembers that she has not cleaned this room for two weeks, what with everything else....

The girl, she can now see, is maybe seven or eight years old. How peaceful she looks, and how unnaturally clean. She has been covered with a rough linen nightshirt several sizes too large for her. Her clothes, still sodden from the rain, lie folded in a forlorn pile beside the bed. Adah picks them up one by one, holding them out towards the light as she examines them. A little black cloak, damp but strangely unstained. A frock that may once have been pink, but is now a blotchy white; a black stuff petticoat, frayed and muddy round the hem; a faded blue pinafore, also adorned with a patch of mud; a flannel undershirt, a little too small for its wearer, with yellowish marks around the armholes, but carefully mended in two places. Adah runs her fingertip over the neat stitches of the mending.

This is no foundling or workhouse child. Someone cared for her; someone cares for her still.

When Adah pushes the hair back from the child's brow, she can see a discoloured patch on the left temple, which seems slightly indented, although the surface of the skin has not been broken. The room smells of soap and herbs and something sour. A clock ticks remorselessly on the wall, and a fly buzzes against the window pane. Outside in the street, a cart rumbles past and a woman's voice gives a muffled curse. And then suddenly the bells of St. Leonard's Church start to pour their cascade of pure sound into the morning air.

Adah lifts the nightgown, and slowly and carefully looks at the girl's thin legs. So thin, she could wrap a finger around the ankle. One knee is marked by a fading white scar. She examines the concave belly and slightly protruding lower ribs. Hungry, thinks Adah, but not starved. Apart from the mark on the child's forehead, there are no signs of injury or violence.

It is not death that is the mystery, but life. A day or two ago, a spark inhabited this small body. An entire world, a universe of sense and memories and dreams. With outstretched finger, Adah lightly touches the belly that will now never swell with child. There are worlds that will never come into being now, world after world vanished as completely as bubbles burst in air. Adah is so intent on the child's lifeless body that she fails to notice Annie enter the room and take her place on a chair at the head of the bed. It is Jonah's voice that alerts her.

'What's your daughter doing here?' he barks.

Annie glances neither at Jonah Hall nor at Adah. She has taken her paper and quill, and is swiftly, deftly, sketching lines in black ink. Adah watches her for a moment, with an odd ache in her heart. Annie's face is calm, her mind and body focused on her task of capturing the image of the child's face on paper. The light from the opened casement illuminates the soft line of Annie's cheek and her downcast eye as she draws. Is it right that one so young should become so familiar with the sight of death? But Adah has never been able to protect her children from death. Not from the deaths of their brothers and sisters, nor from the sight of bodies brought to the ground floor of the courthouse where they grew up, nor from the sight of their own father's body, stretched fully-clothed on the big bed upstairs....

'Mr Hall,' Adah replies acerbically, 'you used to treat me with greater respect when my husband was Beadle. William may be gone, but I'll ask you to remember that I am now Searcher of this Liberty. It is my task to discover who this child was and what befell her. My daughter is helping me. How am I to fulfil my duties unless I have a likeness of her face?'

'It's probably a foreigner,' says Hall dismissively. 'A Portuguee as like as not. Or maybe a gypsy. They're everywhere these days.'

'It ...' notes Adah silently.

Adah straightens the nightshirt, and with her right hand, which looks so large and red and hard beside the child's delicate form, strokes the little girl's head. The hair is surprisingly fine, like strands of wet silk.

Annie's sketch is done already. Adah always wonders at the speed with which her daughter draws portraits. The sketch on the paper is a fair impression of the child's waxy face, though the mouth seems slightly awry. Annie glances up at her mother, who nods and, arm in arm, they leave the room in silence, with a brief gesture to Jonah Hall, standing as stolid as ever at his post.

As always after examining a body, Adah finds herself closing the door of the room very softly, as though anxious not to disturb the sleep of the dead.

Hetty Yandall, the Liberty's scavenger, wears a rusty brown canvas cloak over her dress when she is working. Striding down White Lion Street on this winter's day, her cloak billowing out in the wind, she looks for all the world like a Thames barge under full sail. The impression is somehow strengthened by her unusually large feet, encased in bulky brown work boots.

The rain, which has been pouring down relentlessly for days, has lifted briefly, and a watery light pierces the clouds at the far end of the street, glittering on the ripples that blow across countless puddles in the uneven paving; but above the roofs and chimney pots, another mass of clouds is already gathering. Hetty Yandall's figure, splashing heedlessly through the puddles, is silhouetted by the fleeting shafts of light. She seems vast, mythical, unstoppable. Adah stands on the steps of the courthouse, drawing her own thin black cloak around her shoulders as she watches this apparition approaching.

'Ah, Mrs Flint,' booms the scavenger as soon as she is within earshot. 'A sad business, a sad business. And you, you are well, you and the children? You're managing on your own?'

It is an awkward greeting, and for a moment, Adah is unsure how to reply. She realizes that this is the first time she has exchanged more than a word or two with Mrs Yandall since William's death, and recalls that her dead husband and the scavenger heartily loathed one another.

'We're doing well enough,' she murmurs, 'as well as can be expected.'

But she senses, too, a note of rough kindness in Hetty Yandall's voice.

'That poor dead child,' continues the scavenger, 'just the age of my youngest, by the look of her. It gave me such a nasty turn to find her lying there, cold and wet and alone, first thing this morning. My innards fairly churned over, and they've not righted themselves yet. You'll want to see the spot where I found the poor lamb. Come along.'

And she turns abruptly on her heel and heads down Blossom Street, with Adah almost running behind to keep up with the scavenger's energetic stride. Mrs Yandall is carrying her big hessian sack draped over one shoulder, though the sack is empty, and her greying red hair, so often wild and uncombed, has been tied in a knot under her bulging brown bonnet. A couple of small children pause in the midst of their game of hopscotch to watch nervously as she passes, and Adah remembers how William used to say to their own little ones, 'Look at that sack. You know what she's got in there? Bad children. Children who don't do what they were told. Taking them to throw in the Thames, she is.'

On the corner of Blossom Street, a little wizened man has set up a wooden crate on which he is carefully arranging a pathetic array of wares – a handful of potatoes and onions that seem almost as shrivelled as the man himself. Nearby, an old soldier in the ragged remains of a red jacket sits in a doorway with one hand stretched out to passers-by while the other sleeve hangs empty over a missing arm.

How quickly things have changed since William's death.

Hetty Yandall seems to read Adah's thoughts, for she glances back with a sardonic half-smile.

'Your William would have had *them* off the street before they could give him the time of day,' she observes, 'but this new beadle Beavis is a puzzle. Speaks to me so soft and gentle that I can barely hear what he's saying, and lets all sorts of riffraff set themselves up in the street to make mischief, but I've heard say that he has a devil of a temper when he's crossed. Not that I've seen it myself, yet …'

‘He’s always been perfectly polite to me,’ responds Adah, a little stiffly.

‘Polite enough to turf you out of your own house and home so that he can be lord of courthouse,’ retorts the scavenger. ‘You should stand up to him, Mrs Flint. Your William and his father turned that house from a ruin into what it is today. And you’re Searcher now, aren’t you? You’ve got the right to live there, you and your children.’

Adah falls silent. Unlike William, who always spoke scornfully of ‘that rag-and-bone woman’, she feels an uneasy admiration for Mrs Yandall. There is something powerful about the scavenger’s tall, broad-shouldered frame, her steady gaze and her refusal to bow and curtsey to her superiors. She manages her brood of children – is it nine or ten? – in the same forthright manner that she drives hard bargains with the Norton Folgate trustees and puts the officers of the watch in their place if they dare to cross her. Of a Mr Yandall, there is no sign. Some say he ran off to sea to escape his wife, or that he’s languishing somewhere in a debtors’ prison. Others say there never was a Mr Yandall, and that Hetty’s brood are the children of many fathers. None of which seems to worry Hetty Yandall in the least. She keeps the streets clean, and makes a handsome income from the treasures that turn up in her sweepings. As far as she is concerned, people may say what they like. Adah wishes she shared the scavenger’s self-sufficient confidence. But she doesn’t want this woman’s sympathy, and cringes to think that her affairs are talked about by strangers. The fact that Mrs Yandall’s words echo her own thoughts only makes matters worse.

The cobbles of Blossom Street are slippery after the rain, and little rivulets of water the colour of ale run down either side of the road. Mrs Yandall is still holding forth about the new beadle, but her words are drowned out by the clatter of the shuttles from Loom Court, the cries of a sand man and the frantic barking of a pair of brindled mongrel dogs who are fighting over something that looks like a chewed slipper. As they pass the windows of the charity school, a chorus of girls' voices mindlessly chanting a lesson adds another thread to the texture of sounds. Adah glances uneasily at the grimy brick walls of a small tenement on the left: the place into which she and her six children will somehow have to cram themselves in two weeks' time, when they leave the courthouse forever. The very thought of the impending move fills her with a leaden sense of exhaustion and dread.

Before they reach the Blossom Street almshouses, Hetty Yandall turns down Magpie Alley and stops by a battered fence, from which a wooden gate hangs precariously, half on and half off its hinges. Beyond, a muddy path leads between the backs of houses into the gardens and waste land between Blossom Street and Bishopsgate. It is a dank and unappealing corner. A heavy smell of rotting greenery hangs in the air as they squeeze their way through the broken gate but Hetty Yandall strides confidently ahead, thrusting through the overgrown privet that almost chokes the pathway.

Beyond is a row of walled gardens, where Adah can glimpse the bare branches of fruit trees and the withered stems of beans still clinging to their bean poles. The place has a strange, stifling feel: an island of wildness penned in by the stern brown brick walls of the rows of houses on either side. After the clamour of Blossom Street, it is suddenly silent here. The only sounds are the liquid notes of a song thrush perched on a dead tree branch, and the soft tap of the rain which is beginning to fall again.

'It's pure luck I came here first thing today,' says Mrs Yandall. 'I don't come every day, nor even every week, to be honest. But I was passing and saw the gate off its hinges and thought, maybe someone's been in here. You get tramps and tinkers and all sorts now and then, and who knows what mess they may leave behind. Thank God I came. To think that poor child might have been left lying there for days, weeks … horrible!'

Where the gardens end, they come to an overgrown space which must once have been a livery yard, but is now a jungle of rank grasses and littered with empty barrels and broken cart wheels.

'If I had my way I'd clear all that lot out,' says Mrs Yandall, gesturing at the decaying mass of timber, 'but they tell me it belongs to old Hodges that works for Mr Tillard, and I'm not to touch it.' And then, more softly, 'Here it is. Here's the very place where I found her.'

Adah can see at once how the grass is pressed down and crushed in one spot. She can almost trace the imprint of the small body that lay there. The ground beneath is soft and muddy, but when she bends and parts the tangle of damp grass, she glimpses something pale concealed amongst its stems. Cautiously, so as not to cut her fingers on the razor edges of the lush leaves of grass, she runs her hands through the hollow in the vegetation, and reaches down to feel among its earthy roots. Her hands touch stone; smooth, worn sandstone. A largish lump of weathered stone lies concealed by the riot of weeds that have reclaimed the abandoned yard. Perhaps an old mounting block. In her mind's eye, she can see the scene all too clearly: the child, probably lost, running through the grass, and then slipping, or maybe catching her leg in some snare of weeds; falling forward, her head cracking against the rounded corner of the stone block. It would, at least, have been very quick, she thinks.

For a moment, she and Hetty Yandall stand side by side in silence, looking down at the child-sized impression in the grass.

'How long do you think she'd been lying here?'

'Most of the night, I'd say,' replies the scavenger. 'Her clothes were soaked through with the rain when I found her. And look, let me show you something else.'

In a corner of the wasteland stand the ruined remains of a stable block. The roof is caved in in places, and blackened beams like the ribs of a dead animal stand exposed to the elements. But when Adah fights her way through the long grass to the building, she can see that the wooden stalls are still standing. In a couple of them are mounds of straw, mouldering but quite dry. After the sour odour of the muddy pathway, the straw smells warm and sweet.

Adah steps cautiously into the stable. The floorboards beneath her feet sag and creak, threatening to give way at any moment. A broad shaft of hazy light slanting through the broken roof only serves to cast the recesses of the building into deeper shadow. Drops of rain glisten on a huge cobweb that hangs like a curtain from the central timber beam, dividing the visible stalls at the front of building from the impenetrable darkness beyond. A little way inside the entrance, she sees what the scavenger is pointing at. A mound of straw has been freshly disturbed, piled up into a heap and then pressed down into a makeshift bed. To a small lost child on a rainy night, this would have been an appealing spot, the straw warm and the fragments of remaining roof providing some shelter from the weather. The child would have slept here, and perhaps been startled by something, woken confused in the night or in the half-light of morning, stumbled out into the long grass, tripped and fallen …

Adah bends down and prods carefully at the straw, hoping that there might be some trace of the child's presence: a kerchief or a bundle of possessions that might give some clue to her identity. But there is nothing. Just a few scuffed muddy marks and the churned straw, seeming somehow to emit the last fading warmth of the child's vanished life.

A sharp rattling sound startles her. Deep in the darkest corner of the stables, something has stirred: a sound like a small pile of wooden poles being knocked awry.

'Who's there?' Adah calls.

There is silence; a silence so intense that, for a moment, she can sense some other living being in the recesses of the stable keeping absolutely, unnaturally still. She gets to her feet and moves very cautiously towards the darkened rear of the building. When she steps from light to dark, the blackness is total, and the floorboards beneath her feet sag more alarmingly than ever. Her own breathing sounds too loud, and she holds herself very still to see if she can hear the breath of another living creature, but the silence is as thick and heavy as the darkness itself. Very gingerly, she takes a step forward, and then another, and at that moment, her foot cracks right through a rotten board, badly scratching her ankle. She yelps with surprise and pain, and at the same instant, a scrawny tabby cat hurtles out of the interior darkness with a snarl and shoots past her into the wilderness outside the stable door. Laughing ruefully, Adah hobbles out of the ruined stable, rubbing her ankle.

The scavenger pats her arm sympathetically. 'Drat them stray cats,' she says. 'The bane of my life, they are.'

Now that she looks more closely, Adah can clearly see the line of crushed grass leading from the stables to the spot where the child died. At one point, where the grass is thinnest, she can even make out the blurred and watery outline of a small footprint.

'Well, at least it's no mystery how that child died,' she says.

'You think not?' replies Mrs Yandall warily. And then, after a short silence, 'But that was an odd thing about her cloak.'

'Her cloak?'

The scavenger looks askance at Adah. 'They didn't mention the cloak to you? I told the officer of the watch all about it when I brought her body in.'

'Nobody told me anything,' replies Adah. Her heart tightens with anger. She has been made a fool of again.

'The child wasn't wearing her cloak when I found her, you see. That is, it wasn't fastened round her. It was lying over her. As though someone had tried to cover her up.'

'Cover her up how? You mean, hide her body?'

'No,' says Mrs Yandall thoughtfully, 'not to hide her, because her head wasn't covered. The cloak was just pulled up to her neck, as though someone had tried to keep her warm, to make her comfortable, like.'

Baffled, Adah bends down again to touch the patch of crushed grass where the child died, running her hands down into its roots, and over the surface of stone beneath. Her fingers encounter nothing unexpected. But lying almost on the surface, just concealed by the edge of a drooping dock leaf – how did she not see this before? – there is something.

Something about the size of a coin, slippery with rain and mud, but too white to be a coin. Not a coin, but a shining disc engraved with convoluted patterns. Very gingerly, she picks it up between her thumb and forefinger and holds it out in the light: gleaming, pearly white, its round surface polished smooth, but then etched with fine writhing lines. Adah can make out a curling tail, claws, a snarling mouth, an eye – a dragon, perhaps? She turns the disc over. The back is more roughly hewn and, sure enough, has a little nob with a hole for the needle and thread to pass though.

Not a coin but a button. A single, ornate, exotic button.

Darkness

Adah lies on her back in the big bed in her room above the courthouse, staring into darkness. Since William died, she has spent many nighttime hours like this. The room is quiet, save for occasional snuffles from the little ones, Amelia and Caroline, curled together in a tangle of warm limbs in their shared wooden cot, and the soft fall of crumbling ashes in the hearth. The last glow from the embers of the fire has faded, though the thick odour of woodsmoke still fills the room. If she opens the shutters, a faint flicker of light will shine in from the gas lamp in the street below, but with the shutters tight closed and no candle burning in the room, she cannot see her hand in front of her face.

The darkness above her is thick and furry, but Adah finds that if she stares at it for long enough, something strange happens. She starts to feel that she is no longer looking at the sooty ceiling of her bedroom, with its pattern of stains and cracks like the map of some unchartered continent, but is instead gazing out into the night sky, as though the roof has been lifted off the courthouse and she can see into the very depth of the murky London firmament, into the limits of the heavens themselves. In this unbounded night, the city shrinks to a mere pinprick, and Adah floats as though on a small bark adrift on limitless oceans of darkness. Beyond this city, beyond the globe, a vast black void stretches infinitely far until it comes to … what? Adah stares and stares into the darkness, but she never finds an answer.

She has been sleeping fitfully ever since William's death. Even now, when she falls into fretful slumber, she sometimes wakes, expecting to find his broad warm back pressed close to her body and, feeling only the cold and the emptiness, wonders where she is. Then the coldness and the emptiness and the sense of guilt catch hold of her heart, but with them comes something worse, something she cannot acknowledge to even herself: a sneaking sense of relief.

With no William here, there will be no sudden clanging of the bell that links this bedroom to the watch-room below. No stumbling out into the cold at five in the morning, after a night interrupted by feeding babies, to answer the summons of the imperious bell by lighting the fire and heating water for William's washing bowl and tea, while William himself struggles into the beadle's uniform she has laid out for him, bad tempered as always at this hour in the morning: 'My hat, woman! Where have you put my hat?'

Now William is gone, she can lie in the big bed until the grey wash of dawn appears in thin lines through the cracks in the shutters, or until the little ones crawl, snotty nosed and tousled with sleep, under the covers to join her in the big bed.

The snuffling in the cot beside her turns into hiccupping sobs, the first sounds of little Caroline working towards a fit of howling that will wake Amelia and probably the rest of the children too. Wearily, Adah slides out from under her warm coverlet and lifts the youngest to her breast. Caro is too old for the breast, but suckling seems to soothe her, and now there is no William to scold her for indulging the child. After a few minutes of nuzzling, Caro's warm downy head sinks quietly into her mother's bosom, and Adah cautiously lifts the sleeping child back into her cot.

But sleep seems further away than ever. So many months after William's death, she had hoped that her nighttime awakenings were starting to subside. But the last two nights she has found herself lying awake thinking, not of her dead husband, but instead of the nameless dead child.

When she closes her eyes, she sees again that small sallow face with the mark on the forehead. Sometimes she seems to see the child lying on her cloak on the pile of straw in that god-forsaken stable. Again and again she envisages the child rising from her makeshift straw bed, stumbling out into the darkness of the livery yard, running, tripping, falling, lying still … and then the shadow of another person – is it a man to a woman? – steps out of the stable to spread the small black cloak over the child's motionless body.

Why? Why not go in search of a doctor? Why not call the officer of the watch? Or, if this unseen other person is an evil-doer, a child-stealer, why not flee the scene? Why stop to cover up the child's body in an odd gesture of gentleness? And where are the child's parents? Is there, somewhere in this vast city, a woman lying awake in the darkness at this very moment praying for the safe return of the child she will never see again: the child whose small body was taken out of the watch house yesterday to a lonely pauper's grave in a corner of Bunhill Fields? And what is the meaning of the curious button, which, carefully washed clean of mud, now lies on one corner of the window ledge?

The darkness of the night seems to fill Adah's mind. She can see no glimmer of light; she has not the slightest idea where to begin a search for the child's name and family. And yet it is terrible to think of that child lying under a pile of earth, unmarked and unmourned, as though she had never existed at all.

Her new role as Searcher, bestowed on her by the trustees of the Liberty in a moment of sympathy following William's sudden death, requires Adah to examine the bodies of those who die in unexplained circumstances, and to decide when further investigation is needed. There is no training for this task, and she has received precious little advice from the local officers, who view her with a mixture of pity and irritation. But all those years of marriage to the Liberty's Beadle have not been wasted. She remembers how meticulously William investigated every case, hunting down even minor miscreants with a single-mindedness that seemed almost chilling. Surely, if she could only imitate his logical patterns of thought, she would be able to make sense of this small tragedy, and at least give the dignity of a name to the dead child.

The child is a stranger, not from the Liberty. That much seems sure. Her dark hair and sallow skin may or may not suggest foreign origins. Jonah Hall is convinced the girl was foreign, maybe Spanish or Portuguese, and Adah is half tempted to use her own special connection to the Portuguese community to make some quiet enquiries. But no, she pushes that thought aside as resolutely as she can. Raphael DaSilva has been only the shadow of a memory in her life for the past four years or more, and ought to remain a shadow. Better, surely, to approach total strangers in the search for information than to risk exposing the obscure undercurrents of emotion that even the thought of his name threatens to stir. Besides, Raphael is as much an outsider to his community and his own earnest mercantile family as he is to the close-knit world of the Norton Folgate worthies. She will have to look elsewhere for a starting point.

Now that the fire has gone out, the damp winter cold is seeping into Adah's bedroom from every side. The darkness is oppressive, and Adah feels the need for fresh air. She gropes her way along the bottom of the bed and treads carefully over the uneven wooden floor in the direction of the window. Her fingers touch the metallic chill of the bolt that holds the shutters closed. Very slowly and softly, so as not to wake the sleeping children, she prizes the bolt open and pulls the shutters back.

The new gas lamp by the corner of White Lion Street seems not so much to light the space around it as to make the darkness come alive. Its flame flickers in the wind that sweeps down the empty street, and as it does so, the shadows move and dance, shooting out long tongues of darkness across the wet pavement and then retreating again. Apart from the shadows, and a fragment of some white stuff bowled by the wind along the street, everything is still. But then the flying clouds above part for a moment, and light from the full moon falls on the tall face of the silversmith's house across the road, and something moves.

A little patch of darkness separates itself from the other shadows, flits swiftly from one doorway to another, and then vanishes – something too small to be an adult human, too large to be a cat or dog. Adah stands very still at the window, wondering if she is imagining things, and waiting in vain for the dark shape to reappear.

Then the scratching begins. It is a small but insistent sound, and it seems to be coming from the front door of the courthouse, almost immediately beneath her bedroom window. Something is tapping and scratching at the door, as though a small animal is trying to get into the house. Adah leans her head out of the window as far as she can and tries to look down at the street below, but from this angle, the doorway beneath is invisible. The sound stops, and she is about to close the window and go back to bed, when it starts again.

Scratch, scratch, rattle. The sound of small nails against woodwork.

Her mouth dry and her heart beating too fast, Adah creeps out of her bedroom and, feeling her way cautiously along the bannister, quietly descends the darkened staircase towards the front door. The polished wood of the old staircase is chilly and slippery beneath her feet. At the bend in the stairs, she passes the spot where William died and, as always, instinctively mutters a word of prayer under her breath.

The hallway below is pitch dark but for a thin crack of light which comes from beneath the door of the watch-room on the far side of the hallway. I am not alone in this house, thinks Adah. I have no reason to be afraid. The officer of the night is on guard in the watch-room, always alert, always ready to apprehend any night prowlers who disturb the peace of the Liberty.

It seems foolish to summon the officer simply because she has heard a strange noise, but something about this noise makes her heart feel tight and cold. There is a peculiar fear and urgency in that scratching.

She walks across the dark hallway and opens the small interior door that leads to the watch-room, words of apology for the intrusion already on her lips. But the words remain unspoken. The watch-room is dimly lit by a fire in the hearth which has burnt low, and by a candle on the table whose gleaming molten wax overflows in sculpted rivulets from its battered pewter candleholder. At the far end of the room, Adah can just make out the shape of the little truckle bed where the body of the child lay until yesterday. At the near end, Jonah Hall lies slumped across a chair, the mountain of his belly rising and falling slightly beneath his officer's uniform, fast asleep.

Adah pauses on the threshold for a moment, uncertain whether to wake him, but then turns away and returns to the chill darkness of the hallway and listens intently. Moments pass. She recalls standing in the ruined stables near the spot where the child died, listening to a silent and unseen presence in its cobwebbed darkness. Now, in the dark of the courthouse, she feels that presence again.

Scratch, scratch, scratch. Like small nails on the other side of the latched and bolted front door. A silence, and next, a sound like breathing, and a soft whimper. A terribly human sound.

Adah stands frozen, waiting for the sound to come again. Then she forces her shaking hands to fumble with the big iron key, which slips in her unsteady grasp, and to pull the heavy front door ajar. At once, a blast of wind flings the door open, almost knocking her off her feet. It takes her a moment to recover her balance and step out into the night, and by the time she looks down the street, there is only a distant dark shape, about the size and shape of a small child, vanishing like an eddy of the wind itself into the shadows of Bishopsgate.

The cold damp air strikes Adah's face. The winter chill scours the empty street. The moonlight disappears behind clouds.

Everything is silent but for the voice of the wind and then, far away, ghostly and utterly un-consoling, the clear tones of the town cryer calling, 'Five of the clock, and all's well.'

Standing in front of the synagogue later that morning, light-headed from lack of sleep, Adah still hears in her mind that sound of scratching nails and human breath, and the little whimper. She hears them still so clearly that she doubts her own senses. Did her troubled imagination conjure them up from the depths of last night's half-waking dreams? But surely the dark hallway and the feel of the wind on her face were real?

She has left Annie in charge of the other children, and another part of her mind is distracted by everyday anxieties – will little Caroline have another fit of screaming? Will Annie remember to light the fire under the washing copper?

Adah has never ventured down this alleyway nor seen this building before, and it is completely, almost shockingly, different from her imaginings. She expected the Spanish and Portuguese synagogue to be something dark, rich and mysterious, full of deep reds and midnight blues and gold, with patterns as ornate and exotic as the dragon on that strange white button. Instead, she is confronted by a plain, four-square building of brownish brick which looks very much like the New Church in Bethnal Green where, in her childhood, pious Aunt Dorcas used to take her, muttering out of one corner of her sour-plum mouth if five-year-old Adah yawned or sneezed during the sermon.

The windows of the synagogue are tall and arched, with square panes of plain glass that allow broad beams of sunlight to flood the space within. Inside, Adah can see a row of well-polished oak benches. The sight of them brings back the damp smell of plaster and brick dust from the Bethnal Green church of her childhood. It must be thirty-five years or more since she last inhaled that unmistakable smell, but now it suddenly assails her nostrils again. The only ornate or exotic things in the synagogue seem to be the great brass candelabras that hang from the ceiling, trapping gleams of light in their golden orbs. Adah wants to go closer and peer deeper into the interior, but she senses that such open displays of curiosity might give offence. Although there is no-one else in the street, somehow she feels as though she is observed. She turns away and walks briskly along the alleyway. The house she is looking for is just a few doorways down from the synagogue. Its dark blue door is adorned with a shining brass knocker in the shape of a lion's head.

The very thought of approaching these people whom she knows only by name makes her body feel awkward and angular. Perhaps she should have tried speaking to Raphael DaSilva first. He at least might have been able to provide introductions, and tell her what to expect. But it's too late for that now, and having come this far, it would seem craven to return home without attempting to find a starting point to her quest. She knocks, somehow expecting to be greeted by a solemn-faced man with a skull cap and white beard, but again she is taken by surprise. After a long wait, and just as she lifts her hand to knock again, there is a flurry of soft steps inside, and a tall, well-built young woman with her face framed by curling chestnut hair appears in the doorway. She is wearing a plain but elegant grey-striped muslin dress and a matching shawl, and her green eyes are frank and inquisitive.

'I would like to speak to the Rabbi Meldola,' says Adah.

The young woman stares at her for a moment, and then turns back towards the interior of the house and calls out some words in a foreign language.

For a moment, Adah wonders whether the people in this house understand English, but then the young woman opens the door a little wider, and says, in the perfectly modulated tones of the London gentry, 'Please do step in off the street, Mrs …'

'Flint,' says Adah.

'Mrs Flint. I am sorry if our household appears to be in some disarray. Our housemaid was taken ill this morning, but my mother will be able to assist you.'

The mother, who appears from the dim recesses of the tiled hallway, is almost an exact older replica of the daughter. The strong face is more severe and already lined with the marks of age; but her expression is equally open and quizzical. She exchanges a few words with her daughter in a lilting language that Adah does not understand, and then speaks to Adah in musical but heavily accented English.

'You wish to see my husband, the Haham? What is your business with him?'

'I am the Searcher of the Liberty of Norton Folgate. A young child was found dead in our Liberty, and I am trying to find out who she was. She was …' Adah hesitates. She was going to say 'dark-skinned', but suddenly feels full of doubts. It was Jonah Hall who had suggested foreign connections, and encouraged Adah to ask the Rabbi of the Spanish and Portuguese synagogue whether any of the families in his congregation have lost a child. But looking at this green-eyed, chestnut-haired young woman and her mother, the logic seems very tenuous. The people who worship at this synagogue are clearly not all dark haired or dark skinned, and the child's colouring was not even obviously foreign. She might just as well have been a dark-haired English or Welsh child. This is a fool's errand: a desperate attempt to find some thread to follow, however tenuous.

'We thought the child might be Spanish,' Adah concludes lamely.

The two women observe her in silence for a moment, then the mother says, 'My husband the Haham is very busy. Perhaps he has no time to see you. But I ask.'

They leave her standing in the hallway. While she waits, her eyes adjust to the dim interior, and she picks out a line of sombre family portraits along one wall, and, at the entrance to the black and white tiled corridor beyond, a beautiful brass candelabra: a miniature version of the ones she had glimpsed inside the synagogue.

It is the daughter who returns as last, and says, with grave courtesy, 'My father apologizes for the fact that he is very busy and can spare little time, but he will see you for a few minutes. Please step this way.'

Adah follows her down the corridor and into a large room whose windows are filled with dim green light from a garden bordered by dark yew hedges. Every wall is lined with rows of books – velum covers in countless shades of beige and brown, olive green and faded red. The man who rises to greet her from his seat at the big desk by the window is middle-aged and round-shouldered, and has a rather lugubrious long face with skin sagging in wrinkled folds beneath his eyes. He wears not a skull cap but a yellowish, old fashioned peruke. His desk is covered with stacks of papers, perilously piled one on the other. On a small table in the centre of the room stands a quill and ink-well and a dish with a peeled, half eaten orange. Adah wonders whether this confusion is another sign of the maid's indisposition, or whether the study always looks like this.

'Mrs Flint, what can I do for you?'

The Haham's voice is soft, and the expression in his eyes is at once searching and strangely mournful.

Adah explains her quest – the dead child in the waste ground beyond Blossom Street, the lack of name or identification, the dark hair, the feeling that this was perhaps a child of foreign parents. Meanwhile, her eyes roam the bookshelves. She sees titles in gold embossed characters that she cannot read, and others in Latin, which she cannot understand, but her gaze is caught by a book in a row on the shelf nearest to her, whose title contains, in particularly vivid golden letters, the words: *Animal Spirits*. The meaning is enigmatic, but the words are alluring.

The Haham is slowly shaking his head. His English is accented, but his voice has, when he speaks, the same intonation as his daughter's.

'I am sorry, Mrs Flint. This is a sad story, but alas, I cannot help you. I know of no lost child from our congregation. We are a small community here, and a very close one. I would surely know if any child was missing, but I have heard of no such thing.'

There seems nothing more to say.

Muttering thanks and feeling foolish, Adah is about to turn and leave when the Haham continues pensively, 'Perhaps you might have better luck in Shadwell or Wapping. There are people of all nationalities there, and you might be surprised to learn how often women and even children come into the docks from all parts of the world on those ships. I heard tell a year or two ago of a Siamese child brought in on an East Indiaman who was found wandering lost in Billingsgate market. But you should send one of your officers of the watch to make inquiries there,' he adds, 'the docks are no place for a lady like yourself.'

How little he knows about me, thinks Adah. But the Haham's gaze is penetrating. Perhaps it is the expression in his eyes, or perhaps it the title of that strange book on animal spirits which prompts her, almost without thinking, to blurt out, 'Rabbi Meldola, may I ask you something?'

He nods silently.

'Do you believe in ghosts?'

The Haham is quiet for a while, observing her as though looking for the answer to some unspoken question. His ink-stained fingers toy with a corner of his slightly faded blue waistcoat.

At last he says, 'You have had some strange experience. Connected with this dead child?'

She nods.

'Mrs Flint,' says the Haham. 'You are a Christian, are you not? You should ask your own pastor these things. He is the person who will be able to help you.'

Adah thinks of the Reverend Henderick at St Leonard's, with his stern and disapproving frown as he reluctantly baptized her two youngest, after roundly scolding her for leaving them in peril of hell-fire for so long. She has already been marked out as a sinner; whatever would Reverend Henderick think if she were to tell him she had started seeing ghosts?

'As for my own thoughts,' continues the Haham, speaking as much to himself as to her, 'in our faith we do indeed believe that troubled spirits may walk the world in the dark of night, and that we mortals are wise to be aware of their presence, and to take steps to guard against their influences. But I also think that our mortal minds may seem to play tricks on us, and yet those tricks have their own meaning. It is for us to discover that meaning.'

He smiles at her, and Adah notices that, even though his lips smile, his tawny eyes remain profoundly sad.

THE CHILD'S STORY

April 1817

When spring came, she was allowed out to play in the garden. There was a long pebble path which ran between two rows of dark trees, ending at a green wooden door in the garden wall. The pebbles were endlessly fascinating – smooth and round, some bluish and veined like water, others white, others dusty faded rose.

The child sat on the path and picked up the pebbles one by one. She rolled them in her hand. They were hard and yet soft, and held the warmth of spring. The sky above was very high, and streaked with thin wisps of cloud. A bird floated across her field of vision, a speck of darkness on the rim of heaven. Sometimes she imagined that there was another child sitting beside her – a child with no name who was just the same size as herself. She smiled at the imaginary child and held out pebbles towards her, and then snatched them back again to add to her own pile.

The woman she called Sully stood beside her, wearing heavy, black laced boots. The hem of her shiny black gown was stained with rusty brown marks.

Sully bent down to her level and picked up a pebble with her fat red fingers.

'One pebble,' she said, setting it carefully on the line of bricks that marked the edge of the path.

Then she picked up another, a grey-blue one. 'Two pebbles,' said Sully, coaxingly.

'Three pebbles.' Sully added another yellowish pebble to the line.

The child liked this game. She picked up her own pebble, rolled it between her fingers, and then slowly and deliberately added it to the row.

'Good girl!' said Sully. 'Four pebbles.'

The wooden gate at the end of the path was closed, but if it were open, the child would have been able to look out and see the whole world. Far below, beyond the woods rose two stone towers, and beyond the towers again flowed the long lazy curve of the river. The river was a living stone, grey but veined with faint lines of white.

'Pebble,' said the child slowly. She could taste the round sound of the word, like a pebble in her mouth.

'Good girl! Good girl! See, you can say it! Five pebbles!' cried Sully, excited.

Now the child started to pick them up, faster and faster, adding to the row.

'Pebble,' said the child. 'Pebble. Pebble. Pebble.'

She could have continued forever, but Sully suddenly seized her arm.

'Enough!' said Sully. Her mood had changed, like the sun going behind a bank of cloud. She pulled the child roughly to her feet and propelled her towards the house. Down the path. Across the yard where grass sprouted between the uneven bricks. In through the kitchen door to the smell of soup bubbling on the huge black hob. Up the back stairs, arm aching from the grip of Sully's hand. She was dumped on the nursery floor while Sully fetched a ewer of water and a flannel, and hastily scrubbed her face and hands and the back of her neck with freezing sloppy water.

'Time to see Mamma. You want to see Mamma, don't you?' said Sully.

In Mamma's sitting room there was a sweet smell of woodsmoke. A fire was burning in the hearth. Its amber light glowed behind the bars of the grate, and spilled patterns like flames onto the carpeted floor. The floor was soft and covered in squares of red with darker red flowers and curling leaves at the centre. Mamma sat on her rocking chair by the fire, next to a table whose feet had claws like a bird's talons. She reached out her long thin hands and drew the child into the folds of her satin skirt, which smelled of woodsmoke and tea and lavender.

'Cara, cara!' *said Mamma.*

The book was lying on her lap. The child could see its familiar fraying green cover. She leant in close, peering at the picture on the page. She loved this picture: mysterious, terrifying. It showed a huge creature with pointed ears and uplifted snout staring at a diminutive man with a beard and a crown on his head. While Mamma read from the book, the child sat at her feet, tracing the flowers on the carpet with one finger. The words were music, flowing endlessly and soothingly with rhythm and cadence but without meaning.

'Dovete adunque sapere, donne mie care,' *read Mamma,* 'che Galeotto fu re di'Anglia, uomo non men ricco di beni della fortuna che di quelle dell'animo; ed aveva per moglie la figliola di Matthias re di Ungheria …'

The fire crackled softly in the hearth. The wind rattled the window panes. The pile of the carpet was soft beneath the child's finger. When she looked at the dark red flowers one way they were flowers, but if she looked another way they were strange beasts, with the deepest red spot in the centre a half-open eye. The little golden clock on the mantle-shelf chimed the quarter hour.

When the flow of music stopped, Mamma bent forward and stroked the child's hair with her soft hand.

Sully, who was sitting nearby with her black boots blotting out the flowers on the carpet beneath her chair, said, 'Say goodnight to Mamma, dear. Goodnight, Mamma!'

But the girl was looking at Mamma's feet, white and gold next to Sully's hard black boots. Mamma wore white cotton stockings and apricot coloured satin slippers fastened by buckles decorated with tiny round green stones. The child cautiously reached out to touch one of the stones.

'Say "goodnight, Mamma,"' repeated Sully, bending down so that her sourish breath puffed against the child's face.

The child still stared at the stones on Mamma's slipper buckles.

'Pebble,' said the child, 'pebble.'

ADAH'S STORY

January 1822
From the Courthouse to the Green Dragon

THE DAY SHE HAS been dreading has arrived. Adah takes off her apron, and pauses for a moment in front of the blotched green looking glass which still hangs on the bedroom wall, smoothing her hair. A strange, distorted face gazes back at her from the depths of the mirror. The looking glass is one of the things that will have to be left behind.

Young Will, as usual, has left the house first thing in the morning after wolfing down a lump of bread and a tankard of ale. Whenever she asks where he is going, he always says 'work', but he rarely seems to bring home any money. Adah knows she should take him aside and talk to him seriously, but can think of nothing to say. Her husband's death has built a wall of silence between her and her eldest child.

Nine-year-old Richard has been doing his best to help Adah and Annie move crates of clothes and crockery down the stairs and along the slippery cobbled road to their poky new home in Blossom Street, but has to stop repeatedly to cough and catch his breath. The boxes and bags seem unending. Adah did not know they had so many possessions until it was time to move them: the cauldron and the wooden spoons, the candlesticks and the chamber pots, even the half-full coal scuttle and a bucket of soda ash, too precious to leave behind. There is so much to remember. In the confusion of the move, she almost forgot about the strange white button which she found in the grass where the child's body had been lying. It was only by luck that she spotted it on the window ledge where she had left it, and carried it carefully over to their new house, where it sits now amongst the confusion of salt cellars, vases, cotton reels, candle ends and sealing wax on the corner table in the dark little bedroom that she will have to share with her four daughters.

Now, with most of the moving done, Richard is sitting in the back room, coughing quietly into a handkerchief. Caro and Amelia are rolling around happily on the patched green rug in front of the kitchen fire, while Sally runs about in wild excitement, managing to get under everybody's feet.

Pausing to watch her for a moment, Adah notices how Sally's hair, which looked almost fair when she was a baby, is rapidly darkening as she grows. Her head, shiny like a dark horse-chestnut, is starting to stand out amongst the other children's straw coloured mops.

Mr Cansdell the assayer and three other trustees arrive in a body: an invading army. Mr Cansdell is a stout man with a fob watch and a mottled red blob for a nose. With his leather-bound book and quill in one hand and an inkwell in the other, he reminds Adah of the hanging judge she saw on her visit to the Old Bailey to watch William give evidence in the trial of that poor mad John Stafford. I should not dislike this man, thinks Adah.

Mr Cansdell reaches out a soft white hand and tries unsuccessfully to pat Sally's head as she whirls past, imagining that she is a huntsman riding his horse after the hounds. The surveyor turns to Adah with an unctuous knowing smile and asks, 'And she is one of your little ones too? What lovely dark locks!'

Adah tries to pay attention as the trustees tramp though the half-empty house, sucking their lips and tut-tutting over cracks in the plaster walls, while their boots leave muddy footprints all over the floors that she and Annie assiduously mopped all day yesterday. But her mind is elsewhere.

Wherever she looks, small objects catch like hooks in her memory, dragging out images from its depth.

When they move the heavy wooden sea-chest from the big bedroom, she finds behind it, half jammed under the wainscot, a yellow, broken-toothed ivory comb, and has a sudden recollection of William's long-dead mother Elizabeth wringing her hands in distress as she hunted high and low for that comb. The day after Christmas, it was. How many years ago? Fifteen, twenty?

Seeing that room stripped of most of its furniture, Adah sees herself, for some reason, as she was the first day she arrived in the courthouse, a new bride, awkward and uncertain in this building which at that time seemed so huge and dark and cold compared with the warm earthy chaos of her father's cottage in Fulham. It is strange to remember. Now these rooms are home, filled with the familiar smells of a multitude of memories, sweet and alluring and bitter.

While the uninvited visitors tramp around on the floorboards above, muttering and measuring and recording things in the leather-bound book, she cannot help slipping quietly down the stairs to the landing, and gazing again at the spot where she found William on the bleak night of his death. She can see precisely the place where his head was lying, although the stains that were left on the wood have been scrubbed away. He was still alive when she found him, but she knew the moment she saw him that he would not live long. The doctor later said that it was apoplexy, but everyone else said it was the drink. Even now, when she stares at the spot where he lay, it all seems unreal.

'Mrs Flint!' calls a breathless voice from below.

It is the new beadle, Benjamin Beavis, fresh faced, bright eyed and out of breath.

He looks little older than young Will, she thinks.

The beadle has been hurrying, and his cheeks are flushed, either with exertion or embarrassment. In one hand he carries a small parcel wrapped in grey paper and untidily tied with string.

'I am so sorry about the intrusions,' he murmurs, 'so very sorry, but alas …'

His hand holding the parcel waves vaguely in the air as he searches for words.

'No need to apologize, Mr Beavis,' replies Adah, hearing the tightness in her own voice, 'this is your home now.'

'I brought you this. A small present.' The beadle thrusts the grey parcel into her hands and retreats up the stairs to join the trustees.

Adah unties the string. Inside, neatly folded, is a limp strip of linen embroidered in cross-stitch with a pattern of pink and blue foxgloves. She has no idea what it is meant to be used for.

This in return for a home, she thinks. But the beadle's intentions are good. They are not unkind, these people. Only they see her as a problem. They made her Searcher merely out of pity after William's sudden death, and when she began to assert herself – asking to be allowed to stay on in the courthouse – the pity turned to irritation. All of them bar one will be glad when she has left, and would be happier still if she would quietly relinquish her role as Searcher. But that she will not do; not, at least, until she has found the dead child's name.

Suddenly she is immensely tired. She struggles up the flights of stairs and wanders into her empty bedroom, desperate for somewhere to sit down and rest her feet. The only furniture left in the room is a single upholstered chair, which stands near the window, and she sinks into it with an involuntary sigh. She can distinctly remember her father-in-law buying a pair of these chairs for two pounds, which seemed a terrible extravagance at the time. Mr Cansdell insists that they are only worth one pound four shillings the pair, and she is too exhausted to argue.

Weak sunlight shines through the open shutters onto her face. Outside in the street, an infant is wailing with that abandoned utter grief that we all feel from time to time, but which only the very young are allowed to express. Then a dog starts to bark, and a man's voice from across the road shouts, 'Stop that damn racket,' though she can't tell whether the words are addressed to the infant or the dog.

She stares at the blank face of the silversmith's house across the road, remembering that strange moonlit night when she saw a dark shape moving in the street below. Today, in broad daylight, it seems impossible to imagine. A carriage rattles past, and a couple of children bowl a hoop over the cobbles, yelling with panic and delight as it escapes from their hands and careers unaided towards the gutter. Everything seems normal, calm, bathed in sunlight. Yet in her head Adah can still evoke those strange midnight sounds that she heard from the door below: the rattling, the scratching of nails and the little whimper …

There it is again. She catches her breath. A scratching sound, and the sound of a sigh, somewhere close at hand. Her heart begins to race, but almost at once she realizes her mistake. This time, the sound is not coming from an invisible being in the street below, but from someone who is standing just outside her bedroom door. The door is barely ajar, so she can see nothing but the dark shadow of a man on the landing outside. Not one man but two, their heads bent together, speaking quietly to one another.

'It's Jonah Hall,' says the soft voice of Beadle Beavis, 'he will have to go.'

The reply is an inaudible mutter from one of the trustees.

Adah is conscious of eavesdropping on a conversation she is probably not meant to hear, but is too tired to move.

'It's the drink,' continues Beavis, 'just like poor Flint in his last days. There'll be another tragedy if we don't act soon.'

'I thought Hall seemed such a sober man,' murmurs the other. 'He's a regular at church on a Sunday, and I've never seen him have more than half a jug of ale. Are you sure of this?'

‘I found him asleep on the watch at five this morning,’ says Beavis, ‘fast asleep. I could barely rouse him. It’s the second time. Thursday it was the same story, but today was worse. His mind was wandering … Talking of ghosts.’

‘Ghosts?’ says the other sharply.

‘Ghosts in the street at dead of night, is what he was saying. Muttering. Incoherent.’

Beavis drops his voice to a whisper, which somehow only serves to make his words carry more clearly.

‘He was muttering about that dead child. Says he saw that dead child’s ghost in the street. Swore to it, hand on his heart. “I saw her face in the lamplight. The same child,” he said. I’ve no doubt he believes it himself. It’s drink or delirium. He’ll have to go.’

Jemmy Harbottle, the landlord of the Green Dragon, flings the used tankards into the water butt with an energy driven by anger. Small waves of grimy water slop over the side of the butt, creating a gradually spreading stain on the flagged floor. The air is full of the smell of spilled drink, pipe smoke and stale urine.

The fire in the big open hearth is barely alight, and the room is growing cold. Jemmy ought to poke the fire and put on more logs, but he can’t be bothered. He is angry at the emptiness of his inn, which by this time of day should be beginning to fill with men off the ships, angry with his wife Betsy who has been making eyes at that evil-faced lodger next door again, and particularly angry at the young woman who has been sitting in the corner of the bar for the past hour, staring silently at the bottle of gin on the table in front of her. He has no idea who the woman is, but secretly blames her for the fact the inn is still empty at four o’clock in the afternoon. She’s bad luck, that woman.

The only other living creature in the inn is the mangy, ageing mongrel dog who sleeps, snoring audibly, amongst a jumble of baskets and empty barrels under the battered oak settle. The smoke-darkened walls of the room are lined with shelves which bear an assortment of bottles, jugs and bowls, a cage containing a moulting stuffed parrot, an array of scrimshaw brought back by a sailor from the Azores and the skull of a baboon, whose hollow eyes stare balefully out over the empty room. The tattered cloth which hangs from the blackened rafters above was once decorated with an image of St. George impaling a curling green dragon, but is now so frayed and faded that only a faint trace of scales and horse's hooves remain.

The woman who sits in the corner is thin and gaunt, with wisps of pale dry hair falling over her eyes. Her bony hands are cupped around the gin bottle, from which she occasionally takes a tentative swig. Most of the time, though, she just sits and stares. Jemmy observes that she might be pretty, if her face wasn't so bony and so streaked with tears. Too bony to appeal to him. She sits absolutely still, making no sound at all, with the tears rolling steadily down her cheeks, creating slowly expanding damp marks on the threadbare green shawl around her shoulders.

Jemmy's mood is not improved when the door swings open and another woman walks in: a smallish, plumpish, middle-aged woman with curling hair under a blue bonnet. She looks completely out of place in the Green Dragon, and Jemmy's anger rises another notch.

'What do you want?' he asks sourly, staring at the woman's freckled face and her slightly faded frock and gown. Not really poor, he thinks, but not rich, either. Jemmy prides himself on being able to make these judgements in an instant.

'Give me a drink of clean water, and I'll give you a penny,' says the woman, returning his stare. Her eyes are grey and surprisingly shrewd.

'Water?' exclaims Jemmy in disgust. 'Ain't yer got no water at home? What are you here for, if not for the drink? Looking for a lost husband?'

'No, looking for a lost mother. I am the Searcher of the Liberty of Norton Folgate. We have had a dead child brought to our courthouse. I am trying to find who she was and where she came from.'

The Green Dragon is the fifth inn in Shadwell that Adah has visited today. Her feet are sore from walking, and she is growing nauseous from the sour smells of the inns, and weary of hostile gazes from landlords and patrons alike. But the further she goes, the deeper the urge becomes. She cannot stop now. Somewhere in this city is someone who knows the name of the dead child, and she is going to find that person. I am haunted, she thinks. Ghost or no ghost, I am haunted by that child.

'If you're from Northing Falgate,' says Jemmy, 'what are you doing in these parts? More likely the child's from your end of town.'

'She looked as though she might be a foreigner. Perhaps a child off a ship, or her father might be a Spaniard. They told me I should try Shadwell.'

Jemmy Harbottle gives a snort. 'That's right – Shadwell. We've got 'em all here, all right. Spaniards, Laskars, Malays, Chinese, mongrels, brindled, take your pick. Some of 'em probably lose a child from time to time, I shouldn't wonder.'

He turns back to his tankards, flinging them into the water butt with deliberate viciousness. His back is still turned as his speaks again, and she can't make out his words. When she asks him to repeat himself, he turns and mutters, half-reluctantly.

'Unless it's got something to do with that madwoman.'

'Madwoman?'

'Mad or drunk,' says the landlord, 'or probably both. Screeching at the top of her voice, over and over.' He puts on a horrible falsetto in mimicry. '"They've stolen my child again, they've stolen my child again! Take me out to the ship!"' Then, returning abruptly to his normal register, 'But she didn't say nothing about Northing Falgate. Just "Take me out to the ship! Take me out to the ship!" She wasn't no foreigner, either, far as I can tell.'

'She wasn't mad.' It is the woman in the corner who has spoken, suddenly and clearly, lifting her tear-stained face.

Adah turns and looks at her more closely. The woman is probably not much more than twenty, but seems older. There are dark shadows under her eyes, and the nails on her fingers have been bitten down to the quick.

Adah walks over and pulls up a chair to the young woman's table.

'Tell me,' she says softly, 'do you know this woman who says her child's been stolen? Where can I find her?'

The landlord gives another snort, and speaks before the young woman has a chance to respond.

'Davy Jones's locker is where you'll find her. Jumped in the river and drowned herself yesterday evening, she did. The officers of the watch are still out looking for the body.'

'Poor soul,' murmurs the young woman. 'God rest her. She wasn't mad, just troubled. She'd lost a child years back, she said, and now another one had disappeared. I don't know why, but she was sure that a sailor's wife had stolen it. A little girl, she said. She was wild with grief, but she wasn't mad. I think she meant to swim out to one of the ships, but they say she just sank like a stone.'

'You didn't see this happen?' asks Adah.

'No, I wasn't there. Just heard about it from the girls I live with. Two of them was on the quay, not more than a dozen yards away when it happened. But I'd spoken to the woman right here.' She points to the settle at the other side of the room, where the dog is still wheezing and twitching in its sleep. 'Right here, she was, two days ago. She'd had a bit to drink, but she wasn't drunk, nor mad, neither. Said she'd loved her little girl. Hunted for her for days. "My little Rosie," she called her. I felt sorry I couldn't help her. Told her so. She said, "Never mind, dearie. It's just good to talk to someone with a kind face."' The young woman gives a wry laugh. 'That's funny. There's not many as think I have a kind face.'

Rosie. Adah repeats the name quietly to herself, thinking of the child's waxy face in the shadows of the watch room. Rosie.

'And the mother, did she tell you her own name? Did she have a husband, other children?'

'I don't know about that. She didn't speak of no husband, nor of children, except that she'd lost another one years ago. But she did tell me her own name. Catherine, she was called.' The young woman pauses. 'Catherine something or other … It's gone. Catherine … something beginning with C.'

Adah reaches out and takes the young woman's cold hand in her own. The hand is stiff and unresponsive, but the young woman doesn't draw it away.

'Thank you, my dear,' says Adah. 'Thank you, you've been very helpful. Is that why you're crying? Are you crying because Catherine drowned?'

'No,' says the young woman, with such finality that Adah feels she can't pry further.

Most mysteries, she thinks, have no answers. That's something she learnt from living with William for twenty years. Most puzzles are never solved. You find one answer, and then it just proves to be the start of another mystery. And the biggest mystery of all is the least solvable of all.

Rosie. That might be the child's name. But then again, this mother's tragedy might just be a coincidence. The child who died in that abandoned stable yard might have been this lost Rosie, or she might not. And anyway, the mother is dead, and no-one here seems to know any more about her. This door has closed as quickly as it opened.

Adah puts down the penny on the landlord's counter, even though she can't afford it, and he never bothered to give her the glass of water.

She is about to leave the inn when the young woman in the corner suddenly lifts her head again and says, 'Creamer.'

'What?' asks Adah, confused.

'Creamer,' says the young woman. 'That's what she said her name was. The mother. Catherine Creamer. Or it might have been Cramer. But I think she said Catherine Creamer.'

*

The river is close to flood, its turbid dark waters frothing and splashing against the cobbled quay as Adah makes her way home in the rapidly gathering darkness. The wind has risen, and threatens to blow the cloak from her shoulders. The figures who pass her by move swiftly, hunched against the gale, hurrying towards the warmth of their homes or of neighbouring inns. Lamps on the ships moored in midstream toss in the dark, sending reflections like flames dancing across the furrowed surface of the water.

At the far end of the quay, a group of people has gathered around the dark mound that lies on the ground. One of them holds a lantern high, while the rest peer down at the shapeless form at their feet, speaking to each other in low voices which reach Adah only as wisps of sound snatched away by the wind. Two of the men hold long grappling hooks, and as she approaches, she sees their small skiff drawn up against the stone jetty.

There is no mistaking the shape on the ground. The circle of light from the lantern falls on dark, sodden cloth, from beneath which extend strands of long black hair and a white, claw-like hand and arm, streaked with river mud. The body of the drowned mother has been found.

For a moment, Adah hesitates, wondering whether to join the group around the dead woman, to ask questions, to peer at the woman's face, looking for some resemblance to the dead child. But the very sight of that white lifeless arm chills her. Instead, she turns away and heads homeward, listening all the while to the long-forgotten words which sprang unbidden into her brain the moment she heard the dead woman's name.

Catherine Creamer.

It is like some snatch of tune that you have heard long ago and forgotten, and hearing it again, find it circling maddeningly in your brain, like a fly in a closed room.

She can hear her husband William speak that name. She can see him in her mind's eye, sitting before the fire, pipe in one hand, talking to someone. When would it have been? Six, seven years ago. Maybe more. Adah can remember nothing else. Who was William talking to? What else did he say? Nothing returns except those two sentences, spoken in the pitying but slightly smug tone that we use when speaking of others' misfortunes.

'*Poor* Catherine Creamer,' William is saying, and she can hear again the very rise and fall of his voice as he says it. '*Poor* Catherine Creamer, just like *poor* Mrs Dellow. Whoever would have thought it could happen again?'

THE CHILD'S STORY

June 1819

In the days when old Father Sheehan came to call, Sully and the child used to play the hiding game. Sully would take her down to the little scullery at the back of the kitchen, which always smelled of mildew and onions, and they would sit there, listening to the footsteps and distant voices that came from the priest and Mamma as they spoke in the room above.

'Let's play at being as quiet as mice,' Sully would whisper, feeding her little pieces of cheese, and the child would giggle silently into her pinafore.

But then Father Ambrose, new to the district, arrived, and it seemed that they didn't need to play the hiding game anymore. She and Sully could go up to Mamma's drawing room, and stand in the corner of the room next to the black and gold cabinet that she loved more than anything else in the world. When she was smaller, the cabinet was so high that she could not see the top of it unless Mamma lifted her up. But once she grew taller, she could gaze in wonder at all the things laid out on the shiny black lacquered wood: the strange and beautiful things brought back by the Captain from the Indies and the Fijis and the coasts of Tartary.

'Look, this is an elephant,' Mamma liked to say, 'see his long trunk? The Captain brought this picture all the way home from Bengal.

And this is a seashell from the Sandwich Islands. Listen – put it closer to your ear. Can you hear the sound of the sea in the shell?'

When the child put the big pink mouth of the shell to her ear, she could hear a faint roaring sound, but she didn't think that it sounded like the sea.

Best of all was when Mamma let her hold the translucent round white thing that lay on the centre of the cabinet. When she touched it, she could feel the pattern that curled and writhed across its surface. 'That's jade,' said Mamma, 'a Chinese jade button, all the way from Canton. Can you see the curly dragon on the button?'

Then one day there were other things on the cabinet that the child had never seen before: two pewter candlesticks and two little silver bowls. She had been dressed for the occasion in a new white dress with stiff white lace around the collar, and a big white bow tied in her hair.

'What lovely brown eyes,' said Father Ambrose, gazing down at the child. 'Just like her mother.' And Mamma clapped her hands and laughed delightedly.

The priest had a soft, plum coloured face and wore a long black robe with a large golden cross hanging on his chest. The centre of the cross was decorated with a green stone. The child couldn't keep her eyes off it.

'What's your name, little one?' asked Father Ambrose.

'Grace,' said Sully.

'Grazia,' said Mamma at the same time.

'Grace! What a perfect name. A grace from God to be sure,' cried the priest, then paused and added, 'she's very quiet, isn't she?'

'As good as gold, our dear little Grazia,' said Mamma, 'never the least trouble.'

'We have a fine little chapel now,' continued Father Ambrose, 'might it not be better to wait a week or two and do it there?'

'Oh no!' cried Mamma. 'Such a weak chest has little Grazia. So often ill. We cannot take her all that way. The wind and the chill, they would be bad for her.'

'It should certainly be done as soon as possible. Why ever did Father Sheehan not arrange it earlier?'

'He was away in Rome when she was born. It has weighed on my mind so long. I am so happy that you can do it.'

'And you, little Grace,' asked the priest, 'are you happy too? Are you happy to enter into the family of Our Lord Jesus Christ?'

The child nodded, her eyes never leaving the golden cross on the priest's chest.

Sully brought a taper, and the priest lighted the two candles on the cabinet, filling the room with the sweet smell of beeswax. The priest placed a gold-embroidered stole around his shoulders, and Mamma put her white lace kerchief on her head.

'Quid petis ab Ecclesia Dei?' Father Ambrose asked the child, who gazed back into his eyes, silent and uncomprehending.

'She doesn't understand the Latin,' whispered Mamma, 'I will say it for her', and then, more loudly, 'Fidem.'

'Fides, quid tibi praestat?'

'Vitam aeternam.'

While the priest and Mamma spoke, and the priest bent over to breathe on her with breath that smelled of sugar, and pressed his soft thumb into her forehead, the child wondered about Mamma's words – about her chest and the wind and the chill. Why would Mamma say she could not walk in the wind? The child loved the wind.

Sometimes at dusk, when few people were about, Sully would take her out of the little green door in the wall of the garden, and they would walk along the narrow road that wove its way through the woods beyond. As they reached the corner of the road, she would see the river far away, flowing endlessly seawards, and beyond the river the murky outlines of a great city. The wind that rose up from the river blew against her face and through her hair. You could see tall ships on the river, raising their canvas sails towards the sky.

'That one's bound for Jamaica,' Sully would say. Or, 'See her: she's the Northumberland, bound for the Indies. The Captain used to sail a ship like her.'

On those rare days when they ventured out of the green gate, Sully herself seemed somehow to swell in the wind. Wisps of her hair would blow loose, and in place of her normal silence, the words started to flow. She told the child stories of her own childhood in Greystones, across the sea in Ireland, and of the Captain's travels. She would describe how the Captain and Mamma first met at a ball, far away, in the port of Naples, and how they fell in love and were married that very week so that the Captain could bring Mamma home to live with him here in Westcombe. The child loved those stories almost as much as she loved the strange tales Mamma would read her from the story book full of mysterious words and pictures.

'Oremus,' *the priest was saying*. 'Omnipotens sempiterne Deus, Pater Domini nostri Iesu Christi, respice designare super hanc famulam tuam, *Grazia* …'

The priest picked up one of the silver bowls from the cabinet and, with a tiny silver spoon, scooped out a little pile of something white and held it to the child's lips. She clamped them firmly closed. Her heart was beating in her chest like a butterfly.

'It's all right, cara mia,' said Mamma gently. 'Open your mouth. It's only salt.'

Slowly, she parted her lips, and the spoon darted in onto her tongue. The taste of salt filled her mouth. Salt like the salt wind from the sea where the Captain's ship disappeared over the horizon.

It was summer, and the light lasted long in the evenings. At the end of that day, after the child had eaten sweet black cake full of currants, rubbed her hair to remove the clammy feel of the water that Father Ambrose poured on her head, taken off the stiff new white dress and put on her old blue dress and grey pinafore again. Sully quietly took her left hand, and they walked down the garden path to the green door in the wall. In her other hand, Sully held a small bunch of white flowers, their stems wrapped in a damp cloth which dripped water onto the pebbles of path. The child quietly opened and closed her own right hand, imagining that it was grasping the hand of an invisible girl who walked silently beside her.

The air was still. The long shadows of the trees fell across the lane, but when they reached the corner and looked down at the river, she could see that its water still held the silvery light, treasuring it, reluctant to surrender day to night.

Far down in the direction of the sea, a tall, three-masted ship was silhouetted against the fading sky.

'Where do you think that one's going?' asked Sully.

'India,' said the child. India was a dark purple-blue word. Like the night sky itself, dotted with tiny stars.

'India!' said Sully, giving her hand a little squeeze. 'Sure enough, India is where she's bound.' And then, pensively, 'It's India the Captain was bound for when he was lost, you know. Your poor dear Mamma

watched and waited so many days, believing he would come home. There are days when I think she's watching and waiting still … And then that other sorrow …'

She fell silent for a moment, and then squeezed the child's hand again and said more cheerfully, 'She is so good to you, your mamma. Isn't she good to you, my dear?'

'Good,' said the child.

'You're the light of her life, you know,' said Sully.

And the child looked at the light on the river, silver grey and barely rippled by the wind – shining like the silver grey silk that covered the great bed in Mamma's bedroom.

Further along the lane, there was a little latched gate which led through an old wall into a wide space, almost like a forest, full of cedar trees and big stones. In the evening light, the whiteness of the stones stood out amongst the trees whose dark branches curved downward, nearly touching the ground. Long grass and rosebay willow-herb grew thick in the patches of open ground. The willow-herb was tall enough to brush against the child's cheeks as they made their way quietly through this garden of stones. A flock of birds, settling down for the night, chattered briefly in the branches of one of the great trees, and then fell silent.

Sully led her firmly towards two stones which stood together before a lichened stretch of the wall. One stone was grey and taller than the child herself. On it were words, and a picture of a sailing ship, carved into the stone. The ship had three masts, with sails unfurled on two of them. Stone waves curled around its hull.

The other stone was white, and very small, so small that the child had to squat down to touch it. The stone felt like the jade of the dragon button all the way from Canton. On this stone there were six words and a little engraved flower. In front of it stood a tiny alabaster vase, almost hidden by the grass. Sully bent to put her bunch of flowers in the vase, and then closed her eyes and folded her hands, her lips moving silently.

The child reached out one finger and ran it over the smooth white stone. She felt the folds of the carved flower, traced the outlines of its petals. A drop of water had fallen on the stone from the cloth that Sully was carrying. It ran down the stone and formed a droplet on the tip of one of the stone petals. The child touched the smooth globe of water, feeling its coolness, and then gently wiped it away.

ADAH'S STORY

February 1822
The Artist

THE DOORSTEP OF THE house in Spital Square looks the same as ever, its surface slightly stained, and dandelion leaves pushing up through the cracks between the stones. But the brown paint on the door is more faded than it was before, and has peeled away in a patch above the door handle.

Adah vividly recalls standing on this doorstep for the first time, years ago. She had been sent here by William with some trivial message about a meeting of the trustees. The message is long forgotten, but the moment will always be remembered. And then, much later, standing here again with her heart pounding, wanting to lift the brass knocker but lacking the courage. And today, here she is once more, and her heart is hammering as hard as ever, and her hand still trembles as she lifts it to knock on the door.

It is the manservant Stevens who answers, his face ageless and as sour as ever. He must surely recognize her, but gives no sign of doing so.

'Please could you tell Mr DaSilva that Adah Flint would like to speak to him briefly?' Adah is astonished at the steadiness of her own voice.

She steels herself for a blank refusal, but after a wait that seems to last forever, Stevens returns and gives a small sardonic nod. 'The master will see you upstairs,' he croaks.

The floorboards creak as she follows the old servant slowly up the stairs. Stevens seems to have grown slower and even more bandy-legged since she was last here. His breeches hang loose over his bony legs, and the seam in the back of his olive-brown jacket has split. Upstairs, though, the rooms are just as she remembers them.

The study, lined with orderly rows of books, and with its two watercolour paintings of Jamaica beside each doorway, opens into the chaos of the studio beyond. Every flat surface of the studio is covered with a jumble of sea shells, gourds, vases and shrivelled flowers. Raphael DaSilva has set up his easel in front of a cupboard door, and is painting a picture of the cupboard and the clutter within. She can see the faint outlines of scrolls of parchment, a glass of water and a tasselled cap appearing on the square of canvas. The air is heavy with the smell of pomanders and turpentine.

Adah waits while the artist pauses, brush in hand, putting a few further touches to his painting. While he does so, she looks up at the paintings of Jamaica that hang on either side of the study. She has loved these since the first moment she saw them. Even the name Jamaica sounds like music when Raphael pronounces the name of his birthplace. In one of the watercolours, a black woman and a fair-skinned man sit facing one another in an arbour covered with luxuriant tropical vines; in the other, a small dark boy holds out a bowl full of sugar to a man in a tricorn hat. In the background of this painting, through an open window, you can see tall palm trees and a glimpse of turquoise sea. Is the sea really that colour in Jamaica, Adah wonders idly. I must ask him sometime.

At last Raphael turns from his easel, wiping his paint-stained hands with a rag. His long thin face is unsmiling. His dark eyes gleam as brightly as ever, though she notices that there is now one vivid streak of grey, indeed almost of pure white, in his otherwise black hair.

'Mrs Flint,' he says gravely, 'it has been a long time. I heard about your husband William. I am so sorry.' She had forgotten the lilt of his voice, the unusual musical rhythm and soft burring of the letter R.

He motions her towards one of the big velvet-covered chairs in the study.

'Mrs Flint will take tea,' he says to Stevens, without asking her wishes. Perhaps he remembers that she always liked a cup of tea.

But once the servant has shuffled away, he bends towards her and says more gently, 'How are you, Adah? Are you in any trouble? And how are the children?'

He means Sally, of course, but she replies carefully, 'They are all well, very well. Except for poor Richard and his coughing. We have had to leave the courthouse, but we have lodgings nearby, in Blossom Street. It's small, but comfortable enough. Did you hear that they made me Searcher after William died?'

'I did indeed.'

'It was kind, of course,' she continues, the flow of words seeming unstoppable now they have started. 'But still I cannot help but feel they do not really trust me. They have given me only little tasks until now, but now … now we have a mystery of a dead child. Poor thing. Poor little thing. She was perhaps seven years old. Mrs Yandall the scavenger found her in the old stable yard behind Magpie Alley, just a week ago today. She had fallen and struck her head on a stone. It seems a simple enough story, but …'

She is startled to find tears welling up in the corners of her eyes as she speaks. How along ago is it since I last cried, she wonders. To stop the tears that seem to be rising relentlessly through her throat, she turns away, fumbles with the strings of her little striped purse, and from its depths fishes out the button with its curling engraved dragon.

'Did you ever see the like of this before?' she asks.

Raphael takes the button and holds it carefully between his thumb and forefinger. His brown fingers are patterned with shadows of blue paint. She notices again how the knuckles show paler beneath the darkness of his skin. His face is the face of a scholar, but his hands are the hands of a labourer. He walks to the window and holds the button up to the light.

Adah recalls him standing just like that, his back to her, silhouetted by the light from the window, the last time she was here; and those other times, when she sat in this room, while Raphael turned the pages of a book with those paint-stained fingers, coaxing her to read the difficult words on the page.

He turns back towards her, shaking his head.

'Chinese jade,' he says, 'but that is all I can say.'

'I found it where the dead child was found, lying in the grass. But oh, poor child. No parents came forward to claim her. We had to bury her in an unmarked grave in Bunhill Fields. I have hunted high and low to find her family, but all I can find is a story of some poor, half-crazed woman who was seen in the inns around Shadwell, looking for her missing child, and by the time I heard that news, the woman was already dead, drowned in the river. But strangest of all …' No, she cannot bring herself to speak about the ghost. The words die on her lips. 'Strangest of all, when they told me the name of the woman who died looking for her child, I seemed to know it. I am sure I heard William speak that name, some years back now. Catherine Creamer, she was called.'

'Catherine Creamer,' says Raphael slowly, 'Catherine Creamer … Yes … Yes … It seems familiar to me too. But where I have heard it, I cannot tell.'

The crockery rattles as Stevens hobbles into the room carrying a tray laden with the curious teapot with its pattern of cabbage leaves, two mismatched mugs and a plate of aged-looking muffins.

They are silent for a moment as Raphael pours the pale China tea. The steam rises thickly from her mug, and Adah suddenly realizes how cold this room is. She wraps her fingers around the pottery mug to warm them.

'Do you remember anything more that William said about this woman, this Catherine Creamer? Does Beadle Beavis know anything of her?' asks Raphael, once Stevens has gone.

'I don't like to ask Mr Beavis,' says Adah. She finds it difficult to explain, even to herself, her reluctance to share this story with the beadle and the other officers. 'As for William, for some reason, all I can remember him saying is "Poor Catherine Creamer, just like poor Mrs Dellow."'

'Ah!' exclaims Raphael. 'Now I see it! Dellow, of course. I don't quite remember the story of Catherine Creamer, but surely you too must remember the case of Thomas Dellow?'

Once he says the words, of course she does. Thomas Dellow. The little stolen child. Such a famous story. How could she have forgotten?

'Wait,' says Raphael. 'Let me see what I can find. When would it have been? Perhaps eight years ago now?'

He turns to the long row of brown covered volumes of the *Aldwych Almanack* which fill one shelf of his bookcase.

While he thumbs through one volume after another, Adah, out of nervousness, crumbles the muffin on her plate. It is dry and tasteless, and in any case, she does not feel hungry. She promised herself that she would never come to this house again, and she has failed in her promise. Mr Cansdell's sly glances are bad enough, but worse still are the memories of William's long silences in the last months of his life, when he would sit alone at the table, not reading the papers in front of him, drinking one glass of gin after another, the bubble of his slightly pompous pride deflated, his raucous laugh turned to ponderous sighs. He never said what it was that troubled him. When Sally was born, he had been delighted with the new baby, chucking her under the chin and holding her in the crook of his arm. They had continued to lie together in bed, and only little by little, as Sally grew and began to walk, the silences had grown, and he had come to bed either drunk and half asleep or wakeful, staring wordlessly into the darkness. Perhaps it had nothing to do with Sally's birth. Perhaps it was something entirely different. She will never know how much, if anything, he suspected.

'I have it,' says Raphael, turning towards her, his face suddenly animated with excitement. 'Here is the story. Just as I remembered. Let me read it to you.'

He draws his chair closer to hers, sets the 1815 volume of the *Aldwych Almanack* on his knee, and begins to read.

THE STORY OF THOMAS DELLOW

In all the dark annals of crime which have disturbed the sentiments of the citizens of this and neighbouring boroughs these past years, some of the very darkest chapters have concerned the heinous act of child-stealing. It will perhaps be recalled in this regard that a curious failing in the laws of the land was brought to light a mere four years ago by the pathetic case of Master Thomas Dellow.

Young Thomas Dellow and his little sister Rebecca, having been left in the care of a neighbouring shopkeeper while their mother sought the attentions of a physician for a minor ailment, were playing (as children are wont to do) about the doorstep of the premises, when they were accosted by a female person who tempted them away with promises of apples and penny plum cakes. No sooner were the children beyond sight of prying eyes than the woman seized the little boy and made off with him, leaving his sister alone in the street, whence she was soon rescued by the shopkeeper. Imagine the horror of the unhappy mother when she returned soon after to find her precious only son had vanished, as it would appear, into thin air!

Hand bills were printed, and Master Dellow's uncle, a Mr Shergold, in the employ of the East India Company, made inquiries far and wide, distributing the hand bills in the company of officers. At first it seemed that a happy conclusion to the mystery might soon be at hand, for several shopkeepers in the neighbourhood of St. Martin's Lane and Fish-street Hill (where the felony had occurred) attested to having seen a certain lady in the company of the two Dellow children at the very hour when Master Dellow disappeared. From such information, the child's uncle went to No. 7 Trafalgar Place, where he found a lady whose visage and deportment answered to the description given by witnesses. Indeed, when this lady was brought to the Town Hall, young Rebecca Dellow, asked to point out the person who had given her plum cakes and who had stolen her brother away, pointed without hesitation to the lady in question. Yet here, as it would soon appear, the investigation had taken a false turn, for when this lady was sent to trial at the Old Bailey, it quickly transpired that the memories of the witnesses were mistaken, and that the accused was a respectable person of impeccable character. Moreover, the law as it existed at this time possessed no remedy for the crime of child-stealing, so the suspect could only be tried on the charge of stealing Master Dellow's clothing, of which she was found to be innocent.

But what of the child himself? His loving parents were perhaps close to despair when, a full year after his mysterious disappearance, a wholly unexpected development occurred. A citizen of Gosport, having chanced to read the hand bill which described certain identifying marks upon Master Dellow's body, recognized him as being the boy whom one Mrs Harriet Magnis, the wife of a Gosport sailor, was claiming as her own son. The case by now had made an immense sensation in the metropolis, and this sensation was only heightened when the circumstances of Mrs Magnis's crime were revealed.

It appeared that, while her credulous husband Richard Magnis was away on one of his long voyages, the artful wife had sought to extract money from his savings by persuading him (through her letters) that she was with child, and that a long hoped-for first born offspring would soon be born. The ruse was well planned, and Richard Magnis generously sent his wife a sum of no less than 300 pounds in preparation for the happy event. Compounding the deception, Mrs Magnis next announced to her spouse that his first born son had indeed arrived in the world. All this while, Richard Magnis remained at sea, and even upon his homecoming, the innocent husband was persuaded to believe that his infant son was alive and well, and merely temporarily absent, having been sent away with a nurse for his health. At length, however, the deception became impossible to sustain, and so Mrs Magnis betook herself to London in search of a likely child. It was the misfortune of the Dellow family that her eye fell upon their son Thomas, who was spirited away to Gosport and disguised as the child of Harriet and Richard Magnis.

Happily, his discovery by the sharp-eyed acquaintance resulted in his being returned, unharmed, to the bosom of his own family. But once again the weakness of the law was made clear. Harriet Magnis was committed to Winchester Gaol on the charge of having stolen Master Dellow's clothing, but escaped even the small punishment that this charge would have incurred, because her counsel protested that, the crime having been committed in London, her incarceration in Winchester was unlawful.

The public anger which this case provoked led to the passing of new laws, allowing the prosecution of child-stealers, and these were soon put to use, for

> in October 1814 (a mere half-year after the new laws had reached the statute book) another heinous crime occurred which was remarkable for its similarities to the case of Thomas Dellow. This time the victim was a poor woman by the name of Catherine Creamer of Swan's Court, Cowheel Alley in Golden Lane *['Ah ha, here she is', exclaims Raphael, 'here is Catherine Creamer.']* who was begging in St. Paul's churchyard with her infant twins in her arms, when she was approached by a woman who lured her away with promises of money, and then seized one of the two babies from its mother's arms. Once again, the issuing of hand bills led to the discovery of the miscreant, and once again the child-thief proved to be the wife of a gullible common sailor, whose vessel was moored upon the Thames. But in this case justice prevailed, and the offender, one Sarah Stone, was sentenced to seven years' transportation.

Raphael falls silent for a while, and then says, 'That is it. I remember this story clearly now. This was much talked of at the time, this story of Catherine Creamer and Sarah Stone.'

But Adah, disconcerted by the abrupt end to the story, can only seize upon the word 'twins.' 'Twins. Of course. Why did I not see this at once? Not a ghost but a twin.'

THE CHILD'S STORY

December 1821

MAMMA WAS ILL. SHE sat propped up in the big bed, her hands moving restlessly on the surface of the grey silk counterpane. Her hair, falling loose around her shoulders, had lost its shine. Her cheekbones protruded above her sunken cheeks, flushed with a strange colour.

'Come closer, little Grazia,' she said softly to the child. 'Let Mamma touch your hair.'

But the child was afraid, and as she slowly approached, Mamma was seized with a fit of coughing, and turned her head away.

Sully took the child firmly by the shoulders. 'Come away, dear,' she said. 'Mamma must rest now.'

The house, always quiet, seemed more silent than ever now. The child walked from one room to the other. She sat in the scullery and played at being a mouse. Then she wandered into the sitting room, where the fire was dead in the grate, but the golden clock still ticked on regardless, chiming the quarter hours. She looked through the long windows into the garden. She would have liked to go out, but the rain was falling as though it would never stop. The last time she walked down the pebble path and through the green gate at the far end, she had seen how the river below had grown swollen and brown, swallowing up the meadows on either bank.

The child heard the sound of a carriage in the driveway, and a sharp tap at the front door, then Sully's rapid footsteps, and the sound of subdued voices.

'She's no better, Doctor,' said Sully, 'I am glad you came. I'm so afraid …'

The child picked up the big shell on top of the cabinet and held it to her ear. The roaring sounded louder than ever, not like the sea but like the sound of an angry river in flood. There was a fine bluish layer of dust on the top of the black lacquer cabinet, and when she put the shell back in its place, little filaments of dust drifted up into the still air.

After the doctor had left, the child waited to see if Sully would come to find her. She was feeling hungry. The golden clock chimed one o'clock, but no-one came. She walked softly up the curving staircase and stood outside the closed door of Mamma's bedroom. She could hear low voices inside, but could not hear what they were saying.

She was about to turn away when Sully's voice behind the closed door suddenly cried out, 'No! No! I cannot do it!'

She had never heard Sully speak to Mamma like that before.

'You must,' said Mamma, firmly but more quietly. 'You must try to find her. It's the only way.'

Suddenly frightened, the child ran down the stairs and back into the sitting room. She pressed her hands and face against the cool black surface of the cabinet. She ran her fingers over the objects on its surface. The painted Indian elephant gazed at her patiently with unwinking eyes. She picked up the white jade button engraved with its writhing dragon, took it to the window seat, and curled herself, as small as she could, into one corner behind the heavy brocade curtain, gazing out at the rain that swept in waves through the branches of the leafless trees beyond. A robin landed on a branch just outside the window, puffing its body to shake the rain from its feathers, and then flew away and disappeared over the garden wall.

'We're going in a carriage,' said Sully, first thing the next morning. 'You'd like to go on a carriage, wouldn't you? You've never been in a horse carriage before, have you? At least, not that you'd remember.'

They were in the child's bedroom, putting clothes into a portmanteau. The child picked up the white dress with the stiff lace collar, but Sully shook her head. 'That's too small for you now, dear. Besides, it will never fit in the bag. We'll have enough difficulty shutting it as it is.'

There was something wrong with Sully's face. It had gone a red blotchy colour, and her voice sounded strange, the way it sometimes did when she had a fit of sneezing.

The child had tucked the jade button into the waist of her petticoat. She could feel its round surface pressing into the skin of her stomach. It was uncomfortable, but comforting at the same time. Only she knew that it was there.

'Go and say your goodbye to Mamma, dear,' said Sully. 'We'll take a little journey, so you won't be seeing her for a wee while.'

This time, Sully didn't go with her into Mamma's room. The room smelled of medicine and something strange, and the curtains were drawn. Mamma's eyes were closed at first, so the child waited by the bed in the half-dark room, uncertain whether to speak. She touched the grey silk counterpane very cautiously, feeling its coolness. There was a big porcelain jug beside Mamma's bed, and a cup with dark liquid in it. Then Mamma's eyelids flickered, and her eyes opened just a little, as though she were still half asleep. She didn't raise her head, but her hands fluttered on the silk bedspread like butterflies. Mamma was smiling.

'Luce della mia vita. Luce della mia vita,' *said Mamma.*

'Goodbye, Mamma,' said the child.

It was warm inside the carriage. Sully and the child had a fur rug wrapped around their legs. The seats of the carriage were made of red leather, shiny and cracked with age. There were two horses, one dappled grey, and the other the colour of ginger biscuits. The child liked the ginger horse better. She liked the way it tossed its head, making the harness jingle. At first she looked out of the window at the tall houses and the bare leafless trees on either side of the road and the glimpses of the river beyond, but soon the creaking and rocking of the carriage made her feel sleepy. She dreamed that she was being held in someone's arms, and the person holding her was running. Her body was rocked back and forth, faster and faster, and as they whirled round a corner in the street, they came face to face with an elephant, which winked at them …

It was the coachman's voice that woke her.

'That's the start of Golden Lane market,' he barked, glancing back over his shoulder at his passengers. 'That's as close as I can take you. You'll have to find the rest of the way on foot.'

Golden Lane. The name sounded full of light, but when the coachman opened the door of the carriage to let them alight, the child felt the blast of cold wind outside, and did not want to go out into the strange noisy street where nothing seemed to be made of gold.

'Come along, my dear,' said Sully. 'Wake up. Down you come. Help me carry the bag.'

Outside in the street, everything was grey and icy, and the world swirled around her like an eddy in the river. There was roaring and shouting and banging and clattering. A cart pulled by huge black dray horses thundered past, laden with barrels. The ground was littered with horse dung and cabbage leaves. There were people everywhere. Strange people. Staring people.

People shouting, 'Mind out of my way there!'

'Who'll buy my fine apples?'

'George! George! What you got in that sack of yours?'

'Twelfth-day cakes! Buy my twelfth-day cakes'.

Wherever she looked, there were people and houses and walls and doors. An ancient crone with a black bonnet and a withered hand sat grinning in a doorway. Cows were mooing and milk-churns clanging in a dairy, where the sickly smell of warm milk mingled with the smells of dung and yeast and soot from a hundred chimneys. Through the window of the building next door, the child could see a pinch-faced tailor with his mouth full of pins, staring at an armless, half made jacket. The armless jacket seemed as maimed and frightening as the black-bonneted crone. Until now, the child had known only the stillness of the house and the garden, and of the quiet evening walks along the lane through the woods. This world of Golden Lane seemed more terrifying than any tale of dark magic from a storybook.

'Hold my hand tight,' said Sully.

The child wanted to close her eyes, but she had to keep them open to watch the ground she was walking on. They passed a dead rat, with something spilling out of its stomach, dark red like patterns on the carpet in Mamma's parlour.

'Can you tell me the way to Cowheel Alley?' said Sully to a passing woman carrying a basket full of chickens. The woman jerked her free thumb in the general direction of the dairy, and then spat into the dirt at their feet.

Round behind the dairy, the streets grew narrow. Bricked up windows stared blindly into the alleyway.

'Wait here just a moment,' said Sully, letting go of the child's hand. 'I won't be two minutes.'

The child's mouth was dry with horror. She wanted to say, 'Don't leave me,' but no sound came out.

Three children were squatting by the side of the alleyway, throwing something like small handfuls of pebbles into the air and watching them fall on the ground. As Sully hurried off through a narrow archway into the courtyard beyond, all three looked up and stared at the child with strange expressions on their faces.

The child closed her eyes and put her hands over her ears to shut out the world with all its sights and sounds. She thought about the dragon button, pressed against her skin under the band of her petticoat. She waited, staring at the darkness behind her own eyelids, for what seemed like eternity.

Then a hand tapped her softly on the shoulder, and she turned her head.

And opened her eyes. And saw that her imaginings were reality, and her dreams had become flesh.

ADAH'S STORY

March 1822
Golden Lane

She chops the turnips hastily into rather clumsy chunks and throws them into the big cauldron of soup for their supper. The fire is burning strongly in the hearth, and she has brought in a scuttle of coal from the shed at the back, and scrubbed her hands roughly clean of coal dust. At least the tenement into which they have moved is so small that there's not much cleaning to be done, though it is difficult to find space to hang all the washing, and Adah worries about the grey mouldy marks that keep appearing on the back wall. She has gulped down her mug of scalding tea too quickly, and can feel a blister of scalded skin forming inside her cheek.

Sally has the croup and is curled up under a blanket, unusually subdued and snivelling.

'Don't go out, Mammy,' she whines.

'I won't be long, my love. Annie, keep an eye on her, will you? I should be back by six or not long after.'

But no sooner has she set out to walk to Golden Lane than Adah finds her way blocked by a diminutive but furiously angry figure. It is the little wizened man who sells fruit and vegetables on the corner of Blossom Street. She has passed him several times, and once (out of sympathy) even bought a string of mouldering onions from him, but has never learnt his name and never seen him standing up before. Today he is on his feet, and she sees that his thin legs are like crooked sticks: one sagging outward at the knee, the other with the lower leg bent as a strange angle. The poor man can barely walk.

His face, usually ashy pale, is now scarlet with rage, and his tufty grey hair stands on end. He is pointing a shaking hand towards the far end of the street.

'That varmint! That wretched thieving urchin!' he yells. 'She's gone and stolen my apples. Catch her! Catch her!'

Adah can just see the blurred shape of a small child who is running at full tilt across the cobbles and has already reached the far end of Blossom Street. There is no-one else around, and the poor man is obviously incapable of running himself, so Adah hitches up her own skirts and sets off in pursuit of the fleeing figure, but has only gone a few dozen yards when she realizes that the chase is futile. The little girl is so quick on her feet that she has disappeared round a corner before her pursuer is a third of the way down the street. Adah can no longer run as fast as she could in her younger days. By the time she gets to the end of Blossom Street, the girl will already have vanished into the thronging crowds on Bishopsgate, or into the maze of alleyways beyond.

But the image of that small fleeing figure remains burned into her brain as she walks slowly and breathlessly back towards the street vendor, who stands, still cursing and shaking his arms in the air, beside his depleted pile of apples. The apple-thief is just the height of the dead child who was brought to the courthouse; just the size of the dark shadow she saw flitting along the nighttime street beneath her bedroom window.

Ever since Raphael read her the stories of Harriet Magnis and Catherine Creamer, one word has preyed incessantly on Adah's mind: *twins*. Not one child, but two. Two children, of just the same age and appearance, who have perhaps run away or been stolen away together. But only one child is dead. If there were two of them, then maybe the other is still out here somewhere, lost, abandoned, terrified, confused.

'You stupid, stupid woman,' Adah berates herself silently, as she straightens her skirt and the bonnet that has slipped sideways on her head as she ran. 'To believe in ghosts, at your age.'

It is dreadful to think that the little scratching she heard at the door may have been the sounds, not of a ghoul or ghost, but of a poor lost child, alone in the cold and dark night. But for her own ridiculous fears and superstitions, Adah might have opened the door at once, let the child in, fed and comforted her.

'Call the officers,' yells the street seller, still trembling with anger. 'I'll have her arrested. The varmint. Thieving from a poor man like me. That's the third time she's done it. The last two times it was carrots. Now it's my apples!'

'Just a moment,' says Adah.

She opens the bag she is carrying over one arm and carefully extracts a roll of paper, tied up with a frayed blue ribbon. Unrolling the scroll, which contains Annie's ink sketch of the dead child, she holds it up for the old man to see.

'Is this what she looked like, the girl who stole your carrots and apples?'

The man squints and peers closely at the curling page. His rheumy eyes seem to be almost as blind as his legs are crooked.

'Hmmm,' he mutters. 'Well, her hair's not like that. It's all long and wild, like a little savage. But the face … Maybe. Yes. I think that looks like her … Mouth's not quite right, though.'

Adah carefully rolls up the paper again and returns it to her bag, and turns to set off towards Golden Lane.

'Oy,' shouts the man. 'Where are you going? Call an officer! Arrest that urchin!'

Adah turns back reluctantly, and then fishes in her bag and brings out a threepenny piece which she put on a corner of the poor man's crate.

'Don't worry,' she says. 'I am the Searcher of the Liberty. I'll find that child.'

Adah makes her way along Primrose Street, peering into every corner she passes. Wherever she looks, she half expects to see a face identical to that of the dead girl staring at her from a doorway. But she sees no familiar faces, nor even many children of the right age. Meanwhile, her mind again rehearses the story that has been running through her brain for the past three days. If she tells herself the story over and over again, somehow perhaps the stray pieces will come together, and then everything will begin to make sense. But the pieces never seem to match up. There is always something that doesn't fit. It is not so much that there is a gap in the picture, but rather that there always seems to be one piece too many.

There were two children: Catherine Creamer's twins. One child was stolen by a sailor's wife almost eight years ago, when she was just a baby, but the kidnapper was caught and sent for trial, so surely the baby would have been returned to the Creamer family. Yet Catherine would have endured days, perhaps months, of fear and grief, from the time her baby was stolen to the time it was returned. The memory of that fear and grief could explain the mother's frenzy – her certainty, when it all seemed to be happening again, that her child or children had once more been stolen away, perhaps even by the same miscreant.

Could two identical twins have run away together, or been lured away and then escaped from the clutches of a would-be child stealer, and found themselves lost in an unfamiliar part of town? Could they both have taken shelter in the ruined stables behind Magpie Alley, and then one of them, little Rosie (or perhaps it is not Rosie, but the other still nameless twin) tripped in the dark and struck her head on the stone and died? Might the second twin – confused, frightened, perhaps not even recognizing the sight of death when she saw it – have placed her cloak over the dead child's body to keep her warm? Worse still, might the sounds that Adah heard in the abandoned stables have been the sounds of a child, cowering frightened and confused in the darkness?

If so – oh, the poor living twin! How terrible it would be to have lost her sister, and to find herself alone in this strange world, not knowing where to ask or who to turn to for help. Like a ghost indeed.

It all makes sense. But something does not fit.

The hateful, sneering voice of the innkeeper at the Green Dragon still rings in Adah's ears. She can hear him mimicking Catherine Creamer's voice: 'They've stolen my child again, they've stolen my child again! Take me out to the ship!'

Not 'my children', but 'my child'. If twins had gone missing together, why did Mrs Creamer not say 'my children'? Why only 'my child'? Why speak of 'my little Rosie' and never mention the other twin's name?

Is it possible that little Rosie ran away from home first, and her twin went in search of her after Catherine Creamer herself had already set out on her frenzied quest for her missing child? Yes, that could be it. But when did Rosie go missing? And when did Catherine set out in search of her daughter? Adah curses herself for not having asked more questions in Shadwell, while she had the chance.

The shadows are lengthening as she passes the Artillery Ground, and she can see how the limbs of trees torn down by the winter gales still lie scattered on the grass. But today, for the first time since the start of the year, there is a faint feeling of approaching spring in the air. The sky is clear and dappled with pale clouds, and along the edges of the playing field, the plump green spikes of crocuses and daffodils are pushing their way up through the earth. After the rainy winter, spring will come early this year.

Adah's tongue probes the scalded spot in her mouth, which is not as painful as she thought it was going to be. She quickens her step towards her destination. If there are any answers to be found to her questions, they must lie there, with the surviving members of the Creamer family. She recites the address once more to herself to make sure that it is firmly fixed in her mind: Swan's Court, Cowheel Alley, Golden Lane.

Beyond the Artillery Ground, Adah passes the corner of Bunhill Fields, where William and his parents and grandparents lie buried. But today she is not thinking of them. Instead, she thinks of the small child buried in the unmarked grave in the darkest and outermost corner of the graveyard.

Rosie – is that your name? Or are you the other child, Rosie's twin? Or some other child altogether?

Then she turns into Chiswell Street, and the leaf-shadowed silence of park and graveyard give way to the clamour of the city again. The street is hemmed in by the great soot-streaked walls of the brewery, and Adah's senses are overpowered by the smell of yeast and hops. The air rumbles and reverberates with the roar of the brewery and the clatter of the long line of dray horses pulling their empty drays back into the brewery at the end of the day's deliveries.

By the time she reaches the Golden Lane markets, darkness is starting to fall, and many of the stall-holders are already packing up their wares, but the streets and alleyways are still crowded with people. Adah passes a fortune-teller's stall, where a shabbily-dressed woman and her little son are peering intently at the stall-holder's wheel to see what their future holds. A tinker, his shoulders laden with pots and pans, pushes past, shouting over the clattering and clanging of his wares, 'Who'll buy my saucepans? Last chance for the day!'

Adah stops to ask a boot mender the way to Cowheel Alley. The man scratches his balding pate with a grimy hand and then gestures towards to the end of the lane.

'I'm new here meself so I can't be sure,' he says, in a strong Irish accent, 'but I *think* it's somewhere over yonder, behind the dairy.'

The dairy, with its mooing cows and cloying smell of warm milk, takes Adah's thoughts back to the days of her childhood, when her father would send her out with a pail to fetch milk from the Fulham dairy. She remembers the sense of pride and importance she felt, aged perhaps seven or eight – just the age of that dead child – as she strode down the narrow way between high banks covered with cow-parsley, pail in hand, and as she watched the thick creamy milk froth into the pail, and then solemnly handed the dairyman the penny that her father had tied into a knot in her shawl for safe-keeping.

Behind the Golden Lane dairy, she finds herself in a confusing rabbit-warren of little narrow alleyways, cast deep in shadow by the fading light. Here and there a candle glitters behind a grimy uncurtained window. To her right, on one side of a narrow archway, she can just make out the painted words WAN'S COUR. The first and last letters have been weathered away by the years. Inside the archway is an enclosed cobbled space, its pavement slippery with moss. As Adah enters the courtyard, a door swings open and a woman flings the contents of a pail of slops out onto the cobbles. The windows next door have been boarded up, but beyond, at the far end of Swan's Court, Adah can see a gleam of light behind a partially open window on an upper floor, where washing hangs from a pole above a rickety front door. She goes to the door and hammers on it as loudly as she can, and almost at once, the window above is flung wide open and a woman's face appears in the gloom above.

'What is it?' shouts the woman.

'I'm looking for the Creamer family. I heard they live in this court,' says Adah.

'They do,' replies the woman. 'At least, they did. You won't find them. They're gone.'

'Gone where?' asks Adah.

'Liverpool,' snaps the woman, slamming the window shut.

Adah feels her heart sink: the answer to this mystery is disappearing again into darkness.

Desperately, she hammers on the door once more, shouting up at the window, 'Please! I need to talk to you!'

Rather to her surprise, the window opens again and the woman's head reappears above her.

'What now?' barks the woman.

'Please,' implores Adah. 'I have some very important questions about the Creamer family. I must speak to you.'

There is a loud clack as, without answering, the woman slams the window shut again.

Adah stands on the doorstep, feeling lost. It seems futile to try knocking a third time. A large marmalade cat slinks out from the neighbouring doorway and starts to rub its furry body against Adah's legs, and then to lick her left boot. She is tempted to kick it away, but lacks the heart to do so.

Then suddenly the door swings open, firelight from the room within floods out into the street, and there stands the woman. She has a face as big as a cooked ham, which is surmounted by a wild mass of grey curls, and she is wearing what seems to be a man's greatcoat tied around the waist with a length of red tasselled rope that looks as though it came from a bell-pull.

'You'd best come in. Never mind the mess,' says the woman.

The room inside is indeed one of the untidiest that Adah has ever seen. Every table and chair and spare corner of floor in the cramped space seems to be covered with bulging sacks and piles of ancient clothing of every colour of the rainbow. Perhaps the woman is a rag picker, thinks Adah. There is a slightly rank smell in the air, but the fire is burning brightly in the hearth and a blackened kettle, hung over the flames, is boiling merrily. The woman lifts an armful of clothes from a stool and dumps them unceremoniously onto one of the random piles on the floor.

'Sit down, sit down. Make yourself at home,' she says, 'It's not often I have visitors these days.'

'You must know the Creamer family well, Mrs …' hazards Adah.

'Murray's my name,' says the woman breezily. 'Elizabeth, but you can call me Lizzie. Everyone does. Lord, yes. I've known poor Catherine Creamer for years, ever since we were both newly-weds.'

For an uneasy moment Adah wonders if the woman knows about her neighbour's untimely death, but her doubts are soon allayed, for Lizzie Murray continues with barely a breath, 'Poor Catherine. Drowned in the river I heard. What a terrible end! How can the good Lord send one family so many misfortunes? First little Molly taken away, then little Rosie goes missing, and now Catherine. They may not be angels, them Creamers, but they never deserved this. Catherine, she was never quite right in the head again after her baby Molly was stolen. She kept thinking that child-stealer Sarah Stone was going to come back and snatch her other children. Many's the time I've said to her, "They've sent that Sarah Stone to Botany Bay, where she belongs. She ain't going to come back here no more, dear," but she'd never listen. And then when little Rosie vanished – just before last Christmas it was, when we had all that rain and them floods by the river – well, it seemed like poor Catherine was losing her wits altogether. I said to her, "Just you wait and see. Little Rosie'll be home any day. Run off for a lark, she has, just like my Tom did when he was that age, the rascal." He had me that worried. But sure enough, he was back again two weeks later, my Tom, soon as he started getting cold and hungry. "Your Rosie'll walk right in through that door any day now, you mark my words," I said. But no, Catherine wouldn't listen. Kept saying that the woman who stole little Molly had come back again.'

She pauses for a moment as a fit of coughing robs her of breath, and then continues. 'It was the strangest thing, you know. She kept saying said she'd seen that child-stealer again, right here in the street, the very day little Rosie vanished. "She's come back and stolen our Rosie. It's God's punishment for my sins," she kept saying. "Nonsense, my dear," says I. "You've done no wrong. You're no more a sinner than the rest of us. And that Sarah Stone is ten thousand miles away in the colonies, getting the punishment she deserves." But Catherine was past listening by then. She had to go out to the docks, day after day, hunting for Rosie. But she never found her, did she? Just fell in the river and drowned, God save her. Poor Matthew (that's Catherine's husband, but no doubt you'll know that), well, he was in such despair when he heard the news. Didn't know where to turn. So as soon as they'd laid Catherine in her grave last week, he was off to his family in Liverpool. I said to him, "You should bide here," I said, "Who knows but little Rosie might yet come home looking for you. She doesn't know her own mother's dead, poor dear. You should stay in case she comes home." But he wasn't having none of it. Rosie'd been gone for almost two months by then, and he'd given up hope that she'd come home. As soon as Catherine was buried, he was off to Liverpool where he comes from, taking the other children with him, except the eldest boy, young Matt. He's still about here somewhere, as far as I know, but you'll be lucky to find him. Always was a harum-scarum rascal, that one—'

'Mrs Murray,' Adah breaks into the torrential flow of words. 'I am afraid I am the bearer of bad tidings. My name is Adah Flint, and I am the Searcher of the Liberty of Norton Folgate. We had the body of a dead child brought to our watch-house last month. I fear it may have been the body of little Rosie Creamer.' As she speaks, she bends down to her bag and brings out Annie's portrait of the dead girl. 'This is a likeness of that child. Can you tell me, does this look like Rosie?'

As soon as Lizzie Murray sees the unfurled portrait, she gives a little shriek and, snatching up a ragged apron at random from the pile of clothing nearest to her, holds it to her face.

'Oh dear Lord in heaven! That's Rosie Creamer as ever was! Oh no! Not poor little Rosie too! Brought to the watch-house! Never tell me she was murdered!'

'No, no,' says Adah gently, 'nothing like that. It seems it was just an accident. The poor child had been wandering the streets and sleeping in an old stable, and she tripped and hit her head on a stone. I'm so sorry to distress you, Mrs Murray.'

Tears are running down the other woman's face, and the hand that clutches the tattered apron is shaking.

'Oh my dear Lord! Poor Rosie dead too! What will poor Matthew say when he hears the news?'

'Mrs Murray,' says Adah, 'do you know how I can contact him? Did he leave an address of the place where he has gone?'

But the woman shakes her head, and smears away her tears.

'Liverpool. That's all he said. Didn't leave no address. He never was much of a one for reading or writing, Matthew Creamer. I suppose young Matt, his son, might know where they've gone, but I don't know where he's got to, either. I can speak to them if any of them come back, but God alone knows if they ever will. Oh Lord! It's one tragedy after another. I blame that harlot Sarah Stone for this. If she hadn't stolen little Molly, all them years back, none of this would have happened. They should have hanged her, if you ask me, or worse. The gallows was too good for the likes of her. They hang 'em for stealing a chicken or a silk handkerchief, don't they? Why don't they hang 'em for stealing a child?'

Lizzie is seized again with a fit of weeping that gives way to wracking coughs.

Adah waits for a moment or two for the wave of grief to subside, and then asks, 'Mrs Murray, can you tell me about the infant who was stolen? Little Molly. She was Rosie's twin, wasn't she? Were you here at the time when she was stolen?'

'Oh heavens, yes,' replies Lizzie, 'I was here that very day. I'll never forget it. Out in the street, I was, looking for my eldest, Tom, who was up to some mischief again. I saw poor Catherine walk into the lane that very morning with her two little twin babies in her arms. Such bonny babes, they were, little Molly and little Rosie: very alike except Molly was a bit bigger than her twin, and her hair a bit paler and thicker. Just three or four weeks old, the pair of them. And Susannah,

Catherine's older girl, was with them too. Four or five years old she would have been at the time; little Susannah, running along behind them. Well, poor Matthew Creamer, he was down on his luck that year. Hadn't had no work for weeks, and had gone off north for a few weeks to look for a job. And Catherine had all them mouths to feed. Twins had come as a shock, of course. She hadn't expected two new mouths at once. So she'd been going out begging. Some days she'd come back with next to nothing, but some days she'd been down to St. Paul's Cathedral and sat on the steps there, and the people going in and out had given her a shilling or more. "I'm off to St. Paul's again, Lizzie," she said that day.'

'Do you remember exactly when all this happened?' asks Adah.

'Well, I couldn't tell you the day or the month. Autumn it was, seven or more years ago. But I'll tell you what I do remember. It was just around the time they had that great beer flood. You'll remember that, surely? When that great barrel of beer burst open down Tottenham Court way, and all them people was out in the streets scooping up the beer in their pails and buckets. Just before that beer flood, it was. Well, I saw Catherine go out with the children, and later that day – I remember it was getting dark – I said to my Tom, "That's funny," I said, "I ain't seen Catherine come home yet. Wonder why she's so late." Well, not long after that she comes home in a terrible state. Crying and shaking, and little Susannah crying too, and the one baby in her arms, little Rosie, bawling fit to wake the dead, but little Molly nowhere to be seen. "She's stolen my Molly! She's stolen my Molly!" says Catherine. "Who's stolen Molly?" I asks, and she tells me the story. Dreadful, it was. You wouldn't believe such things could happen in broad daylight—'

Lizzie Murray suddenly breaks off, as a thought strikes her.

'Wait,' she says. 'I've got something to show you. The magistrate gave them to Catherine, after the trial was over, and Catherine gave one to me. I've got it somewhere here, I'm sure, if I can lay my hands on it.'

She disappears into a corner of the room and rummages about in one of the piles of belongings. Adah hears the clatter of falling saucepans and muffled curses, and then Lizzie Murray appears again, proudly bearing a tattered scroll of paper.

'I can't read them long words too well myself, but this'll tell you all about it,' she says.

The corners of the hand bill are dog-eared, and a large stain of uncertain origin covers a section of the print, but the words are still clearly visible in the flicking firelight that fills the room.

Adah holds the paper to the light and reads:

20 POUNDS REWARD

Whereas about 3 o'clock on the AFTERNOON of Friday last, the heinous crime of child-stealing was perpetrated by a female in the Commercial Road, who Feloniously Kidnapped and Stole away the infant daughter of one Catherine Creamer, wife of Matthew Creamer, labourer – whoever may give such information as may lead to the apprehension and conviction of the said felon shall receive a Reward of Twenty Pounds from the Lambeth-Street Magistrates office.
NB – The female in Question, who first accosted the victim in St. Paul's Churchyard and lured her to the Commercial Road on False Pretences, was about Forty Years of Age, dark, with a pockmarked visage, and had on a Red Spotted Gown, a White Shawl and a Black Bonnet.

17 October 1814

* * * * *

John W. Nelson, printer, Whitechapel

CATHERINE CREAMER'S STORY

'It was the rummest tale you'll ever hear,' says Lizzie Murray, as Adah peruses the hand bill, 'and I was there when Catherine told it to her Matthew. We was the first to hear it, except for the magistrates. She'd been sitting in front of St. Paul's, she said, and it was a gloomy, windy day, not many people about, so her begging bowl was empty. Then along comes this woman and drops a shining new penny into the bowl. Well, Catherine was so surprised, because this weren't no grand lady, she said, just a commonish looking woman. Then this woman starts speaking to Catherine, all sweet and friendly like. "Such a cold day to be sitting in the street begging. How are you going to feed your bonny babies with hardly a penny in your bowl?" Sweet words like that. Then this strange woman starts to spin a yarn about how she knows a fine lady who lives in a big house with a garden and just loves little children, and if this fine lady could see Catherine and her bonny babies, she'd be sure to give them money enough to buy strawberries and cream for a year. "No point sitting here in the cold," she says to Catherine, "why don't I take you to meet this kind lady in her fine house?" Well, Catherine'd never heard such a story before, but she thinks, it can't do no harm. So off she goes with the stranger, carrying both the twins in her arms, with little Susannah running along behind, and they walk and walk, right through Leadenhall Market and down towards Whitechapel way—'

'Didn't Catherine ask the woman her name?' interjects Adah.

'She did, she did, and the woman gave her some name or other, but then what with all the confusion that happened after, she'd forgotten it. And anyway, everything that child-stealer said was just a pack of lies. Then, when they got to somewhere around the start of the Commercial Road, says Catherine, her arms was aching from carrying the twins and the wind was blowing her cloak off, so this stranger offered to carry little Molly for her. By then the older child Susannah was getting tired and starting to whine, so the woman says to Catherine, "Look, here's an inn. Why don't we sit a while and have something to drink? Don't you worry, I have the money to pay for it." Well, Catherine didn't want no drink. She wanted to meet this fine lady and show her the twins and find out how much money the lady would give her. And now she's starting to feel there's something odd about this woman and her fancy yarns. Then they walk on a little further, and the woman says, "Wait here a moment. I'll be back in no time," and she turns down one of them lanes behind the Commercial Road. Well, Catherine had her suspicions by then, and she weren't about to let this woman out of her sight, so she starts to follow her down the alleyway. They was building all new houses along that road back then, and there was bricks and wood and piles of dirt everywhere, and they hadn't gone far down the lane when little Susannah trips over a pile of bricks and grazes her knee and starts howling. So of course Catherine turns round to comfort her, and when she looks up, that evil woman has gone! Run off with baby Molly, she has, just like that! Of course, Catherine sets up a hue and cry and goes running after her, but the woman's nowhere to be seen. So poor Catherine, she's screaming and crying and yelling, and she goes running back to the inn on the main road and calls out for the men in there to come and help her search for her baby. But by then it was too late. That child snatcher's run off with the baby and vanished into thin air. So in the end, one of them men took poor Catherine and the two little ones to the Lambeth Street Magistrates Office. The magistrates were proper gentlemen, Catherine said. Gave her and Susannah milk to drink, and sent out the officers to hunt for little Molly. But of course they couldn't find her—'

'Mrs Murray,' interjects Adah, 'would you let me borrow a copy of this hand bill, just for a week or two? I can promise to return it to you. By the by,' she adds, 'who had the hand bills made up? It must have cost a pretty penny to have them printed.'

'Lord, yes,' replies Lizzie, 'you can keep *that* for good. What use would I have for it now they're all gone? It was the magistrates what had them hand bills made. She was taken to see the chief magistrate himself. Sir Daniel, he was called, so Catherine said. He told her how there'd been this other child stolen away to Gosport by that wicked woman Harriet Magnis, and how the magistrates had printed hand bills, and brought that little boy back. "It's a piece of luck for you that they've made a crime of child stealing now," he said to Catherine. "No-one's going to get away with that crime again, like Harriet Magnis did. We'll find your Molly, even if we have to hunt the length and breadth of England for her."'

Sir Daniel, notes Adah. This woman may be strange and garrulous, but she seems to know her story well; for the chief magistrate at Lambeth-Street is indeed a Sir Daniel. She remembers William speaking of him rather sourly, and also (unusually for William) with a faint note of fear.

'But it was a whole six weeks before they found little Molly,' Lizzie Murray continues. 'It seemed like everyone in London was talking about the crime. We had all sorts wandering into the yard and asking questions. Somehow they'd found out Catherine's address, and they all wanted to come and see the poor woman whose child had been stolen away, just like that little boy what Harriet Magnis stole. And all that while Catherine was in despair, crying every day, and not sleeping at night, thinking she'd never see her baby again. In the end, when they found her, that poor little babe was on a ship in the Thames where she'd been taken by this wicked sailor's whore. They took Catherine out to the ship, and of course, the moment she saw little Molly, she knew her, and knew the woman who'd stolen her too. But by that time – six weeks to the day after Molly was stolen, it was – well, by then the poor baby was no more than skin and bones.'

'But they brought her home safe and arrested her kidnapper, did they not?' says Adah. 'So where is little Molly now?'

Elizabeth Murray is frozen into sudden silence. She stares at Adah, her mouth half open, as though she suspects the Searcher of having taken leave of her senses.

'Good Lord! What a question!' she says at last. 'Little Molly's dead, of course.'

'Dead?' says Adah. 'But, when did she die?'

'I thought you knew,' says Lizzie Murray. 'She died back then. A couple of months after she was stolen.'

Now it is Adah's turn to be dumbstruck.

'I … I don't understand,' she stammers.

'They brought her home,' says Lizzie, 'but not safe and sound. Like I said, she weren't nothing but skin and bones when they found her. That whore Sarah Stone pretended it was her baby. Trying to cheat her stupid sailor husband, just like Harriet Magnis did. Except that Sarah Stone and her sailor weren't even married. It all came out at the trial. They were living like man and wife but they were living in sin. She told all her family she was having a baby, but she was lying, of course. So she didn't have no milk, did she? Hadn't fed that poor baby proper. That Molly, she was such a bonny little thing when she was stolen, but when Catherine got her back, she was already half wasted away, and her lovely hair all thin and patchy. We tried everything to bring her health back, Catherine and me. Got her cow's milk from the dairy, and made her pap. And of course Catherine still had her milk. Her twins was only two months old. But poor little Molly wouldn't take the breast no more. She just faded away. She was dead already before that Sarah Stone was sent for trial. I was there in the room when that poor baby died in her mother's arms. They buried her right here in the Golden Lane burial ground, but you won't find the grave now. It's all overgrown. Them Creamers never could afford no headstone. That's why I say they should have hanged that Sarah Stone. She weren't no better than a murderess. Caused little Molly's death as surely as if she'd killed that poor baby with her own hands. And now her poor twin dead too …'

The tears well up in Lizzie's eyes again, and she wipes them away with the back of one big hand.

'But what am I thinking of,' she continues, gulping back the tears, 'not offering you a morsel to eat or drink, when you've come all this way from Norton Folgate. There's not much food in the house, but I think I've got a twist of tea somewhere, and the kettle's boiling. Would you take a cup of tea?'

'No, thank you,' replies Adah. 'I must be getting home. If any of the Creamers come back, you can contact me through the Norton Folgate courthouse. The officers there know where to find me.'

She rises from her uncomfortable seat on the stool and is about to say her farewells when a thought strikes her, and she opens her bag again, and brings out the little jade button, with its curling outline of a dragon, and holds it out on her hand for Lizzie Murray to look at.

'Have you, by chance, ever seen this before?'

But the other woman only shakes her head. 'Never seen anything like it in all me born days,' she says.

Adah has hardly ever travelled in a Hackney carriage before, and can barely afford to hail one this evening. But as she leaves Golden Lane market, the church bells are tolling seven, and she thinks of Sally lying sick and fretful in bed, and of her other children waiting hungrily for their supper.

Besides, she has suddenly been overcome by a strange dizziness. She hails a passing cab and sinks gratefully into its seat.

The lamps are flaring brightly outside the gates of the debtor's prison as they clatter past. With the coming of darkness, the air has suddenly grown very cold.

I should be relieved, thinks Adah. I have found the answer to my search. I know the dead child's name: Rosie Creamer. It's a sad and strange story, but my part in it is complete. A story of family tragedies: first the baby Molly stolen, and returned half-starved a month later, only to die in her mother's arms. Then the surviving twin Rosie, barely seven years old, goes missing. Then Catherine herself dies in the frenzied search for her daughter. At least Catherine's death has saved me the terrible task of having to tell her of her daughter's death. As soon as the thought enters her head, Adah chides herself for her selfishness.

As the carriage jolts through the dark streets, she remembers the words of the Rabbi Meldola: 'Our mortal minds may play tricks on us, but tricks have their own meaning. It is for us to discover that meaning.' Rosie's twin Molly is long dead. The scratching Adah had heard at the door of the courthouse was probably just a cat. The dark shadow she glimpsed in the street was surely just a shadow. The ghost that Jonah Hall saw was doubtless only a vision created by his drunken brain. The little girl who stole the poor man's apples must simply have been an urchin whose face happened to look a little like Rosie Creamer's.

But however hard she tries to suppress them, Adah Flint cannot banish those other words of the Rabbi's. What were they? 'We do indeed believe that troubled spirits walk at dead of night, and that we would be wise to be aware of them, and guard against their influence.' There is a chilling vision that arises unbidden from somewhere deep in her mind, and closes like a hand around her heart: a vision of the ghost of the dead baby Molly Creamer, growing silently and invisibly alongside the living child Rosie, watching over her sister like a small guardian spirit, following her invisibly as she wandered lost through the streets of the city, and, in the end, stepping out like a shadow from the darkness of the ruined stable, to cover the body of her twin with a small black cloak.

PART TWO

SARAH STONE

January 1815
The Verdict

On 11 January 1815, the day of her trial, Sarah Stone stands in the dock of the Old Bailey, looking down at her hands, which clutch the polished wooden rail in front of her for support. In the weeks that she has been in Newgate Prison, her hands have changed. Her nails have grown long, and then been roughly hacked back with a knife by the fat, lardy wards-woman whom everyone calls 'Queen Charlotte.' Her fingers have turned purplish and blotchy. A patch of white skin is peeling from one knuckle of her right hand. Her hands no longer belong to her. Her limbs seem to be floating away from the rest of her body. As she listens to one witness after another talking about her to the judge, never turning their faces in her direction, she gazes at her own life from the outside. She has become a stranger to herself, a woman in someone else's story: I am no longer 'I', 'myself'. I am 'that woman, Sarah Stone.'

The men in the front row of the jury benches have twisted their torsos around to engage in heated debate with their fellow jurors in the back row. Sarah watches them intently but dispassionately. One thin, balding man in the back row bends forward repeatedly to argue with the jury foreman, from time to time vigorously shaking his head. The juror at the far end of the bench, meanwhile – a ginger-haired fellow in an ill-fitting brown jacket – seems to take no part in the discussions at all. Instead, he nervously jiggles his feet and glances repeatedly over his shoulder, as though searching for a familiar face in the crowd.

When she lifts her head and looks straight in front of her, Sarah finds herself gazing into a long mirror on the opposite side of the courtroom, which reflects the glaring white wintery light that shines through the big windows on every side. In the middle of the mirror stands a woman with dark hair and a greyish pock marked face, dressed in a grey prison gown, staring back at her: that woman, Sarah Stone.

At length the argumentative juror falls silent, and slumps back into his seat. The clamour of voices from the crowded courtroom gradually subsides into a silence full of anticipation. The jury foreman rises to his feet. He is a solidly built man with a soft, sagging face and a head of silver hair which shines as though it has been oiled and polished. A draper, perhaps, or a wine merchant.

'Have you agreed upon your verdict?' barks the judge. He seems incensed that it has taken the jury a full twenty minutes to make up their minds.

'We have, your Honour.'

'Do you find the accused, Sarah Stone, guilty or not guilty of the crime of child-stealing?'

The foreman opens his mouth to speak, but as he does so, a large black fly lands on his forehead, and he pulls out a handkerchief to brush it away. Watching the plump, beringed hand that clutches the handkerchief, Sarah knows with perfect certainty what he is going to say.

'Guilty, your Honour.'

The court erupts into a roar of applause, and the foreman sits down abruptly and sneezes into the handkerchief. Amid the gleeful, grinning faces and the waving fists, Sarah can see her mother, her head bowed, face hidden in her hands, shoulders shaking. Next to her sits Ned, silent, staring down at his boots. Sarah wills him to look up at her, but he does not move.

The judge's voice is addressing her, but from somewhere that seems to be a great distance away.

'… you have been found guilty of the heinous crime of child-stealing. There can be few acts more cruel than to deprive an innocent mother of her child. Moreover, your own wicked actions, carried out for personal gain, have led to the death of this infant. If I were able to impose a severer sentence upon you I would happily do so, but the law, alas, allows me only to impose a maximum sentence of seven years' transportation. I therefore hereby impose that maximum sentence upon you, and order that you be transported to the colonies for a term of seven years. Guards, take the prisoner down.'

Hands grip her arms on either side. Sarah does not bother to look at the people who are half pushing, half carrying her down the wooden steps from the dock. Instead, she watches herself as though from far away – a small figure in a grey gown being dragged down a stairway, through the arched door from the glittering brightness of the courtroom into the gloom below, from where the stench of the underworld rises up to greet the world above.

As she passes through the archway that leads down towards the bowels of the building, she hears a woman's voice from the courtroom behind her, shouting over the hubbub of the crowd, 'Hang the whore! You should hang the whore!' And then the approving roar of other voices.

The words mean nothing. The roar means nothing. The word 'guilty' is as empty of meaning as the cry of an owl or the bark of a dog. She has heard only one word of the hundreds spoken in the courtroom. Only one word remains, echoing in her head as the gripping hands march her over the slippery flagstones of the passageway, under the iron grill of the birdcage back to Newgate Prison.

One word. 'Dead.' Dead, they said.

The woman Catherine Creamer said it first; lifting her gaunt tear-streaked face and pushing back a strand of her long greasy hair, she looked across at the judge and wailed, 'She's dead. Our Molly died last week.' And then again as he summed up the case and sentenced Sarah, the judge had said it again, but quite coldly and indifferently: 'the death of the infant.' The infant is dead.

At first it all seemed like a dream, or perhaps like one of those slightly cruel japes that Ned's younger brother liked to play on people – tying the laces of visitor's boots together or, on one occasion, putting a weasel he had caught in the laundry basket, so that Sarah's mother, when she went to fetch the clothes for washing, was confronted with a snarling furry face with devilish eyes, and linen covered with weasel droppings.

Surely this too – this mad world of prison walls, of insults and blows and angry faces – is just a cruel joke, or a bad dream.

But perhaps the madness is inside her own head, not in the world around her.

When she was about eleven or twelve years old, Sarah was terrified of her uncle, Josiah. In her earliest memories, Uncle Josiah, with his bulbous red nose and whiskery chops, seemed like a benign and slightly clownish figure, always ready to play games with the children and give the little ones horse-rides on his shoulders, even though Sarah and her sisters did notice that his breath often smelled of gin and he tended to be clumsy, breaking crockery and dropping his knife and fork on the floor. But then one night, coming home late from the inn, Uncle Josiah was knocked down by a post chaise, and lay for two days between life and death. He appeared to recover, but after that his games became stranger, more fevered and alarming. He took to covering his head with the coal scuttle and announcing that he was King George, and he would fly into a fit of anger if anyone laughed or contradicted him.

A little later, the officers came and took him away to Bedlam, with the sleeves of his jacket tied in a knot in front of him. And after he was gone, Sarah was filled with fear that his madness had somehow infected her, and that the world she thought was real was just a dream world like Uncle Josiah's fantasy kingdom.

Now that icy fear has seeped back into her heart.

Sometimes still, although she tries to push them away, memories return of the oddly beautiful late autumn morning last year when she went with her mother and the infant to St. Leonard's to be churched. It was the first time she had been out of doors since the baby arrived, and, if she allows herself to do so, she can still recall how fresh and sweet the air felt on her face when she stepped out into the street. The morning was cold. A skin of ice covered the puddles, and frost glittered on the cobwebs that hung like bridal veils over the hawthorn bushes in the churchyard. The child nestled snugly asleep in her arms, wisps of hair like dark silk just visible beneath the lace of the miniature bonnet that her mother had sewed, and one tiny fist with dimpled knuckles protruded from the folds of a blanket. The sky was high above, and the future seemed full of light …

But perhaps that memory too is no memory, only a madwoman's dream. Her head seems so full of clouds that she can no longer be sure. Even Ned has begun to doubt her. When the officers first took her away to Newgate, Ned was full of confident anger, shouting after them, 'She's done nothing wrong. There'll be the devil to pay for this! Never fear, Sarah, you'll soon be free.'

But when he visited her in prison three weeks later, his manner was changed. His words were still kind, and he managed quietly to press a half-crown into her hand, enough to buy beer and some clean cotton cloth from the turnkey. But he refused to meet her eye, and she could see in his face confusion and horror at the crowded prison yard with its stench of un-emptied chamber pots and its rabble of women who reached through the iron bars of the visitors' enclosure, plucking at his clothes, trying to thrust their hands into his pockets, and lewdly joking and nudging one another all the while.

He stayed only for a few minutes, and has not come back since.

Sarah cannot help envying Eliza Dee, the strange tall woman who dresses in grimy sailor's breeches and a man's jacket, and is accused of hitting her brother-in-law on the side of the head with a skillet, rendering him partly deaf in one ear: an event about which Eliza's only comment is 'he deserved it.' Eliza is visited every Monday by her mother, a wizened bird of a woman with a halo of white hair under her lace cap and piercing blue eyes. Eliza's mother always carries a covered basket over one arm, from which she produces an array of wonders to be squeezed though the bars into her daughter's waiting hands – freshly baked rolls, apples, and once a wad of chewing tobacco and a pack of cards. Although she does not like to ask, Sarah feels sure that Eliza Dee's mother must have spent time in prison too. The old woman seems so comfortably at ease in the surroundings of Newgate, always knowing just when to slip a coin into the turnkey's waiting hand. Sarah's mother has never visited, which, in a way, is a blessing. The very thought of the tears and hand-wringings that would ensue seems too much to bear.

After Ned's one unhappy visit, until the time of the trial, Sarah's refuge was to stand in a corner near the narrow window which looked out into the prison yard and the visitors' enclosure beyond. From there she could see the tradesmen coming in the morning with their pails of milk and bundles of firewood, and sometimes, surprisingly grand gentlemen in satin waistcoats or ladies with fine feathers in their bonnets, who would arrive to inspect the prison, all with their faces stern and their noses lifted resolutely away from the squalor around them. Some of the other women in Sarah's cell would squeeze their skinny arms through the windows or the barred doorways, snatching at the sleeves of the passing visitors and whining, 'Give a poor woman a penny, ladies! I'm as innocent as the babe unborn.'

But Sarah only watched the procession of passing faces, and when the visitors had gone, she watched the sparrows and pigeons pecking for crumbs between the grimy cobble stones, and the bony, sly black cat that sat, poised and taut, in a patch of shadow, waiting for unwary sparrows that strayed too close.

Once, as she was gazing out of the barred window, Sarah felt the touch of a hand on her leg, and looked down in surprise. It was Tom, the small son of Catherine Wells, accused of jewel theft. Little Tom, who spent his days crawling at will amongst the prisoners in the ward, receiving treats and curses as they came, had crept close to her, and was touching her leg and gazing up at her with wide blue eyes and a bewitching smile on his grimy face.

'Hello, young Tom,' whispered Sarah, 'have you come to watch the birds? Shall I lift you up to look at them?'

The blow from Tom's mother's fist that struck her as she bent down towards the child sent Sarah sprawling on the floor, her ears ringing so that she could hardly hear the shouted words that followed.

'Keep your thieving hands away from my boy, child snatcher!'

After that, Sarah stayed away from the children, and spoke only silently in her head to the cat and the birds, and to herself. 'Innocent,' she whispered. 'I am innocent.' But neither the cat nor the birds seemed to pay the least attention, and the more she said it, the fainter and more uncertain the voice in her head became.

The time for her trial came, and then passed. They said there had been some delay. The prosecution needed more time to make their case. For a moment, a narrow window of hope opened. If they found her innocent, then the memories of that frosty morning in St. Leonard's courtyard could become memories again, and she would again feel the warm weight of the child in her arms, and smell the milky sweet smell of the infant's breath …

But now in a new cell – the ward for the convicted women – Sarah makes her home as far away from the window as she can, in the darkest corner of the room. She is guilty; and the infant is dead. Her memories are the dreams of a madwoman.

The lower parts of the wall, at which she gazes for much of the day, are green with a mossy growth. The damp that runs down in sluggish trickles has made streaks which sometimes look like the outlines of ghostly trees. In one place, about a foot above the floor, some long-vanished inmate has laboriously and unevenly carved the letters 'forg' into the wall.

forg. Is it part of a name? Or a message, unfinished because the carver was interrupted before she could complete her task? And if so, what was the message? *Forgery*? *Forget*? *Forgive me*?'

The letters have been hacked into the thick decaying plaster of the wall so deeply that they are still clearly visible, particularly when a faint beam of morning light slants through the grills of the cell and falls on them, even though the slimy green moss has crept into their crevasses too.

How long ago were they carved? Ten years ago? Twenty? And what has become of the woman who carved them? And all those other women too. Sometimes she thinks of them: that long procession of women who have passed through this room over the years, to the gallows, to Van Diemen's Land, to God knows where …

At night, Sarah lies with her face towards the wall on which the letters are carved. Just a few inches behind her back, Eliza Dee, who sleeps next to her, snores loudly, from time to time waking with a sudden curse, or flinging her left arm out so that the back of her hand lands with a thud on Sarah's shoulder. All of which makes little difference to Sarah, since she lies awake in any case, letting the darkness press against her eyeballs like a great soft hand, and seeing that long procession of ghost women passing before her. Above her head in the darkness, the bells of St. Paul's chime the endless quarter hours with agonizing slowness.

By day, Sarah takes out a little sharp pebble which she found in one corner of the cell, and has carefully hidden in her shoe so that no-one might take it from her. Slowly, laboriously, she scratches away at the moss on the wall, and into the plaster itself, carving the letters that will complete the unfinished word left to her by an unknown fellow-prisoner. An E and then a T. Sarah whispers the letters to herself as she carves. And then she whispers the completed word, again and again. Forget. Forget. Forget.

When a hand grips her shoulder, Sarah turns in startled terror, as though she had been seized by the hand of the hangman himself. But it is only Leah Swift, with her incongruous soft pink and white smiling face and her shining golden ringlets.

'You're a strange one,' laughs Leah, as she squeezes Sarah's arm, 'sitting in the corner muttering to yourself. I ain't seen you take a bite to eat since they put you in this ward. That's no way to behave, starving yourself to death. They may have found us guilty, but we ain't condemned to death, you know. No point doing the executioner's work for him. You've got to live. Seven years' transportation, is that what they gave you? Seven years is nothing. Just keep on eating and breathing, and seven years'll be gone before you know it.'

Leah squats down beside her, fastidiously tucking up the skirts of her dress as she does so. Amongst this crowd of ragged, unwashed, pock marked, care-worn women, Leah Swift stands out like a peacock in a chicken coop. Yet oddly, though they tease her and mimic her airs and graces, the other women accept her presence with an envy tinged with admiration. For she has achieved the almost impossible: she has been brought back from the convict ship which should even now be carrying her away to the Antipodes, returned to the gaol on the orders of the Keeper himself, to help clean his quarters by day and (as everyone knows) to warm his bed on chilly nights.

'Here,' says Leah, opening a small leather flask that she has pulled out from the folds of her skirt. 'Come on. Drink a bit. It's brown ale. Make you feel better. Got it from me good gentleman himself.'

She giggles and thrusts the flask into Sarah's face. Too startled and confused to resist, Sarah opens her mouth and then chokes as the pungent liquid fills her throat. And yet Leah is right. The ale is warm and bitter, but its warmth seems to flow into her cold dry veins. She has not realized until this moment how parched her mouth has become. She grasps the flask and takes another deep draught of the liquid.

'That's the idea,' says Leah. 'Nothing much a good swig of ale won't cure. Finish it off before the other women get their hands on it. Need to keep your strength up for that long journey you'll be taking. There's plenty that doesn't make it to the other shore, so I've heard. '

'What's it like, on the ship?' whispers Sarah. The sharp pebble is still in her hand, and as she speaks, she clenches her fist around it, feeling it cut into her palm.

'Ah, it's no better nor worse than here,' says Leah, 'though below decks it does get mighty gloomy, and they say that once you're out at sea, the ship sways something terrible. There's them that can stomach it, and them that can't.'

'And Botany Bay? Did you hear tell what it's like if you reach Botany Bay?'

'There was a sailor I made friends with who'd made the journey twice. Said the first time he was there it rained for weeks and there was mud everywhere, but the next time he hardly saw a drop of rain. You don't want to go too far into the forests, he said. There's snakes and savages and Lord knows what else. That's what my friend the sailor said. But plenty of fish in the sea, he said, and land aplenty for them as can get it. He met this woman as was sent there for horse stealing, and married a man in the liquor trade, and now she's a fine lady and wears silk every day and dines off dishes with little golden flowers on them. Saw it with his own eyes, he says.' She sighs. 'He was a mighty fine man, that sailor. Eyes like amber and a grand tattoo of the lion and the unicorn, one on each cheek of his arse. I was quite sad to leave him the day they brought me back here.'

Botany Bay, whispers Sarah to herself. Botany Bay. That is where they will send me.

Now when she lies awake at night, she begins to see herself there. There is a great dark forest in front of her, and as she walks into the forest she sees the green snakes that curl in the branches and hears the voices of strange people singing in the darkness, but somehow she is not afraid. She has heard say that Botany Bay is on the bottom of the world, and that everything there is upside down. But even upside down, she keeps on walking until she comes to a place where the trees end, and beyond the land stretches broad and green in every direction, patterned with golden flowers. Land aplenty for them as can get it.

Everything here is upside down now, thinks Sarah. Perhaps if I can survive long enough to reach Botany Bay, the world may right itself again. If I can survive until I reach Botany Bay, maybe I might begin to live again.

The strange noises wake her while the sky is still dark. After weeks of sleepless nights, sleep has begun to come in strange patches, like waves of fog that sweep over her mind, leaving everything blank and silent. She wakes every morning feeling dull and unrefreshed.

But this morning something is happening. It is a sound of clanging and clanking at first: gates opening, chains striking cobbles. Around her, the other women begin to stir. Eliza Dee raises herself on one elbow, muttering, 'Mother of God, what's that racket?' Then comes the sound of horses' hooves and the rattle of cartwheels on the cobbles outside, and then the sound of men's voices.

'How many have we got in there?'

'You'll need another cart to take them all, Ben.'

'Ahoy there, fellows! Bring another cart!'

In the murky gathering light, she can see that the yard is full of people and horses. The door of the cell swings briefly open and a turnkey thrusts a basket of bread and a pail of water into the hands of Esther the wards-woman.

'Better eat and drink while you've got the chance,' mutters the turnkey.

Now all the women are awake, seizing chunks of bread and filling their tankards with water.

'They've come for you. You're going,' the wards-woman announces.

The voices rise like the buzzing of a swarm of angry bees. Muttering and cursing, and then wails of grief rising above the hubbub. Sarah can hear the voice of one of the women, keening louder than the rest, 'Jamie! Jamie! God have mercy, I ain't had a chance to say goodbye to my Jamie!'

There's barely time to wolf down the bread before the door opens again, only for the light behind to be blocked by the massive form of a giant of a man in a soiled blue uniform, who pauses for a moment on the threshold, staring at them, a sardonic grin on his face.

'Pack your bags, ladies,' he shouts. 'You're off on the grand tour.'

It's the sight of ranks of men behind him that produces pandemonium: a crowd of men carrying chains and shackles, for all the world like an army of demons come to drag them to hell. The wailing of the women rises to a pitch that makes it almost impossible to hear the names that are shouted out, one by one.

'Mary Brown! Mary Brown! Which of you is Mary Brown?' yells the uniformed giant, and when no-one responds, the wards-woman pushes poor shaking Mary towards him, to be grabbed and held by two men while they shackle her hands and feet.

'Catherine Wells! Catherine Wells! You're next.'

As the jewel thief is seized by both arms she gives a shriek that echoes round the courtyard.

'Tom!' she shouts. 'What about my boy Tom?'

'Never you mind that. We'll take care of him,' replies a voice, and the little boy, whose screams are now adding to the general chaos, is seized by strong arms and disappears into the swirling crowd in the courtyard.

Sarah sinks to her knees in her corner of the ward, covering her ears in a forlorn attempt to block out the sounds around her and whispering over and over again, 'Forget; forget; forget.'

She hears the clanking of the chains as the women are hoisted up onto the carts, and the sound of hooves as the first cart moves forward. The gaolers are still shouting out the names of the women. 'Martha Gallagher! Come out, Martha Gallagher! Edith Parsons! Where are you, Edith?'

Sarah waits and waits for the sound of her own name. But what she hears instead is the slamming of the ward door, the turn of the key in the lock, the creak of the carts outside in the courtyard and the shouting and cursing of the women.

'May you burn in hell, the lot of you!' shouts a voice. It sounds like Catherine Wells.

'Ha!' retorts one of the men. 'You lot'll get to hell long before we do!'

And then another sound, more terrifying than any that has come before. The roar of the crowd outside the prison walls. They have been waiting for this, waiting to watch and jeer as the cartloads of chained women – the evildoers, the dregs of society – rumble out through the streets of London on the journey to Deptford and the ship that lies at anchor there.

Sarah turns away from the wall and looks around the suddenly silent ward. Uneaten crusts of bread and overturned tankards are lying scattered across the empty floor, amidst the abandoned rags and odd shoes and other detritus of the women's departure. Esther the wards-woman is sitting slumped on the floor near the door, staring down at her hands. Leah Swift, her rosy face calm and smiling as ever, stands by the window watching the last cart disappear through the prison gate, and brushing invisible specks of dirt from her dress. Apart from these two and Sarah herself, the only other prisoner left in the ward is Eliza Dee. Eliza is whistling softly and tunelessly though her teeth and, after a while, speaks into the silence.

'Well, dears. At least there's a bit more room for the rest of us now.'

Sarah tries to stand but finds that her legs are shaking violently.

'Why?' she whispers, to no-one in particular. 'Why didn't they take me? I was ready to go.'

Eliza gives a little laugh. 'Why?' she echoes. 'You're still asking why? Why do they do anything, these gentlefolk? They do what they want, and that's an end to it. Be thankful you've been spared. Perhaps they've got grand things in mind for you.' She chuckles aloud at the thought, and goes back to whistling, picking up the tune of 'My Bonny Lies over the Ocean' in an uncertain and quavering tone.

JUNE 1816

Henry Addingon, Viscount Sidmouth

Lord Sidmouth's hand is poised over the paper to add his signature. The nib of his quill, he notices, needs sharpening, but he doesn't have time to bother with that. And now there is another problem. He has just touched the quill to the paper when he realizes that the clerk has forgotten to add the names of women to the document.

'Murgeson!' he shouts. 'Murgeson, why in heaven's name is this memorandum incomplete?'

There is a rustling and shuffling of papers in the next room, and Murgeson waddles in through the open doorway with exasperating slowness. There are times when Sidmouth could almost swear the fellow is doing it on purpose.

It is already close to noon, and the glorious June sunshine is slanting in through the tall windows of his office. Sidmouth has promised to meet his youngest daughter Henrietta and his sister Charlotte at half past the hour on the far side of St. James's Park. He is going to be late, and he hates unpunctuality, whether his own or anyone else's.

'I beg pardon, your Lordship,' says Murgeson unctuously, peering at the offending document.

'The women's names, Murgeson. There's supposed to be a list of the women's names on this.'

'A thousand pardons, your Lordship. It must be on a separate sheet of paper. I will find it for you without delay.'

'Please do, Murgeson. I have an important appointment and I am already late.'

As the clerk shuffles away ponderously into the adjoining room, Sidmouth glances up at the ormolu clock on the marble mantle-shelf. It is five to noon already.

In an effort to calm his impatience, he picks up a report on the unrest in Cambridgeshire which he has skimmed through already, and starts to read the first page more attentively. The indigestion is beginning to bother him again: that sharp ache that has been plaguing him for more than a month. It troubled him so much this morning that he was unable to eat any breakfast, but hunger just seems to make matters worse.

The year that started so gloriously – with the sweet taste of victory over Napoleon still on everybody's lips – seems to have turned strangely sour. The reports from the counties are becoming more and more alarming: houses plundered, bakers' shops smashed open by the mob. It is as though the coming of peace has loosened some madness in the minds of masses. First Newcastle and Nottingham, now Cambridgeshire. The violence of the mob seems to be seeping up through cracks in the earth in a dark and threatening tide. Heaven forfend that London should be next.

Murgeson is still audibly rummaging among his papers and muttering to the deputy clerk. The clock strikes noon. How absurd, thinks Sidmouth, that with all the weight of the safety of the realm on my shoulders, the thing that I am worrying about most at this moment is Henrietta and her impending season in Bath. If only he could understand his own children better. Why is Henrietta not like other young women that he knows, excited at the prospect of the coming season, and eager to attract the attentions of some eligible young man? But no, nothing seems to rouse her from her perpetual langour, or tempt her to raise her nose from the books in which it is always buried. Poetry seems to be her main interest in life. Not even Virgil or Pope or Dryden, but some recent romantic nonsense. It is bad enough that her sister Frances should have set her heart on marrying that totally unsuitable clergyman. Surely, thinks Sidmouth, I have not climbed to these perilous social heights only to have my offspring marry second-rate clergymen and poets.

'Please forgive me for the delay, your Lordship,' murmurs Murgeson, as he bustles in, as fast as his portly form will allow him, clutching a crumpled piece of paper bearing the list of women's names, 'young Forsyth had placed it in the wrong pile.'

'Good heavens, Murgeson. What is this? Look, the corner's torn, and just look at the smudges on these names. We cannot attach this to an official document. You'll have to copy them out afresh. Hurry, man. Hurry. Fetch a fresh sheet of paper.'

The pain between his ribs is growing worse.

He glances again through the document he is about to sign. This at least is one achievement, one bright spot in the year, one plate in the shining armour that will protect England from the rising tides of disorder and darkness: Millbank.

The rather mundane name, he feels, is at odds with the grandeur of the new penitentiary which, seen from a distance and on a foggy day looks for all the world like a great medieval castle, perched on the banks of the Thames to guard the city from its enemies. Which indeed it will do. Sidmouth is struck by the image of Millbank as a fortress towering over the city, holding at bay the waves of barbarism that threaten to assail the capital from every side. But inside, how far from medieval! How full of order, rationality and Christian charity! Designed by the very best minds in the nation and run by its finest philanthropists, to redeem and cure, not to punish. For some lucky few at least, the squalor and depravity of the convict ships will be replaced by moral improvement and practical education within the walls of this great edifice. He reads through the final sentences of the document he is about to sign again:

H. R. H. the Prince Regent having been pleased in the Name and on the Behalf of His Majesty, to give Directions that the Female Convicts specified herein, now under Sentence of Transportation in the Gaol of Newgate should be removed from there to the said Penitentiary and committed to the Charge of the Governor thereof, I am Commanded to signify to you His Royal Highness's Pleasure, that you do advise the said Convicts, if upon being examined by an experienced Surgeon or Apothecary, they shall be found free from any Putrid or Infectious Distemper, and fit to be removed from the said Gaol, that they shall be removed to the said Penitentiary, and there delivered to the Governor thereof, where they are to remain and continue until they shall be discharged by due course of Law.

Let us hope, he thinks, with a small and slightly wry smile, that some of these females at least feel due gratitude to His Royal Highness.

'Murgeson! I have no time to waste. Just copy the names in the margin and let's have done with it.'

He scrawls an addendum at the bottom of the final page, *For list of Names, vide margin of the forgoing letter*, signs his name below and hands the document back to the clerk, who begins to write with agonizing slowness in the margin: *Jane Dockerill, Esther Horton, Eliza Day (alias Dee), Sarah Stone…*

'Forsyth, check to see whether His Lordship's carriage is at the door,' shouts Murgeson as he writes.

Lord Sidmouth glances again at the ormolu clock, which now says nearly ten past the hour. Charlotte, of course, will be impatient and scold him for tardiness, but Henrietta will have her head in the clouds as usual. Perhaps, he thinks, I am partly at fault after all. Since her mother's death, poor Henrietta has lacked a woman's guiding hand, and in these past tumultuous few years, I have had so little time to spend on domestic concerns …

Sidmouth hurries down the curved staircase towards the double door, already held open in preparation for his departure. Beyond, the sunlit street is patterned with the dappled shadows of the elm trees. Halfway down the staircase, a new thought strikes him. He will suggest a ball for Henrietta at the White Lodge. Charlotte will surely be willing to help with the organization. It will give the guests a chance to glimpse his latest improvements to Richmond Park. It is a pleasing idea, and as Lord Sidmouth steps out into the warmth of the summer's day, his heart lifts. Even his indigestion is feeling a little better. Perhaps he might manage a light collation a little later in the day. One of Brook's pasties would be just the thing. But first the meeting with Charlotte and Henrietta.

The Citadel

Millbank. The name means nothing to Sarah Stone, except for a faint memory of the smell of river mud from some occasion long ago when her brother took her there to buy a bucket of periwinkles. In those days, as far as she can remember, Millbank was nothing but a few tumbledown cottages surrounded by trackless marshland, tangles of tall reeds and thickets of willow.

So she is completely unprepared for the apparition which rises before her eyes as their cart creaks slowly down the Horse Ferry Road in the rain, amid the howls and jeers of passers-by. At first it seems less like a building than some marvel of nature rearing up by magic out of the very heart of the city: a mass of dark cloud on the skyline; a jagged, gloomy mountain range; or perhaps a vast living beast, crouched on the horizon, waiting.

The swirling fog parts for a moment to reveal turrets of brownish brick and slate soaring far above the roofs of the surrounding buildings. Turret upon turret, some nearer, some further away. Then the haze closes in again, and there is nothing to be seen but obscure patches of deeper shadow in the murk of the London sky.

Sarah sits in the third of a line of swaying carts, her shoulders bumping against those of Eliza Dee and Esther Horton who are seated on either side of her, as the rickety wooden cartwheels creak along the rutted street. The chains around her ankles are chafing her skin, and her clothes are damp from the misty drizzle. Uniformed guards occupy the padded seats at the front of the cart, and three more ride on horseback behind them. A well-dressed man with a broad-brimmed hat on his head and a cane in his hand pauses on the side of the road, staring at the passing line of carts and their bedraggled women occupants for a while before directing a string of profanities at them. A moment later a projectile skims past Sarah's ear and lands harmlessly in the dirt on the far side of the cart. But Sarah neither turns her head nor flinches from the shouts and missiles of passers-by. She cannot tear her gaze away from the vision that lies ahead of her.

As they draw nearer, the houses close in around them, momentarily blocking out their view of the penitentiary; but then their convoy turns into the wide open space of Grosvenor Wharf, and the enormity of Millbank is upon them. Soaring round towers with slits for windows and roofs like witches' hats rise from many corners of what seems to be a vast maze of buildings, their walls lined with rows of blank square windows, dark as staring eyes. Surrounding it all is a waterlogged ditch beyond which lies a massive wall built of brick, yellow-brown like the London fog itself. Under the shadow of this outer wall, the carts grind their way towards the arched gateway of the penitentiary, which opens directly towards the river.

Outside the huge wooden portal of the prison, the convoy of carts comes to a halt while the guards engage in discussion through a grating in the wall with the officials within the compound of the penitentiary. Although it is summer, the chill damp of the day is seeping into Sarah's bones, and she feels the rain soak through the coarse cotton of her gown and trickle down her spine. She inhales the breeze that blows from the river, laden with smells of mud and tar, but still seeming fresh after the fetid air of Newgate. Out on the ruffled brown waters of the Thames, a barge lowers its sails as it heads towards the wharf, and a couple of fishermen cast their net into the waters from a boat that looks so tiny and ancient that you might expect it to sink at any moment. Above their heads, the seagulls swoop and circle, mewing plaintively. A shaft of pale light appears unexpectedly through the haze, making the water behind the boat glitter, and as Sarah gazes at it, three seagulls descend through this faint ray of illumination to hover above the fishing net, wings beating frantically, clawed legs stretched out towards some morsel of fish below.

'Get down! Get down!' yells one of the guards. The women begin to clamber stiffly down from the cart, their legs and hands still shackled. Sarah hears the sound of a bell clanging somewhere deep within the walls of the prison compound, and then, very slowly, the gates of Millbank swing open to receive them.

She expects the gateway to lead into an inner courtyard, but instead they find themselves entering a gatehouse built into the thick outer wall itself – a strange, narrow, high ceilinged room across which stretches a long narrow table. At the table sits a very thin man with a high collar around his scrawny neck and a pince-nez balanced precariously on his beak-like nose. A large, leather-bound volume lies on the table in front of him, open at the first page, which is, at first, entirely blank.

'Name and age,' he barks to each of the women as they enter the gatehouse, proceeding to inscribe each answer in the book with a black and gold quill pen which looks as new and unused as the book itself. The outer portal has closed behind them, leaving them in semi-darkness, illuminated only by the dim light from two narrow windows and from candles that stand at either end of the table. As each woman speaks her name, an officer steps forward and removes the shackles from her hands and feet.

Sarah is so intent on watching the scribe as he writes her name and age with an artistic flourish that she fails to notice the other figure who stands in the shadows at the far corner of the room, observing them in silence with his arms folded across his chest. It is only when the recording of names is complete that this figure steps forward and begins to speak to them. His voice is soft and curiously high pitched, almost like a woman's. His face, too, is soft, round and rosy-cheeked, and surmounted by a halo of thick white curls.

'My name is Shearman, and I am governor of this penitentiary ...' he begins.

For some reason, Sarah finds that her body is shaking uncontrollably. Her head is swimming, and she hears the governor's speech only as disconnected words, which seem to loosen themselves from his lips and fly around the room like insects: 'discipline', 'prayer', 'labour', 'mercy', 'obedience'. Only the final two sentences penetrate her brain.

'In this building you will not speak, neither to officials nor to one another, without express permission. I wish you well.'

Beyond the gatehouse they cross an area which looks for all the world like a deserted builders' yard, its soggy ground littered with piles of sand, untidy stacks of timber, and abandoned picks and wheelbarrows. The women are herded up the wide stairs that lead to the oaken inner doors of the prison, and into a long narrow corridor with a vaulted ceiling, like the ceiling of an old church. As they enter the inner precinct, Eliza Dee, who is walking immediately in front of Sarah, turns back towards her and places a finger to her lips, a comical grimace on her face.

'Follow me,' orders their guard, and they file down the corridor to the far end where, with much fumbling and clanking, he produces a large key from the bundle on his key chain and unlocks a door that leads to a dimly-lit spiral staircase. Mounting the staircase in silence, Sarah is seized with a deepening sense of dread whose origin she cannot immediately identify. Her heart is hammering so hard in her chest that she cannot breathe. She reaches out her hand to the central stone pillar to steady herself, and her fingers leave faint damp marks on its freshly-hewn surface.

Part of the way up the staircase, the guard unlocks another door and leads them into a corridor exactly like the one they have just walked along. And at this moment, Sarah recognizes the source of her terror. She has been listening for the sounds of the other occupants of this building – the clatter of footsteps, the clanging of doors, the clamour of voices from the cells. But there is nothing. No sound enters from outside. No sound comes from within. Nothing but the soft shuffling of their own footsteps along this endless corridor, down another spiral staircase, along another corridor, and the sound of the blood pounding in her own ears.

Time too seems to have slipped in some strange way. The vaulted ceilings and windows set deep in the thick walls remind her of an ancient house that she and her brothers and sisters once came upon when the family went hunting for rabbits in Abbey Wood. Haunted by the ghosts of friars, they had said. But this place smells of fresh damp plaster and new paint, and the wood of the endless locked doors is unseasoned. They seem to be the only people in this entire vast citadel. The past has slid into the present.

Perhaps they are the only people left alive in the world.

The room into which Sarah is led is vast and echoing. She has been brought here alone, accompanied only by one wardress. Somewhere in the shadowy recesses of the room, drops of water fall one by one into a pool below. Each plop echoes hollowly around the grey vaulted space: a space dimly lit by the slits of windows on the far side. In the room are four deep circular depressions, like immense cauldrons, set into the stone-flagged floor. Three are empty, but one is half filled with turbid water.

'Take off your clothes,' says the wardress, her voice echoing through the cavernous space.

Sarah pulls off her damp dress and undershirt and leaves them in a pile on the flagstones. The air of the room is chill and moist, and the pool of water, when she steps into it, is tepid. The wardress pushes a metal saucer full of soft soap towards the rim of the bath with her toe.

'Scrub yourself all over with this,' she instructs.

Since she entered the crowded Newgate cells with their limited buckets of water for washing, Sarah has never removed her clothes to wash her body all over, and now that she sees her limbs in the hazy water of the bath, they seem entirely foreign to her – darkened with grime and wasted close to the bone, like a beggar-woman's limbs, she thinks. As she scrubs these strange appendages, she is suddenly blinded, deafened and almost drowned by the bucket of chilly water which the wardress tips over her head.

'Now get out,' orders the wardress, as soon as Sarah catches her breath.

The wardress hands her a threadbare round towel with which Sarah wipes the water out of her eyes and rubs her hair and body as best she can, and as she does so, she sees that an elderly man dressed in a long black jacket and wearing an old-fashioned wig on his head has entered the room and is gazing at her intently, as though she were a specimen of some very rare creature which he had never chanced to observe before.

'Raise your arms,' says the man, 'higher.' His voice is hoarse and has a faint lisp.

Sarah stands in the centre of the echoing bath hall like a participant in some pagan sacrifice, while the wardress and the man gaze at her in absolute silence.

Then the man approaches her so closely that she can see the small white wart on one side of his nose, and the patterns of crowns on the brass buttons of his coat. He gazes into her eyes, and she gazes unblinkingly back. The man's eyes are pale grey and entirely without expression.

'Open your mouth,' he says.

When she does so, he whips out a wooden file and thrusts it into her mouth, pressing down her tongue.

'Now close your mouth and breathe in.'

'Turn round.' Sarah turns slowly in a circle.

As she comes face to face with the wardress, a tall thin woman with sunken cheeks and a protruding chin, Sarah sees the light flash on the sharp knife which the other woman holds in her hand. Before she has a chance to cry out, the wardress has seized her by the hair and is hacking the damp locks from her head. They fall to the floor like coils of damp weed.

'Keep still, if you don't want me to cut you,' cries the wardress, pulling tighter on the remaining strands of hair as her barber's blade skims closer to Sarah's scalp.

When the operation is over, Sarah runs her hand unsteadily over the uneven stubble of her bald pate, doubly naked.

'Have you, or has any member of your family, ever been insane?' asks the man.

Sarah feels a wave of dizziness sweep over her.

'No,' she murmurs.

'I can't hear you.'

'No,' she repeats more loudly, and her lie echoes around the domed ceiling of the bath hall.

But at that moment she understands that she has become invisible. These people are staring at her body, but they cannot see it. They cannot see her wasted legs, or her swollen breasts, or the marks on her stomach. They are looking towards her, but they are looking through her, as though she were made of glass.

The man turns away and starts to write something in the book that he has been carrying under his arm, and the wardress thrusts a coarse, rust-brown dress into Sarah's hands.

'Put that on,' she orders.

Every fibre of the dress rubs against the nerve-ends of Sarah's newly washed skin. Its fabric feels like glasspaper.

She is marched down one long corridor, and then another, and then down a spiral staircase and along another corridor. A door is opened, she is pushed through into the room beyond and then the door closes behind her.

Sarah stands just inside the threshold, looking around in disbelief. The small room is decorated like a parlour. There are pink velvet curtains on the windows, two brocade armchairs in a deeper shade of pink, a patterned rug on the floor and a glass-fronted cabinet containing an array of porcelain tea cups. A bright fire burns in a fireplace at one side of the room, beneath a mantle-shelf adorned with two china statuettes of shepherdesses. Sitting at a table in the centre of the room is a diminutive woman with her greying hair swept back into a knot at the back of her neck. The only thing on the table is a glass vase containing a huge bouquet of pink roses which fill the room with an almost overpoweringly sweet smell.

The woman smiles at Sarah and motions to her to sit on a wooden chair by the table. Sarah grips her hands tightly together on her lap to resist the sudden impulse to reach out and touch the roses, whose petals look so silky that, but for their scent, she would have believed them to be made by human hands.

'I am Mrs Chambers,' says the woman, with the air of someone imparting important secret information, 'and you are Sarah Stone.'

Sarah nods.

'You are a child-stealer,' continues the woman, without losing the smile on her face or changing the tone of her voice. 'You committed a very dreadful crime by taking away an infant that belonged to another woman.'

'*She was my child!*' The words burst from Sarah's lips in an explosion of sound before she can check them.

She cowers back in her chair, expecting a repetition of the rain of blows which descended on her head when she spoke those words in the Lambeth-Street Magistrates Office. But no blow comes. The woman's smile does not waver. She just leans in a little closer across the table and says in the same calm and gentle voice, 'No, Sarah. She was *not* your child. She was the daughter of Mr and Mrs Creamer. You stole that baby. What made you want to do such a wicked thing?'

Sarah's voice falters. Her hands squeeze tighter and tighter together, so that the nails of one hand dig into the knuckles of the other.

'I can't remember,' she whispers. And indeed, the fog has descended on her mind again, and nothing is clear. All she can remember is that one wintery morning, when frost clung to the cobwebs on the bushes like bridal veils, she went to St. Leonard's with Mother, and with a tiny child snuggled in her arms, and the vicar bent over and pushed the cap back from the baby's brow, and said, 'What a pretty little creature she is!'

Mrs Chambers is still leaning across the table towards her.

'But you are sorry for what you did, are you not, Sarah?' she continues. 'You are surely sorry for stealing that baby.'

And – perhaps because the words are spoken softly, almost gently – Sarah is suddenly convulsed with uncontrollable sobs. All the pain, all the confusion, all the terror of the past year rise up like a drowning wave from within her, and her body is wracked by the grief that turns to water as it reaches the air, and pours unchecked down her face.

Mrs Chambers watches her impassively, with the air of one who has seen such things many times before. The minutes pass, and at last Sarah's tears begin, little by little, to subside. Mrs Chambers walks over to the hearth and pokes the coals in the fireplace. A small explosion of sparks bursts from the coals and vanishes up the chimney. Mrs Chambers returns to the table and gives Sarah's hand a brief and tentative pat.

'Calm yourself, Sarah,' she says. 'I can see that you may indeed be repentant. Remember that God loves nothing more than the penitent sinner. However black your sins, our dear Lord can wash them white as snow. That is why you are here: to reflect on your evil deeds, repent and be forgiven. You will learn a useful trade here, and if you truly examine your conscience and make the most of the opportunities which will be given to you within these walls, you may yet be rescued from the path of sin and perdition, and learn to walk on the path to paradise. You would like that, wouldn't you?'

'Yes,' replies Sarah very quietly.

IN THE CASTLE OF THE GIANT DESPAIR

Sarah's first impression was wrong. This place is not silent. The building speaks to itself. At night it groans and murmurs, as though plagued by troubled dreams. From time to time, it gives a little shudder.

For some reason, her tiny solitary cell never grows completely dark. Even in the depths of night, a hazy flickering light shines through the small barred window far above her head. By day, no sunlight enters. The flickering simply becomes stronger, filling the space with an uneven murky greyness.

When she first entered Newgate, Sarah had been horrified at the thought of having to share a ward with such a crowd of women. But now in Millbank, she misses the warmth of other women's bodies pressed close to hers at night. She lies alone in this narrow space with its vaulted stone ceiling, and if she stretches her arms even a little way out from the straw-stuffed mattress on which she sleeps, they strike the walls on either side. It is like lying in a stone coffin, immured in a church crypt. She no longer knows how long she has been in this place. It might be two weeks; it might be a year.

The warders arrive late this morning. They come after dawn, with an unusual racket of shouting and banging and a clattering of metal. Some of the cell doors, it seems, have become jammed shut, and have to be prized open with crowbars and hammers. When the doors burst open, the women flock out into the corridors, clamouring and cursing in alarm.

'Silence!' roars one of the warders. 'I will have silence here!'

The women's voices subside, and they shuffle meekly in single file to the workroom, as they do every morning, to take their places on the long wooden benches and resume their sewing.

The sewing is endless. Red-brown hessian sailcloth, to be sewn into sacks, or into sack-like clothing for their fellow prisoners. As always in the mornings, Sarah feels light-headed with sleeplessness and hunger. She keeps her eyes fixed on her needle as it ploughs endlessly through yard after yard of brick-coloured cloth. The tips of her fingers have become reddened and hard from pushing the coarse needle through the coarse fabric.

As the prisoners sew, one or other of Mrs Chambers's two daughters, seated in a high-backed chair at the head of the room, reads to them from a sacred book. On the grey stone wall behind the reader's chair hangs an embroidered image of a huge eye, surrounded by leaves in variegated shades of green, so that it appears to be staring out from the depths of a jungle. Above the eye, the words *Thou, God, Seest Me* are embroidered in ornate script sewn in wool the colour of dried blood.

The daughters are as unalike as two siblings could be, the older being tall and bony, with dark hair tied in tightly braided coils over her ears, while the younger is a plumper and softer version of her mother. But they have almost identical voices – sing-song and monotonous, as though reciting an incantation in a language they do not fully understand. They have read the story of Cain and Abel, Martha and Mary, the parable of the lost sheep, and Jonah in the belly of the whale. Today it is Christian and Hopeful in the Castle of the Giant Despair.

If she sits long enough sewing, Sarah finds that her mind drifts quietly away from her body. It floats upward and through the barred windows, until she comes to rest in some completely different place, a place from her childhood, or perhaps some dream landscape that she has surely never visited in reality, but that seems oddly familiar. Today she is in a great field of red-brown earth that stretches endlessly towards a distant flat horizon. As she watches her fingers mechanically stitching the cloth, she sees them, not stitching, but ploughing. She is turning over the earth with a tiny plough, moving ever closer to the horizon, but even as she does so, the horizon recedes, remaining as far away as ever. While her fingers plough the earth, she hears the sing-song voice that seems to come from somewhere above her head.

"'Brother," said Christian, "what shall we do? The life that we now live is miserable: for my part I know not whether is best – to live thus, or to die out of hand. My soul chooses strangling rather than life; and the grave is more easy for me than this dungeon.'"

There is no end to this furrow that Sarah follows across the red-brown earth. Yesterday, today, tomorrow, a thousand tomorrows, it continues, and the horizon endlessly retreats, just as the voice above her head drones on.

"'What a fool," quoth he, "am I, thus to lie in a stinking dungeon, when I may as well walk at liberty! I have a key in my bosom called Promise; that will, I am persuaded, open any lock in Doubting Castle.'"

But here in Millbank all the keys are in the hands of the warders. For the prisoners, there is no promise: only the endless corridors, each identical to all the rest, down which they walk in silent procession, day after day. Sarah's eyes droop a little as they focus on the furrow that she is ploughing across the field. There is one lone tree standing on the furthest edge of the field, near the horizon. A squat dark oak tree. Although it is so very far away, Sarah can somehow see each of its leaves perfectly distinctly, and hear the wind whispering in its branches …

A blow on the shoulder from one of the warders startles her into wakefulness. The sailcloth sack in front of her is almost done, and the elder Miss Chambers is still intoning:

Out of the way we went; and then we found
What it was to tread upon forbidden ground:
And let them that come after have a care,
Lest heedlessness makes them, as we to fare;
Lest they, for trespassing, his prisoners are,
Whose castle's 'Doubting' and whose name's DESPAIR.

On that triumphal note, Miss Chambers slaps the fat book shut and looks up at the assembled women.

'You may eat your breakfasts now,' she announces.

They set down their work on the tables in front of them. As they raise their bent heads, Sarah finds herself looking straight into the face of Eliza Dee, who sits at the bench opposite her. Eliza gives her a broad wink.

'Eliza Dee,' snaps the sharp-eyed Miss Chambers, 'What is that expression I see on your face?'

Eliza bows her head repentantly. 'So sorry, ma'am', she murmurs. 'It's the palsy in me right eye. Had it ever since I was a little girl, ma'am.'

Eliza, astonishingly, always seems to persuade them. Her shorn hair has grown back soft and straight, and the man's clothing that she sported in Newgate had been replaced with the drab uniform gown worn by all the Millbank prisoners. She looks like a penitent sinner from some old stained-glass window. In chapel on a Sunday she can bury her head in her hands with such a heart-wrenching gesture of remorse for wrongdoing that everyone seems convinced, except for Sarah, who sits close enough to Eliza to see her eyes gleaming with mocking irony as they peer askance from behind her concealing fingers.

Eliza is one of the four prisoners entrusted with the all-important task of collecting food from the kitchen and distributing it to her fellow inmates. Every morning, she tries to fill Sarah's cup of cocoa a little fuller than the others, and every morning, Sarah pushes it away after a couple of sips. She is hungry, but the thick liquid clogs in her throat and she cannot swallow it. The bread that comes with it is equally inedible, being rock hard and gritty, as though made of sandstone. Eliza, seeing Sarah's undrunk cocoa, frowns severely, nudging Sarah and making drinking motions with her hand and mouth, but Sarah simply shakes her head, and pushes the tin cup back towards Eliza, who ends up drinking it herself with such a look of rueful sadness on her face that Sarah finds herself smiling despite the pain of hunger (or perhaps it is something more than hunger) that gnaws incessantly at her belly.

A violent shuddering wakes her in the middle of the night. There is a loud splintering sound just above her head. From somewhere far away, she hears a woman prisoner cry out in alarm – a cry that echoes down the long corridors like the scream of a night bird. Sarah lies in the half darkness, rigid with fear, staring up at the space above her in a vain effort to understand the noises and sensations around her. She lies there for what seems like eternity, until the faint light outside becomes strong enough for her to see what has happened to one wall of her cell.

A crack, which was certainly not there when she went to sleep, has opened up in the cell wall to the right of the window, running vertically, almost from ceiling to floor. Fragments of plaster have fallen to the ground and, in one spot, corners of brown brick beneath the plaster have been exposed. Without moving, or even reaching out her fingers to touch it, she stares at the crack. In places, the fissure is so deep and black that it seems like an opening into a strange infernal world beyond. And in the deepest and blackest point, about halfway down the wall, she can see something shining.

There is a faint gleam of reflected light deep within the recesses of the wall; it vanishes, and then is there again. She cannot tear her gaze away from that point in the wall. If she watches very intently, she sees the gleam again. Light is shining on a smooth, moist surface, a black surface that moves even as she watches it. It darts away into invisibility and then furtively reappears – a point of light focused in her direction. A gelatinous gleam of something that is alive.

There is an eye on the other side of the crack, staring back at her: a dark eye staring out of the wall, like the eye of a frightened horse.

Sarah turns her back to the cracked wall, and lies hunched over, arms wrapped around her knees. She can hear the sound of her own breathing, rasping and ragged. She listens for other sounds. No sounds come; but the eye is still there. It feels closer than ever. Thou, God, seest me. She can sense the disembodied eye's unblinking gaze boring into the back of her head. She tries to turn and look again at the crack, but she cannot do it. The eye watches her. It knows her thoughts. But this is not the eye of God.

This is the eye of mad Uncle Jonah, looking into the darkest corner of her soul …

She hears the sounds of banging and the rattling and screaming before she knows that it is she who is making them. Her hands burn with pain as she hammers at the door of her cell.

'Let me out! Let me out! It's watching me!'

Footsteps pound down the flagstones outside. The door bursts open, and she is seized and muffled by a great calloused hand that is clamped over her mouth. Two warders pinion her arms to her sides while a third stands just outside the door watching the struggle with an expression of faint amusement on his face.

'In God's name, what's this racket?' yells the man whose hand is covering her mouth. 'What's got into you, Sarah?'

She struggles and scratches, wrenching one arm free.

'The eye!' she cries into the stifling hand. 'The eye.'

She waves her free arm towards the crack in the wall.

'Criminy,' exclaims the other warder who holds her, 'just look at that, will you!'

'It's watching,' cries Sarah. Her throat is so tight that she cannot breathe.

‘No-one’s watching you, you madwoman. It’s just this bloody building, cracking apart. They should never have built it on a bloody swamp. Calm down, will you.’

As they drag her back towards the mattress, towards the crack and the all-seeing eye, she summons all her strength to break away, sinking her teeth into a fold of hard skin on the hand that covers her mouth. Her captor yells and clouts her across one ear.

‘Jesus Christ, she may be nothing but skin and bone, but she fights like a cat,’ he says.

‘All right, Sarah. We’ll take you to another cell,’ says the warder who still stands outside the door. He speaks in a perfectly calm, almost indifferent, voice. ‘No cracks in the wall. No eyes watching you. Bring her down to B Ward.’

Still struggling and crying, though she no longer quite knows why, Sarah is pulled and pushed along the corridors and down spiral staircases until she finds herself suddenly flung through a doorway into the windowless space beyond. A door clangs shut, and she is alone, in complete silence and utter, impenetrable darkness.

They are right. There is no watching eye here. Here there is nothing except a faint musty smell. No sounds. No air. Nothing but blackness. The darkness is so total that it seems to press in upon her from without. She closes her eyes to prevent the dense furry dark from seeping into her soul, and remembers the story of Jonah in the belly of the whale. Is the darkness inside a whale as black as this, she wonders, or is it veined with red? The ground beneath her is flagged stone, slightly gritty. When she cautiously reaches out a hand, she can feel nothing, above, below or in front of her.

Because she can see and feel nothing, she is afraid to move, uncertain what might lie around her. She might be sitting on the very edge of a precipice. The slightest movement to right or left might plunge her into the abyss. The gnawing in her stomach has become overwhelming, like a rat biting through her gut. She sinks her head on her knees, and sits quite still, while long dark minutes, or hours or maybe days go by.

She thinks that she is back in the darkness of childhood, in the bed where she slept with her two sisters, with the boys tossing and snoring in their sleep on their mattress beneath the shuttered window. Soon it will be dawn, and her mother will come in and fling open the shutters with a cry of 'Rouse yourselves, sleepy-heads!' Her sisters will be up first, hurrying to the kitchen to fill their bowls with porridge, but Sarah will burrow down under the counterpane, savouring the lingering warmth of the bed a little longer …

And then she is no longer a child but an adult, on the ship with Ned. She is a mother with an infant in her arms. The wind blows off the flat shore across the deck of the ship, which lies at anchor near the mouth of the river. The other women on the ship want to peer at the baby and stroke its soft little head, but she and Ned slip away from them, down the companionway into the dark of the lower deck, where Ned pins her against the door of his cabin and begins to nuzzle at her neck, until she pushes him away, laughing fondly. 'You great fool,' she says, 'you can't do that here.' And when Ned ignores her protests she pushes a little more firmly, saying, 'Watch out, Father Ned, you'll stifle poor baby!' But the babe in her arms sleeps on unawares, while Ned places his hands on Sarah's shoulders and pulls her towards him …

Maybe she has slept and been wakened by the sound, or maybe she has been just sitting in the darkness for days, and it is the sound that has made her lift her head from her knees. It is coming from quite close by, a sound that she has not heard for so long that it takes her a moment to recognize what it is.

A woman singing.

The voice is soft; quite deep, but unmistakably a woman's voice. The tune is one she has never heard before. It is a sad and lilting thing, soaring and falling. The unseen woman sings softly but persistently. She finishes her song, and then begins it all over again. At first Sarah cannot make out the words, but as the woman sings a second and then a third time, they begin to take shape in her mind. 'Sleep, baby mine,' the woman is singing.

Sarah wants to join the singing, but she does not know the song. She passes her tongue over her dry cracked lips, and tries to swallow, but her throat seems half closed.

The pain in her stomach is like the pain of childbirth. Something is pressing against her from within, trying to break out of her body.

'Sleep, baby mine,' sings the invisible woman in the darkness, 'not long thou'lt have a mother, to lull thee fondly in her arms to rest …'

Then the voice in the darkness falls silent. Sarah reaches down into her memory for a song of her own. Her throat is so dry that she cannot believe that it will produce a sound, and yet somehow a husky, faint sound comes out of her mouth. She sits perfectly still in the dark, singing. It is the only song that comes to mind. Uncle Jonah used to sing it to her, in the days before he was knocked down by the post-chaise.

In Dublin's fair city, where the girls are so pretty,
I once met a maid called sweet Molly Malone,
And she wheeled her wheelbarrow,
Through streets broad and narrow,
Singing Cockles and Mussels, Alive, Alive, Oh!

The woman in the adjoining cell has fallen silent, but Sarah can sense that she is listening to every note.

She died of a fever, and no-one could save her (sings Sarah)
And that was the end of sweet Molly Malone.
Now her ghost wheels a barrow, through streets broad and narrow,
Crying Cockles and Mussels, Alive, Alive, Oh!'

When the last note dies away, there is silence from the other side of the cell wall, and then softly, the other woman begins again, singing the same song as before.

Sleep, baby mine – to-morrow I must leave thee,
And I would snatch an interval of rest.

Sleep these last moments, ere the laws bereave thee,
For never more thou'lt press a mother's breast.

The soft deep voice of the woman – a woman she will never see – is still singing its endless lullaby when Sarah slumps to one side, and quietly topples over into the bottomless abyss of darkness.

DELIVERANCE

It is the kindness that takes her by surprise. She lies in a bed covered in white linen, and enveloped in unexpected and inexplicable gentleness. The faces of the women float above her, so that she can barely see them. What she sees are their plain grey gowns, the white cuffs of their sleeves, and their large practical hands, which lift her, straighten her sheets, and sponge her body.

The pain in her stomach is still there, stronger than ever, but it has become so strong that it seems to have separated itself from her body, and to float above her as the faces of the women do. The voice that groans from time to time is her voice, but it sounds as though it is coming from outside. Sometimes she hears other cries and groans too, further away.

'You're in the infirmary, dear,' says the woman to the right of her bed. 'We'll take care of you here.'

The cloth with which they sponge her body is soft, and the water is delightfully cool. There is a sweet smell in the air, like rose petals. While they are sponging her stomach, one of the women suddenly stops.

'Will you look at this mark, Mary?' she says to the other. 'Do you think we should tell them?'

'There's little point,' replies Mary, 'they'd have seen it already, if they'd wanted to. She was looked at by the doctor when they brought her here, like all the rest of them, but there's things they'd rather not see. Besides, it is too late now.'

And then the delightful cooling movement of their hands begins again, and the fire in her body abates a little.

The pain comes in waves, sometimes seeming to lift her body out of the bed with its violent force, and then subsiding again, to leave her for a moment feeling relaxed and empty, as though floating on the surface of a vast warm sea.

She starts to imagine again that there is something inside her, trying to force its way out. She sees herself lying on a floor, looking up at a strange ceiling, where rows of garments are hung to dry. She looks up into the folds of lace and linen, and above them there is no ceiling, but only clear blue sky. Staring at the radiant sky, she imagines that she is waiting for the midwife to come, but the child inside her refuses to wait. A cry bursts from her lips as the pain seizes her again.

The woman on the left hand side of her bed touches her head gently, like a mother stroking the head of a sick child.

'There, there, you poor dear,' she says softly.

The woman on the right hand side of the bed takes her hand, and begins to stroke her fingers, one by one.

'I think it won't be long now,' she says.

PART THREE

FOUND

ADAH'S STORY

May 1822
Spitalfields

On the morning when Annie is due to leave for Fulham, Adah wakes to find that young Will has stayed out all night again. It's the third time he has done this in two weeks, and for a moment Adah is so full of anger that she wishes she could take her son by the scruff of the neck, as she used to do when he was six or seven, and slap him on the bottom with one of her slippers. The idea is absurd, of course, since Will is now head and shoulders taller than her, and must weigh at least twice as much. She was counting on him to help her in this moment of crisis, but now they will just have to manage without him.

'Don't fret, Mammy,' says Annie, when she sees the expression on Adah's face, 'Will's still trying to find his own way of becoming a grown man. He'll settle down soon enough.'

They stand in the dark bedroom of the Blossom Street tenement, Annie folding the clothes that she will take with her, while Adah looks on, trying to make sure that nothing important is forgotten, and suppressing a surprising urge to weep.

When the message about her father arrived two days ago, Adah's first instinct was to rush to Fulham to care for him herself. At seventy-eight, her father is too old to live on his own. His chest is bad, and his knees have been full of rheumatics for years. Even at the best of times, it's as much as he can do to manage a little slow work in the gardens of the big house, and now he has fallen off a ladder and is confined to bed. There is no immediate danger, or so they say, but the old man is dazed and shaken, and seems to have hurt his hip. He needs someone to nurse him, but there will be no-one to care for the children if Adah leaves them here in Norton Folgate, and she can hardly take them all with her to stay in her father's cramped garden cottage. So Annie – who has always loved her grandfather's cottage, and the great expanses of lawn and the cedar trees, herb beds and rose gardens that surround it – has offered to go in her place.

Annie pauses in the midst of her packing, her face turned away from the window, so Adah can barely see the expression on her face.

'I forgot to tell you,' she says. 'Mrs Holloway who brought the message from Fulham says they have a place for a parlour maid at the big house. Perhaps they might take me on there. That way I could stay in Grandpa's cottage and take care of him if he needs me. And earn my own keep too.'

Adah, bending down to pick up a stray stocking that has slipped out of Annie's bag, feels the breath catch in her throat for a moment. She has tried to keep her money worries to herself, but clearly she has failed. It is proving harder than she expected to feed seven mouths and pay the rent from the sixteen shillings a week she receives for her work as Searcher. Annie must have heard her sighs as she counts the money in her purse every evening. They need another wage, but Will, who is best placed to provide it, seems to drink every penny he earns. Annie is right, of course. If she could find a job at the big house it would solve two problems at once. But no, no, thinks Adah, please not that. How will I ever manage without Annie's calm and comforting presence?

Catching sight of the expression on her mother's face, Annie gives a little laugh and reaches out to give Adah's arm a squeeze.

'Don't look like that, Mammy. You're making me sad, too. Anyone would think I was going to America. I'll only be a few miles away.'

Sally trots in through the open bedroom door, bearing a gift of her almost favourite rag doll, which she is determined to add to her older sister's luggage. Annie removes the limp grey creature with its moulting woollen hair, and hands it solemnly back to Sally.

'No, Sal, my love, dolly doesn't want to go in my bag. It's dark and cramped in there. She'd be squashed to death.'

Adah has spent most of the past two days boiling up jars of calves-foot jelly to send to her father. It's the jars that make the bag so heavy. In normal times it only takes five minutes to walk to the Four Swans on Bishopsgate Street, but today, weighed down with luggage, they take twice as long, and by the time they reach the inn, all the other passengers have already boarded the coach. Adah just has time to give her eldest daughter a quick hug and press a shilling into her hand before they heave the bag onto the roof and Annie scrambles up into the one remaining seat.

Then the scowling, red-faced coachman cracks his whip over the heads of his team of black horses who, startled into movement, clatter at high speed out through the archway of the inn and down the crowded thoroughfare beyond. Adah stands watching for a moment, as the coach disappears in a cloud of dust round the street corner towards London Wall. Her head is still full of the final words of wise advice she meant, and failed, to give her daughter.

It is a clear sunlit spring day, with just a soft breeze in the air. Even here in the city streets, the sky above is blue, dotted with small puffs of white cloud. In the Fulham garden, the cornflowers and sweet peas will be in flower, and the buds will already be appearing on the wisteria that covers the walls of her father's cottage... Adah is seized by an aching wish that she could be on her way there with Annie, to hold her father's gnarled brown hands in her own again, and walk with her daughter through the woods and lanes that she loved when she was young.

But instead she slips quickly into the dank and smoky interior of the Four Swans to check whether young Will might be sitting at the bar, and then, seeing no familiar faces, turns down the lane into Spitalfields in search of the liquorice she needs to make a posset for Richard's cough. It is a recipe given to her by the silversmith's wife, who swears that it works miracles.

The bright weather has brought out the crowds, and the lanes around Spitalfields Market are filled with people dressed in spring muslins and straw bonnets. A halfpenny showman has put up an elaborate booth, shaped like some oriental temple, on the fringes of the market, and a clamorous mob of small boys are pushing and shoving around the booth in a desperate effort to be next to peer through the peephole and witness the marvels within. Adah knows that she should hurry home to Richard and the little ones, but this moment by herself in the swirling multi-coloured crowds of the market is too precious to miss. It reminds her of the days when she was newly-wed, before young Will was born, and used to wander through these markets, her eyes wide with wonder at the endless treasures on sale, and at the multitude of faces, clothes and accents of the people who sold them.

On the corner of South Street stands the flower seller, her barrow full of sheaves of golden tulips. The bird man has hung up his array of bamboo cages on a rickety stretch of fencing, filling the air with the sweet warbling of goldfinches and canaries. Beyond, in the market square, Adah's senses are assailed by the smells of onions and cauliflower, lemons and leeks. One table is piled high with an elaborate and perilous array of eggs; another, mountains of cheese in every shape and size.

'*Buy* my onions! *Two* shillings a bushel! You won't find them cheaper! Come on, ladies! First new potatoes! Best you'll see all year!'

But the deafening cries of the costermongers are almost drowned out by the raucous clamour of the hurdy-gurdy man, playing a discordant version of 'Over the Hills and Far Away', while a pathetic shrunken child, whom he has brought along in place of a monkey, performs tumbling tricks in the dust next to the organ.

The drifting scents of the spice stall lead Adah to the far end of the square, where she finds bundles of thyme and rosemary, dishes of peppercorns and dried cloves, shiny brown nutmegs and strings of garlic; and, yes, straps of liquorice, coiled like gleaming black snakes. She is taken aback by the price, which is twice what she was expecting, but she is desperate to find something for Richard's cough, so she buys three ounces of liquorice and a twist of anise seeds from the dark, leathery-skinned woman with long braided hair who keeps the stall.

Adah is almost home, carrying her precious purchases in her blue cotton bag, when she sees an ungainly figure tottering towards her from the other side of White Lion Street. Her heart sinks. It is the wretched little vegetable seller, and she realizes with a sudden sense of guilt that, what with all the other things on her mind, she never got around to telling the officer of the watch about the child who has been stealing the poor man's wares. She knows what the man is going to say even before he opens his mouth.

'Ahoy! Mrs Searcher! Why haven't you arrested that thief?' yells the vegetable seller. 'What's the world coming to when the law can't protect a poor soul like me?'

Adah straightens her back and takes a deep breath. 'My good man,' she says, 'the officers of the Liberty are busy people. They have many serious offences to deal with – murders, forgeries, highway robberies. I am sure they are doing their best to find that thief, but you must give them time to complete their investigations.'

'Investigations, indeed!' snorts the little man indignantly. 'I'll give them investigations! She was here again yesterday, snatching my two best apples from under my very nose. If the officers can't catch a scamp like her, they ain't likely to catch no forgers or highway robbers.'

'I'll be sure to remind them,' says Adah, with as much dignity as she can muster. 'I will ask them to give it their most serious attention. But now, please do let me pass. I have a sick child to attend to.'

The little vegetable seller steps reluctantly to one side, still muttering under his breath.

As she opens her front door, hoping in vain that she will find young Will home already, Adah is still nagged by a sense of unease. She should have reported the poor man's complaints, but she was too caught up in the tale of Molly and Rosie Creamer to think of it. The face of the child Rosie still haunts her every day, and she still prays every night for the souls of the dead twins and their poor mother Catherine, though she never feels confident that her prayers are heard.

She mixes the milk and ale for the posset in the copper pan, consoling herself with the thought that her job was to investigate the death of Rosie Creamer, not to chase apple thieves. And she has done that job well. When she reported her findings to the beadle, Mr Beavis, he was full of praise, pleased and (she couldn't help noticing) clearly surprised that Adah had managed to find the name of the dead girl and determine how she died. There was some talk of sending a message to the Liverpool magistrates, asking them to help find the surviving Creamer family, though nothing seems to have come of that yet.

As Adah adds the liquorice and anise seeds to the steaming mixture, the cramped kitchen is filled with a waft of overpowering smells, at once sweet and astringent. This should at least do some good to poor Richard, whose hacking cough she can hear resounding from the upstairs bedroom.

She has just brought the mug of warm posset to Richard, and is turning to go down the stairs, when she hears the sharp rap at the front door. Will, she thinks instantly. Not young Will himself, because he has a key and would not knock at the door. But someone bringing news of Will. Perhaps bad news … Or Father. Surely not more bad news about Father already? They so seldom have visitors at this time of day.

She flies down the stairs, heart pounding, and opens the door, only to find – to her utter astonishment – Raphael DaSilva's manservant Stevens standing on her doorstep, one hand clutching a stout walking stick, with an expression of injured dignity on his face.

'My master, Mr DaSilva, has requested me to give you this letter,' says Stevens very formally, holding out a folded square of paper towards her in the tips of his long sharp fingers. 'He has also instructed me to wait for a reply.'

Flustered, Adah retreats into the hallway clutching the letter. Raphael has never written her a letter before. She is uncomfortably aware that she should ask Stevens to come into the house, but cannot bear the thought of his disdainful eyes roaming over the threadbare matting and mouldering walls of the gloomy entrance hall. She breaks open the seal of the letter and examines the contents, noticing, with a wave of gratitude and relief, that Raphael has not written in his normal artist's scrawl, but has spelled out the words out in a large and careful hand, so that she can read them easily.

Mrs Flint, (she reads)
I have some information to impart to you concerning the matter that we discussed. Would you do me the kindness of calling at my house around 4 o'clock tomorrow afternoon?
Yrs, R. DaSilva.

That is all. She stares at the words, as though trying to decipher some message hidden in its three lines. An impatient cough from Stevens brings her to her senses.

'Thank you, Stevens,' she says, echoing the servant's formality. 'Please express my gratitude to Mr DaSilva, and tell him that I shall be happy to call upon him tomorrow at the time he suggests.'

Another surprise is awaiting Adah when she arrives at the artist's house the following afternoon, and is again led upstairs by a stern and unsmiling Stevens. The table in the centre of Raphael's studio, which is normally covered with a jumble of paint jars, brushes, shells, wizened fruit and paint-smeared rags, has now been swept clean; the only things on its surface are several large leather-bound tomes and a large green glass vase containing a bouquet of irises.

As they wait in the study for Stevens to bring tea, Raphael paces around the room, seeming almost uncertain how to broach the topic that he has summoned her here to discuss. She waits patiently, twisting her hands on her lap, while he embarks on general pleasantries, telling her about a recent sketching trip to Keswick and his long walks in the mountains there.

'There was rain and mist most days,' he says, 'but when the sun came out through the mist, shining over those distant lakes, it was a glorious sight to see. Like a glimpse of paradise itself. You should go there someday yourself, Adah.'

She smiles politely, thinking how unlikely it is that she will ever have the time or money for jaunts to the north of England, let alone for glimpses of paradise. In return she talks about her father's accident and Annie's departure for Fulham, and a little of her concerns about young Will, who finally returned the previous evening, with dark rings under his eyes, a sheepish expression on his face, and an unlikely story about having been taking carpentry lessons from his cousin.

'And tell me, Adah,' says Raphael at last, 'how did your investigations of the story of the dead child end? Did you determine whether she was in fact the daughter of Catherine Creamer?'

Adah is slightly taken aback. She assumed that Raphael would have heard the end of the story from Benjamin Beavis, or perhaps from one of the trustees. But then she remembers how rarely Raphael spends time with the trustees and officers of the Liberty, and how hard he tries to avoid the popular Norton

Folgate pastime of gossiping about local affairs. So, while Stevens serves tea, she describes, as simply and clearly as she can, her visit to Golden Lane, her meeting with the Creamers' neighbour, and her discovery that the dead child was indeed Catherine Creamer's daughter – the twin of the child who had been stolen and who died more than seven years ago.

As she sips her pale golden tea, Adah notices that this time Stevens has given them matching tea-cups and served freshly baked muffins with strawberry jam. Raphael has been preparing for this visit.

Her host listens to her story thoughtfully.

'Hmmm,' he observes, 'it seems clear enough, though a sorry story indeed. But there is something that troubles me. A week or two after our last conversation, I chanced to be reading some information about a certain court case in the *Newgate Calendar*, and my eye fell on an account of the case of Catherine Creamer and her stolen child. I must confess that I was surprised by what I read there. It piqued my curiosity. Since then, I have been looking for other information relating to the story.' He waves his arm vaguely towards the volumes on the studio table. 'I haven't yet managed to find the Old Bailey's record of the trial, though such a record surely must exist. The story I read in the *Newgate Calendar* about the snatching of the child is much like the tale you heard from Catherine Creamer's neighbour. But I am puzzled by other parts of the case. There are curious details that a woman may be best placed to understand. That is why I wanted to speak to you.'

'Curious in what way?' asks Adah.

'When you were last here, and we read the story of Harriet Magnis and Thomas Dellow together', says Raphael, 'it brought back to my mind the story of Catherine Creamer's stolen child, and how I heard that story talked of at the time. It was a famous case indeed. There was much public anger about the crime of child-stealing that year. I didn't immediately remember, but later, as I thought about the case, the story came back to me more clearly. I recall having a long discussion about it, around the time of the trial of Sarah Stone, with Moulton the gem-cutter and his son who keep that shop on the other side of Bishopsgate. For, you know, the key events in this crime took place very close to here, just across Bishopsgate, in Sun Street. Old Mr Moulton had an indirect connection to the case. He told me that a young servant girl who ran errands for him was an acquaintance of Sarah Stone, and was called as a witness in her trial – though, oddly enough, the account of the trial in the *Newgate Calendar* says nothing about her evidence. I believed then (and I think most others did too) that this was another crime just like the crime of Harriet Magnis – a tale of a wife deceiving her sailor husband while he was away at sea. But it seems that this was a rather different story.'

He puts down his cup and walks over to the table, where he opens one of the large books at a marked page.

'The *Newgate Calendar* tells us that this accused woman, Sarah Stone, claimed to have given birth to the child herself, which of course she would have done, to cover up her crime of child-stealing. But, more surprisingly, it appears that, at the time of the incident, she was living in a room in Sun Street, in Bly's Buildings, with the sailor, a man named Edward Swaine, who claimed to be the child's father. It seems that they had lodged in rooms there for some three months, living as husband and wife, though they had never married. Both Swaine and the accused woman's mother, who was lodging in another part of the same house, insisted that Sarah had indeed been expecting a child in the normal manner, and that the infant was hers. Do you think it possible, or likely, that a woman who was sharing a room with her common law husband as man and wife could fool him into believing that she was pregnant and about to bear a child?'

Adah considers for a moment. 'Possible,' she says, 'but not likely. A very crafty woman might perhaps succeed, but it would be a difficult thing to do. When I was big with child, both William and my mother-in-law would sometimes place their hand on my belly to see if the child was moving. A woman might fool strangers in the street by tying a cushion under her petticoats, but a husband would hardly be fooled if they lay together in bed, unless perhaps the woman pretended to be ill, or to have become strangely coy, so that her husband never came close to her person.'

The words about her own pregnancy slip naturally from her lips, but the moment she speaks them she begins to feel hot and uncomfortable. These things are too intimate to be spoken about here. She looks anxiously at Raphael, trying to read the expression on his face. He appears to be avoiding her eyes.

Feeling flustered, she hastily goes on. 'Why ever were the judge and jury convinced that this Sarah Stone was guilty?'

'Well, that too is strange,' replies Raphael, 'for it seems that on 14 October eight years ago, the very day when the Creamer child was stolen, Sarah Stone set out from home in the morning, to all appearances big with child, and came back that very evening with a new babe in her arms. Her story was that she had gone to Rosemary Lane to sell some clothes, for she was in need of money, and, being heavy with child, had suddenly been taken in labour. She said that a stranger named Mary Brown had come to her aid and brought her to an apartment in White Hart Court, a place called Johnson's Change—'

'Is this near Rosemary Lane?' interjects Adah, trying to picture the scene in her mind.

'Yes, just off Rosemary Lane, I believe. This Mary Brown called a man midwife (so Sarah said) and she was delivered of her child there and then, and sent home to Sun Street in a coach. But when, after her arrest, she took the officers from the Lambeth-Street Magistrates' Office to Rosemary Lane, and pointed out the apartment where she claimed to have given birth, these officers found that there was no Mary Brown living there, only a woman named Elizabeth Fisher, who insisted she had never seen the accused in her life. The officers went to find the only man-midwife who lived nearby, but he too knew nothing of the story. Besides, Sarah Stone's landlady, a woman named Isabella Gray, testified that when she saw the baby, on the very day when the accused had supposedly given birth, the infant looked unusually large for a new-born child. Another witness, who lived in the house across the street from the place where Sarah Stone and her sailor lived, also described how she saw Sarah return home in a coach on the day of the supposed birth. Let me read you the *Newgate Calendar*'s account. This witness said that *the prisoner did not appear as if she had just delivered: she (that's the witness) had had children herself, and did not believe that any woman who had only delivered that afternoon could have walked up the court as the prisoner did.*'

'Well …' says Adah slowly. 'A complicated tale indeed. Officers from Lambeth Street Magistrates' Office, you say. Does the account of the trial give their names?'

Raphael consults the tome on the table again, 'Ebenezer Dalton, it says. Yes, an Ebenezer Dalton and a Samuel Miller.'

'Ah,' cries Adah, 'I know those names. William knew them both. He had little regard for the work of the Lambeth-Street office, but he was on quite good terms with Sam Miller. I believe William helped Miller out with one or two small matters a few years back.' She cannot help wondering what William would have made of this – he who always prided himself on being able to unravel even the most complex criminal mysteries.

'Rosemary Lane is close enough to the Commercial Road, where little Molly Creamer was stolen,' she continues pensively, 'so I can understand why a jury might have doubted the strange tale that Sarah Stone told, and believed her to be the kidnapper. But how did the officers find her and arrest her? I heard from the Creamers' neighbour Lizzie Murray that it was a full six weeks before they made the arrest.'

'The *Newgate Calendar* says that Catherine Creamer had hand bills made.' Raphael pauses, running his eyes over the page again. 'Here's the passage: *Poor as she was, the prosecutrix immediately had advertisements and hand bills published, with a description of the prisoner, for which she paid seventeen shillings*. It seems (although no details are given here) that someone, perhaps Sarah Stone's landlady, Isabella Gray, must have seen the hand bill and given information to the magistrates. Then six weeks after the kidnapping, the magistrate took Catherine Creamer to a ship moored on the Thames, where she saw the baby in Sarah Stone's arms and instantly recognized it as her own infant. Of course, she also recognized Sarah Stone as the woman who had snatched her child.'

'That may be true enough,' remarks Adah, 'but as for the hand bills, Catherine Creamer's neighbour told me they were ordered and paid for by the magistrates. She had kept one of those hand bills, and gave it to me. I have it at home. Printed on fine paper by Nelson's Printery. Where would a woman who had to beg for pennies in a churchyard find seventeen shillings to pay for something like that? Not to mention the reward. The hand bill spoke of a twenty pound reward.'

Raphael falls silent for a while, reflecting on the strange twists in the tale.

'This case is certainly a puzzle,' continues Adah, 'but I doubt that we can solve it. It was long ago now. Catherine and her twins are dead. Sarah Stone must surely be at the other side of the globe, serving her sentence in the colonies, or maybe living as a free woman there, for I suppose her sentence must almost be complete.'

Raphael sighs. 'No doubt you are right. I don't know why it troubles me so. I'll see what more I can find in the records, but perhaps this is indeed a puzzle with no solution. May I contact you again if I discover anything more?'

For the first time today, he looks Adah straight in the eye. She smiles back at him.

'Of course you may,' she says.

And as she rises leave, he adds softly, 'And maybe, if you come again, you might like to bring your daughter Sally with you.'

MAY 1822

Sun Street and Rosemary Lane

She tells herself that they are just taking a little walk. Sally has had another chill, and been playing restlessly indoors for the past few days. The children need fresh air. So, leaving Richard to keep an eye on Amelia, she ties Sally's little brown cloak around the child's shoulders, lifts Caroline into her arms, and sets out along the road with the two children. Yet she knows in her heart where they are going, and wonders what draws her there. My task, she reminds herself, was to investigate the death of Rosie Creamer, who died in our own Liberty, not to re-examine the disappearance of her twin sister, years back and in another part of town. And yet, having become so enmeshed in one part of this tangled mystery, she finds it hard to resist the temptation to explore it further.

They take the long route to avoid the little vegetable seller on the corner of White Lion Street, for Adah cannot face the thought of another confrontation with him. On the way, they pass the rickety gateway that leads into the wasteland where Rosie Creamer's body was found. Someone, she notices, has patched up the gate with a couple of planks of wood, and fastened it shut with twine. They make slow progress along Magpie Alley, for Caro is at that awkward age when she is almost too heavy to carry, but her efforts to walk on her own plump legs are slow and wavering. She insists on walking by herself at first, but halfway down the street she starts to fret, and wants to be carried again, so Adah hoists the child up onto her hip. Caro nuzzles her face into Adah's neck, mumbling something that sounds like 'buzz, buzz.'

'Enough, you're tickling me!' laughs Adah.

The child's warm sweaty skin smells of sugar and salt.

Sally, meanwhile, has to stop every couple of minutes to examine something that she has discovered by the roadside.

'Look, Mammy, lace,' says Sally, holding up a grimy corner of a torn handkerchief that she has found lying by the side of the road.

'Oh, throw that away, my love. It's covered with dirt,' says Adah, at which Sally flings the piece of cloth into the gutter with an expression of disgust and promptly turns her attentions to an equally grimy black feather, which she plucks from a pile of rubbish by the road and begins to stroke lovingly.

As they enter Bishopsgate, Adah seizes Sally firmly by the hand and steers her through the traffic of carts and horses, gigs and hand-barrows that throng the thoroughfare. On the far side, at the corner of Primrose Street, Adah catches a sweet whiff of freshly baked bread and spices. A baker's boy stands at the corner, the tray around his neck laden with gleaming currant buns, still warm from the oven. She's tempted to buy a couple, but then remembers her promise to herself that she will save her pennies until her next visit to the market tomorrow.

Bishopsgate is bathed in sunshine, but when they turn the corner into Sun Street, the shadow of buildings falls across the road, and the air suddenly feels clammy. The cobbles are rough and the street pitted with holes, so even though Caro is squirming and asking to be put down, Adah tightens her grasp around her little daughter's waist. Sarah instantly darts in the direction of the gutter, where a particularly bad-smelling trickle of brown water moves sluggishly between green streaked stones.

'Come away from there, Sal!' calls Adah sharply. She is already wondering whether it was wise to bring the children here.

Bly's Buildings stands halfway down the street on the left-hand side – an ugly tall edifice with ancient timber beams still visible in the upper storeys, but the lower part clad in brown brick which looks quite new, although the windows are grimy and a couple have been broken and patched up with bits of sacking. It feels strange to realize that this place holds the key to the tragedy of little Molly Creamer. No wonder William spoke of the case with such interest – it all happened almost on their doorstep, though just outside the bounds of the Liberty.

Sally has found a sleek black cat with two mewling kittens, and is absorbed in playing with them, so Adah sets Caro on the ground and allows her to toddle over to her older sister.

'Don't pull their tails, mind,' she calls, 'and don't let them scratch Caro. Do you hear me, Sally?'

Adah looks up and down the gloomy street, trying to imagine the scene: Sarah Stone alighting from a carriage, somewhere beside the street corner, and walking to Bly's Buildings, with the infant bundled in her arms. What time of day would it have been? Late afternoon, at the earliest. The hand bill, which Adah has read so many times that she can almost recite its contents by heart, speaks of Molly Creamer being snatched from her mother at about three o'clock in the afternoon. If Sarah Stone was the child thief, she must have set off at two or earlier to walk to St. Paul's churchyard, somehow discarding along the way the cushion or other padding that she was using to make herself appear pregnant – for Catherine Creamer's description said nothing about the kidnapper looking as though she were big with child.

Did Sarah Stone wander the streets for an hour or more looking for an infant to snatch? Or had she already seen poor

Catherine Creamer begging at St. Paul's some days earlier, and marked her out as a target? It seems a strange way to steal a child. Adah remembers how often she has seen infants left by their mothers in a basket outside a shop or an inn, always mentally scolding the parents for their recklessness. How much safer and easier to seize an unattended baby while its mother's eyes were elsewhere, rather than choosing to walk the streets of London with the victim for half an hour or more, giving Catherine Creamer ample chance to observe her face and clothing. But Sarah Stone had chosen this perilous path to crime. And then, having seized the child… What then? She must have wandered the streets around the Commercial Road a little longer, for to return home too quickly with the child would surely have aroused suspicion. Then, somehow, she had found a carriage to take her to Sun Street. Would a woman who lived in a rented room in crumbling Bly's Buildings really have money to pay for a carriage ride?

Again Adah tries to conjure up the scene in her mind's eye. October 1814. Perhaps five o'clock in the evening; already growing dark. The woman who lives across the road from Bly's Buildings saw Sarah alight from a carriage, carrying an infant in her arms; but how clearly could she have seen the figure of the woman with a child at that hour of the day in this gloomy street?

Adah can imagine that figure now: a dark haired, pock marked woman of about forty (as the hand bill records) hurrying through the shadows of the street with a bundle in her arms, furtive perhaps, trying not to be seen. It is a strange thing to live in a city of a million people – the greatest city in the world, William always liked to say. Every day you pass dozens, hundreds, of strangers. You see their faces. Sometimes you look fleetingly into their eyes, or give a little nod of greeting. But you never know what goes on in their minds. Their lives and deaths remain total mysteries, of which you can see only tiny, broken fragments.

Sun Street is so close to the courthouse where Adah spent all her married life that, quite possibly, she may even have seen Sarah Stone in the street, around the time when the child was stolen. What was I doing on that day when Molly was snatched, Adah wonders. But no memories return, not of the day, nor even of the whole month of October 1814. A month of my life vanished into nothing, she thinks.

What makes a woman steal another's child? Somewhere in the cold depths of her mind, Adah knows the answer. She remembers the dark days after her own Sarah Ann, her firstborn daughter, died. She recalls the tiny lifeless form of her dead child, like a wax doll. All the passion and anger and tears in her own body could not breathe life or warmth into that waxy form. And then, the first day she ventured out of doors after Sarah Ann's death, seeing a warm, living, crying baby lying in a basket outside an inn door, and being seized by such an urge to pick up that child and take it home that she had fled from the scene in terror that she might become a child-stealer herself …

Then another thought strikes her. Did Sarah Stone have other children? There was no mention of this in the account of the case that Raphael gave her. But the hand bill describes the kidnapper as being about forty years old. Forty seems an old age to bear a first child – or to pretend to bear one. Is it possible that Sarah Stone was unable to give birth to her own children and, growing desperate as she reached the limit of her child-bearing years, decided to steal a baby and rear it as her own?

The front door of Bly's Buildings suddenly opens, interrupting Adah's musings, and a middle-aged woman with a ruddy complexion – surprisingly well dressed and carrying a parasol in one hand – comes down the steps.

Seizing her opportunity, Adah calls out, 'Excuse me, ma'am. I'm looking for Isabella Gray. I believe she's the landlady here.'

'Good gracious, no,' replies the woman in surprise. 'Isabella Gray moved away years ago. Came into some money and bought a better place than this, in Holborn, I believe. Are you looking for a room? You'll have to ask Mr Patullo about that. He's the landlord now. Lives round the corner in Primrose Street.'

'No,' says Adah. 'I'm not looking for a room.' Having come this far, she may as well continue. 'I am the Searcher of the Liberty of Norton Folgate, and I am making some inquiries about a matter from a few years back. May I ask you if you live here, and if so, whether you have been here long?'

The woman stares at her coldly, clearly resenting the questions, but answers simply enough, 'Yes, indeed. Not in Bly's Buildings, I should say, but in number eight.' She points towards a more substantial looking house on the opposite side of the street. 'We'll have been there ten years this December.'

'And do you, by chance,' asks Adah, drawing a breath, 'recall the events surrounding the arrest of Sarah Stone, who used to live in Bly's Buildings?'

The moment the words are out of her mouth, Adah sees that she will get no help from this quarter.

'Never knew her,' snaps the woman. 'That business had nothing to do with me. It was a matter between the Grays and that Stone woman and her sailor. I bid you good day.'

And she turns abruptly on her heel and strides off in the direction of Crown Street.

At the same moment, Sally utters a piercing shriek and rushes to her mother to cling to her skirts, with Caro tottering unsteadily behind her.

'It scratched me! That cat scratched me!' wails Sally.

'I told you not to pull its tail,' responds Adah calmly though rather wearily. She is long accustomed to these dramas. 'Let me see the scratch.'

Weeping just a little too piteously to be convincing, Sally raises one hand, on which Adah can just make out two faint red scratch marks.

She bends down and gives it a kiss, and her good resolutions falter.

'How would you like a currant bun?' she asks the weeping child.

A small smile appears on Sally's tear-stained face, and she nods solemnly.

Adah hoists Caro into her arms again and takes Sally by her uninjured hand.

'Come on, let's see if we can find one,' says Adah.

This time there is no mystery about the body that lies on the truckle bed in the Norton Folgate watch-house.

Adah is already on her way to the courthouse to give the room its weekly clean when young Sam Sloper, the lad who has replaced Jonah Hall, comes running to meet her.

'We need you to look at a body, Mrs Flint,' he cries, with an air of palpable excitement. 'It's Old Mother Leigh. Found her myself, first thing this morning, in that alleyway just behind the corner of Gun Street. Stone dead, she was.'

And here the old woman lies, strands of her thinning white hair straggling over her wrinkled forehead, her cheeks sunken and her pursed lips clamped tight shut over her toothless gums.

Everyone in Norton Folgate knew Mother Leigh: long widowed, seldom without a bottle of gin in her hand, and slightly addled in the head, though harmless. Her favourite occupation was accosting strangers in the street with unexpected remarks like, 'That Boney's rotting in his grave now, you know', or 'Did you hear that the King's sired seven bastards?' and then she would cackle with glee as she watched the confused expression on the faces of the hapless targets of her wisecracks. The mystery is not that Old Mother Leigh is dead, but how she managed to live so long. She must have been well over eighty.

As Adah takes a knife to cut open poor Mother Leigh's stained and ragged dress, holding her breath against the smell that rises from the dead woman's garments, she wonders at the contrast between this shrivelled sack of bones and the delicate body of Rosie Creamer, which she examined almost four months ago now. Will my body too look like this someday, she wonders. The only marks on Mother Leigh's body are the dark freckles and blotches of old age. There is nothing to show how the old woman died, but Sam Sloper says he saw her just three days back, coughing as though her lungs would burst.

Though it hardly seems necessary, Adah feels that she should at least make the effort to look at the place where the poor woman's body was found, in case it reveals anything more about her death, so she and Sam set out down White Lion Street and through the marketplace towards the far side of Spital Square. As they pass the herb and spice stall, with its rich admixture of smells, Adah reflects that the liquorice posset doesn't seem to have done much for Richard's cough yet, despite all the money she spent on it. But perhaps it needs longer to work its magic.

The alleyway behind Gun Street is a dark and dingy spot, littered with splintered planks of wood and empty rotting baskets.

'A sad place to breathe your last,' says Adah with a sigh. 'Old Mother Leigh's husband Jack was a barber, you know, and they say he left her a fair bit of money, but I suppose she must have drunk it all away.'

There is nothing to mark the place where Sam found the body, except for a crumpled and stained kerchief, perhaps left there by the dead woman.

'Will you come back to the courthouse now, Mrs Flint?' asks Sam, after they have gazed at the place in silence for a moment without seeing anything that adds to their knowledge of Mother Leigh's fate.

Adah performs a moment's mental calculation. She needs a walk, to shake off the gloom of this dark alleyway and to rid her mind of its images of the old woman's lonely death, and it can't be more than twenty minutes on foot from here to Rosemary Lane, where Sarah Stone claimed to have given birth to the child. Eight years on, how likely is it that Elizabeth Fisher would still be living in the same room in White Hart Court? And even if she is still living there and can be found, how likely is it that she would have anything to add to the story she told the judge and jury at the time of Sarah Stone's trial? Not very likely, but it can surely do no harm to take a look at the place.

'No, Sam,' she replies. 'I have a small errand to run first. I'll be back a little later in the day, and thank you kindly for your help.'

But when she reaches the entrance to Rosemary Lane, Adah's heart sinks. She had forgotten what a rabbit warren the place is. The lane itself is lined on either side by rickety old houses with lead-paned windows, every one crammed to the rafters with old clothes for sale. The clothes spill out onto the crooked pavements. They hang from rails along the shopfronts and on poles that protrude from windows on the upper floors. There are once-white sailors' breeches and tattered nightshirts, red and golden silken shawls and fraying embroidered waistcoats, exotic blue pantaloons with embroidered garters that must come from some distant country, and here and there a surprisingly grand velvet gown. Adah picks her way with difficulty between the mountains of boots, shoes and hats heaped on sheets of sacking in the laneway, avoiding the hands that clutch at her cloak, and the wheedling voices tempting her to buy their wares. A mass of tiny alleyways runs to the right and left off Rosemary Lane. The very thought of finding anything or anyone in the midst of this pandemonium seems hopeless.

She asks an elderly boot seller the way to White Hart Court, but the woman just grins and shrugs. 'Ain't no White Hart Court round here, my love,' she says.

Adah presses on a little further before trying again. This time, too, the response is a frown and a shake of the head, but then a little urchin, perhaps ten or eleven years old, pops his grimy face out from behind a stand of tall hats, breaking into the conversation to say, 'Hey, missus, it ain't White Hart you want, it's White Horse. Just down the way on the right, behind the White Horse Inn. Folk around here sometimes call the yard at the back White Horse Court.'

‘And do you know a place called Johnson’s Change?’ asks Adah, feeling that, after all, her journey may not be in vain.

‘Course I do,’ retorts the urchin, as though it were the most ridiculous question he had heard. ‘*Everyone* round here knows Johnson’s Change. C’mon. I’ll show yer.’

And he darts off through the throng at such high speed that Adah is barely fast enough to follow him. There are plenty of inn signs of all shapes, colours and designs on the corners of the alleyways off Rosemary Lane, and it takes her a few moments to find the fading wooden sign with its emblem of a winged white stallion in improbable flight. Just in front of the inn, the lad vanishes into a dark alleyway, and Adah, running and stumbling in his wake, finds herself in front of a gaping brick archway which leads into a huge, dimly lit covered market. Even though it is still mid-morning, the tall windows on either side of the building are so grimy that some of the stall holders have had to hang flickering lanterns on hooks at the corner of their stalls to make their wares visible.

Adah’s young guide has vanished into the gloom, leaving her to make her own way between the trestle tables and packing cases covered with bolts of cloth, pinafores and cheap trinkets. Beneath one window she spots a length of muslin in a lovely grey blue that looks as though it is just the colour of little Amelia’s eyes, and is tempted to stop and ask the price. It would make a perfect dress for her daughter. But she resists the distraction and heads instead towards the staircase that she can see in the far corner of the building.

The stairs, uneven and made of dark brick, lead to the first floor of Johnson’s Change. At the top, Adah finds herself in a wooden-floored corridor which runs along the front of the building, with a row of windows on one side and a row of battered doors on the other. There are no name plates by the doors, but here and there, an occupant has tacked a piece of handwritten paper by the door. *Lucy*, reads one; *Pretty Polly*, reads another.

Adah knocks at random on one of the doors. After a long wait and sounds of coughing and shuffling inside, the door is opened by a frowzled, fair-haired young woman, aged little more than sixteen, Adah guesses. She is dressed in a night shift and shawl, and has clearly just been woken from sleep.

'What is it?' asks the girl sullenly, rubbing her puffy eyes with the back of her hand.

'I'm looking for Elizabeth Fisher,' says Adah. 'I heard she lives in this building.'

'Never 'eard of 'er,' replies the girl with a sniff.

'Can you tell me where I might find your …' Adah pauses, hesitating over the right term to use, 'your landlord?'

'Landlady,' the girl corrects her. 'Mrs Aarons. Lives in Duke Street, the other side of Aldgate. Number five, I think it is.'

As the girl closes the door, Adah distinctly hears her mutter 'stupid cow', and wonders whether the insult is directed at herself or is a comment on the landlady.

Mrs Aarons's house, as it turns out, is just down the road from the home of Rabbi Meldola, whom Adah visited back in January. But the contrast is striking. While the Hahams' house seemed a sanctuary of calm and scholarship, Mrs Aarons's is warm, chaotic, rather shabby and full of the most wonderful smells of baking. The landlady herself is a huge woman, almost as wide as she is tall, with an off-white apron stretched over her bulk, coils of iron grey hair protruding from her cap, and small but bright eyes that precisely match the colour of her hair.

'Come in, come in, my dear,' says Mrs Aarons, even before Adah has time to state her business. 'Would you mind stepping down to the kitchen? I have to keep my eye on the stove.'

The kitchen, down a curved flight of stone steps, is whitewashed and cavernous. Bundles of herbs and onions hang from the ceiling. One side of the room is lined with shelves on which stand gleaming rows of jars filled with preserves and pickles, honey and something white that looks like cream; on the other is a big old dresser filled with blue and white china and copper pots of every shape and size. In the middle of the kitchen, at a long scrubbed wooden table, a young woman with dark ringlets is busy kneading dough. She looks up as Adah comes in and gives her a brief, silent nod.

'Never mind our Rachel,' says Mrs Aarons briskly. 'She's deaf and dumb. But bakes the best bread and cakes in all of Aldwych. Now, what can I do for you, my dear?'

'I am the Searcher of the Liberty of Norton Folgate, and I am making inquiries about an incident that happened some years back now. Eight years, to be precise. It concerns a woman who lives, or used to live, in Johnson's Change, off Rosemary Lane. I think she may have rented a room from you.'

Mrs Aarons's eyes narrow a little, but she continues smiling as she asks, 'And what might her name be, dear?'

'Elizabeth Fisher,' says Adah.

Mrs Aarons is silent for a moment, and then, to Adah's surprise, bursts into guffaws of laughter.

'Elizabeth Fisher!' she exclaims, wiping her eyes. 'Oh dear, no! Someone's been playing a little joke on you, I'm afraid. Elizabeth Fisher indeed! That poor lady would turn in her grave if she heard you!'

'I … don't understand,' stammers Adah.

'Why should you, my dear, why should you, if you're not from these parts? But Elizabeth Fisher, you see, was a very grand old lady. Used to live on her own in that big old house with the turret on the south side of Aldgate. Wore black silk every day for forty years after her husband died. Old Mrs Fisher was a famous figure in this area. She died about eight years ago, maybe nine, at a great age. Ninety if she was a day. The thought of Mrs Fisher renting one of them rooms in Johnson's Change is just too funny.' Mrs Aarons wheezes with laughter again. 'No, someone's been bamboozling you, my dear.'

Adah is silent for a moment, watching the deaf-mute girl pound her dough on the kitchen table as though it represented every grievance and injustice she had ever faced in life.

'How about a Mary Brown, then?' she asks. 'Did you have a Mary Brown renting a room from you in Johnson's Change eight years ago?'

'Mary Brown?' echoes Mrs Aarons. 'Ah well, there's plenty of Mary Browns in the world. But as it happens, yes, there was a Mary Ann Brown who used to rent a room in Johnson's Change. I'm not likely to forget that little hussy in a hurry,' she adds.

'Why?' asks Adah. 'What became of her? Where's she now?'

Mrs Aarons gives a meaningful smile and points at the floor. 'Down there somewhere, I suppose,' she says.

For one dizzying moment, Adah has a vision of the delinquent Mary Ann Brown languishing in a dungeon beneath the flagged kitchen floor, but then Mrs Aarons continues. 'Van Dieman's Land, I believe it was. Transported for seven years. Helped herself to a silver watch belonging to one of her gentlemen callers. One of her *many* gentlemen callers, if you take my meaning.'

'When did this happen?' asks Adah.

'Two years back. No, more like three now. But she'd been living in Johnson's Change for six or seven years before they arrested her. Ay ay ay, the Shrewsbury cakes!'

Mrs Aarons leaps from her seat with surprising agility for a woman of her size, and dashes across the room, cloth in hand, to seize the pan of sizzling biscuits from the hob, and even her daughter gives a little grunt of alarm.

'Ah, we're in luck,' cries the mother. 'No harm done. Caught them just in time.'

As she turns out the biscuits onto a board, her daughter Rachel comes over to peer at them, putting one floury arm around her mother's shoulder, while the mother gives the daughter's waist an affectionate squeeze.

'Just as well I caught them,' says Mrs Aarons over her shoulder to Adah. 'Our Rachel would never forgive me if I allowed her precious Shrewsbury cakes to burn. Let me put on a kettle for tea, and you can have one of these before you go. I'll promise you you've never tasted the like.'

In the excitement about the Shrewsbury cakes, Mrs Aarons appears to have forgotten all about the crimes of Mary Ann Brown, but Adah, watching mother and daughter bustle about the kitchen with the tea cups, is lost in thought. No Elizabeth Fisher, but a Mary Ann Brown, with her gentlemen callers and her stolen silver watch.

Surely this justifies another meeting with Raphael, who seems to have become almost as consumed with curiosity about this case as Adah herself. Is it really the strangeness of the case that intrigues us, she wonders. Or has the story of Molly Creamer and Sarah Stone become a bridge for other feelings…? But these are thoughts she does not want to pursue, so she bites instead into the buttery sweetness of the Shrewsbury cake, which tastes of lemon and caraway and something else she has never eaten before.

'This is delicious,' she says, conscious of speaking too slowly and loudly to the deaf-mute woman, who gazes at her as she eats with an intense gaze, her eyes drawing in the thoughts that Adah cannot put into words.

JUNE 1822

The Star Apple Tree

Sally tugs at Adah's hand as they walk together down White Lion Street.

'Where are we going, Mammy?'

'To see a fine gentleman, my love. So behave yourself, and don't ask too many questions.'

The old soldier who begs on the street corner is out again today, but there's no sign of the poor crippled vegetable seller, and Adah realizes she hasn't seen him for days now. Suddenly curious, she drops a penny into the soldier's extended hand.

'What's become of the man who was selling vegetables here?' she asks.

'Moved away,' mumbles the soldier. 'Said there was too many thieves about in this part of town. Don't know where he's gone.'

Sally is tugging at her hand again. 'Mammy. Mammy. How many questions can I ask? Can I ask three questions?'

'No, three is too many. Only two.'

Somewhere in the back of her mind, for the past five years, she has been imagining this moment, when she will see their faces side by side, and have a chance to compare their features. But in fact – when they enter Raphael's study and he bends down to greet Sally – what strikes Adah most is not the similarity in their faces, but rather the quiet gravity with which Raphael addresses the little girl.

'Well, Sally,' he says, 'I am so pleased to meet you. Your mother tells me that you like to draw. I love drawing too. Would you like to look at some of my pictures?'

But Sally's eyes are focused on the painting of Jamaica that hangs to the right of the doorway.

'Did you paint that?' she asks.

'No, that was painted by another artist. But I like to have it hanging on my wall, because that is where I lived when I was a child, around your age. We had a house that looked a little like the one in the picture, with a terrace facing towards the sea, and a big tree growing next to the terrace that bore shining purple fruit they called star apples.'

'Star apples,' whispers Sally, entranced.

'I had a nursemaid named Falelia, who used to bring me my breakfast to eat on the terrace underneath the star apple tree, while my parents were still sleeping. Falelia would look out at the sea and sing songs to me while I ate.'

Adah listens in silent astonishment. She has never heard the taciturn Raphael speak about his childhood before, and had no idea that his memories were so vivid.

'Can you eat star apples?' asks Sally.

'Not the skin. That's too bitter. But inside there is sweet pink flesh which tastes very good. Falelia used to give me star apple flesh to eat when I had a sore throat.'

But Sally has already lost interest in the picture, and turns away to explore the other wonders of Raphael's rooms, her gaze fastening on a mandolin propped against a cupboard door in the studio.

'Don't touch that!' cries Adah, as the child launches herself in its direction.

'Never fear, Adah,' says Raphael with a laugh. 'It's old and broken already. She won't do it any harm.'

While Sally plucks tentatively and discordantly at the strings of the old mandolin, Raphael fetches a pencil and some sheets of paper which are covered with his half-finished sketches on one side, but blank on the other.

'Could you draw some pictures for me?' he asks.

Sally seats herself on the worn and paint-splashed rug which covers the studio floor, spreading out the papers in front of her, and sucking vigorously on one end of the pencil. Then she removes the pencil from her mouth and asks, 'Have you got a wife and children too, Mr Raphael?'

'That's three questions,' snaps Adah. 'I said you could only ask two.'

But Raphael is already answering, quite calmly, though without looking in Adah's direction. 'I have a wife, yes. Her name is Miriam. But she lives in Jamaica. She is not well, and can't come to England, so I haven't seen her in many years.'

'What's wrong with her?' asks Sally.

Raphael bends down and strokes the child's shining brown hair.

'Now *that*,' he says firmly, 'is one question too many. I need to talk to your mother for a little while, so see if you can draw us a fine picture. If it's truly beautiful, then I will have a little present to give you in exchange.'

'I'm so sorry,' murmurs Adah, flushed with embarrassment, as Raphael joins her at the table which is now laden with a larger pile of leather-bound tomes than before. 'Sally's forever asking foolish questions. She's too young to know any better.'

But Raphael's face, she sees, is infused with a strange happiness. 'It's not foolish. She's a child. Children should be curious. That is how they learn. Now, to this story of the Creamer child and Sarah Stone. I have found the court record of the trial at last. Not only that, I also found a report of the case that appeared in *The Times*, and another odd little reference to the affair in a book published a few years back. And better still, I have found something, or rather I should say someone, even more interesting, about whom I shall tell you in a moment. Where shall we begin?'

'First let me tell you what I discovered,' says Adah. 'I went to Rosemary Lane and made some inquiries of the landlady who owns the rooms above Johnson's Change. There was no Elizabeth Fisher living there eight years ago. Indeed, Elizabeth Fisher, it seems, was a very respectable old lady living in Aldgate, and well known to everyone in the district. But there was a Mary Ann Brown, who was earning her living by disreputable means, and was arrested for theft a few years later.'

'Indeed, indeed,' cries Raphael, with sudden animation. 'I was starting to suspect some such thing. For listen to this. There's a very strange passage in the record of the Old Bailey trial that I could not at first make sense of. This woman who called herself Elizabeth Fisher appeared as a witness at the trial. According to the record, she described how the officers came to her rooms. And then she says this: "I was called down to look at the prisoner; somebody called Brown; I answered; my name is Elizabeth Fisher; that is my real name."'

'Whatever does that mean?' asks Adah.

'I couldn't fathom it at first, but when I looked again at the Newgate Calendar, I understood. It is clear that this woman did indeed answer to the name of Brown when first spoken to by the officers. Her only explanation for doing so is that she was "greatly alarmed by the circumstance of appearing before a magistrate". But soon after, she changed her story to insist that she was not Mary Brown but Elizabeth Fisher. As well she might, if she was living by immoral and possibly criminal means, and wanted to avoid any close inspection of the place where she lived.'

'And did the officers not ask her neighbours or her landlady to confirm her identity?'

'Apparently not. And that is not the only strange point about this trial. The Old Bailey record and *The Times* tell us that Sarah Stone's mother, who was living in the same building in Sun Street as Sarah, insisted that her daughter was pregnant and bore a child that day, and that Sarah gave the infant her breast. And there was another witness, too, who spoke on Sarah's behalf. Do you remember how I told you, when we last met, about old Mr Moulton who keeps the jeweller's shop in Bishopsgate, and how he knew a servant girl who was a witness at the trial?'

At this precise moment there is a sound of knocking at the door downstairs, and Raphael announces, rather with the air of a magician pulling a flock of live doves out of an empty sack, 'Here, I believe, she is. No longer such a young girl, of course, but a married woman. I managed to find her with the help of young Ezekiah Moulton, and have asked to her come and meet us here today.'

The woman whom Stevens, with exaggerated solemnity, ushers into the room is so fragile and slightly built that she looks almost like a child. Her hair is fair, and her skin pale and transparent. She wears a clean but rather faded and threadbare green gown and carries a small purse which she clutches nervously in her hands. She enters the parlour with downcast eyes, only raising them fleetingly when Raphael greets her.

'Thank you for coming to speak to us today, Mrs Perry,' he says. 'This is Mrs Adah Flint, the Searcher of the Liberty of Norton Folgate, who would like to ask you a few questions about your connection to the case of Sarah Stone. Adah, this is Martha Perry, whose maiden name was Cadwell. She was a neighbour of Sarah Stone and, as I was just saying, was a witness at the trial. Please seat yourself here, Mrs Perry. Can we give you something to drink?'

The young woman perches herself on the edge of the armchair that Raphael points to, with her head bowed and her hands folded on her lap. She shakes her head. 'No, thank you kindly, sir,' she murmurs.

'Now I will leave you with Mrs Flint,' he continues, turning with a small smile to Adah, who is utterly taken aback at this unexpected turn of events. 'I think I should see how my young art pupil is progressing.'

And with that, Raphael withdraws into his studio and closes the door, leaving Adah and the newcomer facing one another across the study.

Hardly knowing where to begin, but feeling somehow drawn to this small, nervous young woman, Adah says, 'Mrs Perry, how old were you at the time of the arrest and trial of Sarah Stone? You must surely have been little more than a child.'

'Yes, ma'am,' replies the woman demurely. 'I was twelve years old at the time. My mother and all of us children was living in two rooms at the top of Bly's Buildings, and Mrs Swaine – that's what we called her, though they called her Sarah Stone at the trial – her and her husband lived down in the basement.'

'And did you know them well?'

'Oh no, ma'am. I'd only seen them once or twice, before the day when my mother came to say that Mrs Swaine would like to give me a little job to do, and I was to be paid twopence a week for it.'

She falls silent for a moment, and then adds, by way of explanation, 'I've five younger brothers and sisters, you see. That's now, of course. I had six then. Our Joseph, the youngest, he was born with a withered leg. So our mother sometimes had a hard time to keep us all fed, and for as long as I can remember I used to run errands around the neighbourhood to earn a little money here and there.'

'So what was the task that Sarah Stone – Mrs Swaine – wanted you to do for her?'

The young woman is staring intently down at her hands, and a faint flush has spread across her pale face. 'She wanted me to draw her milk,' she murmurs.

'Draw her milk?' echoes Adah, puzzled.

'Yes, ma'am. The baby was suckling, you see, but it didn't seem to take much milk. It would drink just a little, and then pull its mouth away from the breast and cry, or sometimes just fall asleep in its mother's arms. So Mrs Swaine, she had too much milk, and her breasts hurt. She had tried to squeeze the milk out herself, but she said that just hurt all the more. She wanted me to suck the milk from her breasts. She paid me twopence a week, and I would go to her almost every day to draw her milk. I sat on a stool beside her to draw it. It tasted a little strange. Sweeter than cow's milk …'

Adah gazes at the woman, uncomprehending.

'And you told all this to the court?' she says at last.

'Oh yes, ma'am.'

'But if Sarah Stone had milk, then she must have had a child, or at least carried a child almost to the point of birth!'

'Yes, ma'am. I never doubted that the infant was hers, until sometime later, when our landlady Mrs Gray and her father started saying the baby had been stolen. And even then, even after Mrs Swaine was arrested, I still believed it was her child. I believe so to this day.'

'Was it her first child? She was surely rather old to have given birth for the first time.'

'Old?' says Martha Perry, looking puzzled. 'Why, no. She wasn't old. She would have been just a year or two older then than I am now. As far as I know, little Phoebe – that's what they called the baby – was her first child.'

'But if you were twelve years old at the time of the trial, then you must surely be no more than twenty years old now.'

'Twenty-one, ma'am.'

'Twenty-one!' exclaims Adah, half-rising from her seat in astonishment. 'You mean to say that Sarah Stone was only twenty-one, or a couple of years older? How is that possible? The hand bill that was distributed by the Magistrates Office describes the child-stealer as being aged about forty. And Catherine Creamer, the woman whose child was stolen, walked for miles across London in the company of this kidnapper. How could she have mistaken a person aged little more than twenty-one for a woman of forty?'

But at that moment their conversation is disturbed by Sally, who flings open the studio door and marches into the parlour, triumphantly brandishing her work of art – a sinuous design of curling branches and leaves interspersed with a mass of strange squiggles.

'Look, a *star apple tree*!' shouts Sally, exulting. 'A *star apple tree*!'

'My apologies for the interruption,' says Raphael, looking anything but apologetic. 'My art student is *very* enthusiastic.'

Martha Perry raises her eyes, and for the first time since she entered the room, gives a small smile.

'What a sweet child,' she says, 'and so very like—'

'Mrs Perry's story is extraordinary!' interrupts Adah, conscious of her own bad manners. She can feel her face flushing, and her heart beats with a mixture of emotions that she cannot wholly understand, but the strongest of which, she realizes, is a rising tide of anger. 'How could the court have allowed so many contradictions to go unquestioned and so many questions to go unanswered?'

'But Adah,' says Raphael softly, after Martha Perry has taken her leave, and Adah knows at once what he is going to say, for she has been asking herself the very same question. 'Catherine Creamer recognized Sarah Stone as the child-stealer. More importantly, she recognized the child in Sarah Stone's arms as her own daughter Molly. The court record tells us that even before Mrs Creamer saw the infant, she recognized its crying voice as the voice of her lost daughter. How could she possibly have been mistaken? Molly was a twin. Catherine Creamer could see her twin daughters side by side, perhaps not perfectly alike, but very similar. Is it conceivable that she could have mistaken another woman's baby for her own?'

'I don't know,' replies Adah slowly. 'But just think. Catherine was surely desperate to find her child. Her neighbour Lizzie Murray told me that the child who was returned to Catherine seemed gaunt and wasted, very different from the plump baby who had been stolen from Catherine's arms. I don't know the answer to this puzzle. But I am sure that the magistrates should have employed a woman Searcher to examine Sarah Stone's body for signs that she had borne a child. They did not do so. Why did they arrest a woman little more than half the age of the woman they were seeking? Why did they not question the identity of the woman who called herself Elizabeth Fisher? Why did they leave so many questions unanswered? These are people's lives, Raphael. Whole human lives hung in the balance. How could the officers have treated them with so little care?'

THE LAMBETH-STREET MAGISTRATES OFFICE

Samuel Miller spoons the pease pudding into his mouth with his right hand, while his left hand turns a page of his big leather-bound notebook.

'Too much salt today,' he remarks to his wife Jane, who sits in a corner of the kitchen feeding the baby. 'It was better the way you made it last week.' The only response from Jane is a sigh, but her husband, who is used to her sighs, pays no attention. His eyes are fixed on the notebook, re-reading the pages of detailed jottings and diagrams that he has made on the events of the past few days. His powers of concentration block out all distractions, including the snivellings of his daughter Hester, who sits opposite him at the kitchen table, whining and wriggling because she has been told she must stay in her seat until her bowl is empty.

As soon as he has finished reading his notes for the third time, Samuel closes the book, pushes back his chair, and picks up the bulky bag full of equipment that he has left propped against the wall.

'Where are you going?' asks Jane.

'To attend to some business. I'll be back by dark.'

As he walks through his workshop to the back door, his feet crunching on the wood-shavings that lie thickly over the flagstone floor, Samuel passes the half-finished cabinet that he promised to have ready by last Friday. There was a time, years ago now, when he would have felt ashamed of such unpunctuality: a time when the meticulous task of fitting each joint of wood perfectly, so that there was not the narrowest fissure of space between, was his greatest pride and delight. As a young man, he would spend hours absorbed in the task of studying the grain and colour of different woods – recognizing oak and ash, cedar and mahogany even with his eyes closed, from their smell and texture alone, and eagerly learning exactly which woods to combine into the intricate designs that his customers demanded. But now all that seems petty compared with his greater, more intriguing and more rewarding passion for solving crime and seeing miscreants brought to justice. It is, he often thinks, a craft in some ways similar to cabinet making. It needs the same eye for detail, the same skill in fitting the pieces together into a flawless pattern.

The summer evening is still light, and Samuel has time to walk as far as Rosemary Lane before nightfall, and to take one more look at the yard of the Two Brewers Inn, where the area's most recent robbery took place. It has been a warm day, though now the haze is gathering, turning the sky pale grey except to the west, where a thin line of coppery sunset breaks through the clouds, casting its light over the rooftops of Whitechapel. Even here, so close to the heart of the great city, the onset of dusk brings a moment of quiet to the streets after the frenzy of the day. In the Minories and Rosemary Lane, the stallholders are packing up their wares at the end of the day's trading, their long shadows slanting across the cobbles as they do so. The raucous cries of the vendors have fallen quiet, and the wilder, darker cries of Rosemary Lane by night have yet to begin.

The Two Brewers is a shabby little inn, just off the main street in White's Yard. Samuel Miller remembers the days when this place, then known as the Bunch of Grapes, was always filled at night with throngs of noisy patrons, many of them (if the rumours were to be believed) engaged in criminal pursuits. Gambling, prostitution, trading in stolen goods, even the planning of murders, were all said to take place within the smoke-darkened walls of the Bunch of Grapes. The inn was shut down for a while, but then reopened under its new name, soon after the property (according to yet more rumours) was bought by a close relative of the Chief Magistrate, Sir Daniel. But the new landlord has so far failed to make the place thrive.

The archway at the rear of the inn leads into a courtyard filled with a confusion of empty ale-kegs and mounds of sawdust, and redolent with the smell of stale beer. Two carts stand in the shadow of the inn wall, beneath the upper window through which the thieves apparently gained entry to the premises and broke into the landlord's cash box. The case is a complicated one, for the landlord insists that the thieves were four of his patrons, who had been drinking in the bar below, immediately before slipping out into the night and scaling a ladder to enter his bedroom and steal his savings. When the alarm was raised, all the other patrons rushed out into the yard in pursuit of the thieves, and now every witness seems to have a different tale to tell of who was in the bar at which time, who fled from the scene and who was in pursuit. None of which is helped, of course, by the fact that most of the witnesses were drunk at the time.

The story is that one of the thieves concealed a ladder and other tools beneath the carts in the yard, and that he and his fellow conspirators then crept out when the inn was at its busiest, and used these to gain entrance to the upper window. Samuel has already measured the ladder which was found near the scene of the crime to make sure that it is long enough to reach the window, and examined the marks on the window sill that seem to have been made by muddy boots. The window itself was broken when he arrived on the scene, and the cash box had certainly been forced open. But Samuel does not entirely trust the landlord's story. There are too many contradictions between his tale and the stories told by other witnesses. So, rather than knocking on the inn door, he uses this moment of gathering darkness to move around the courtyard quietly by himself, re-examining minor details that he may have overlooked before. The weather has been dry. The ground beneath the window is hard, and bears few traces of the crime, but, crouching down and studying the cracked dusty earth with its patches of shrivelled weeds, Samuel spots a couple of glints of light. Small shards of glass have fallen from the broken window above. If the glass was broken from without, most of the fragments would surely have fallen inwards, into the landlord's bedroom, but if it was broken from within, to make it appear that there had been a robbery …

I should conduct a small experiment, thinks Samuel, to see how fragments of glass fall when a window is broken. But glass costs money. Where can I find a suitable window to break? Still pondering this problem, he takes out his notebook and carefully sketches the precise position of the glass fragments in relation to the wall. Not, of course, that any of this evidence will ever appear before a court. He knows that his fellow officers, and above all Sir Daniel, consider his methods obsessive and slightly mad. They have a much simpler faith in the power of money and fear to solve all crimes: rewards for information, small gifts to cooperative witnesses, carefully worded threats to the less cooperative. Samuel values his work as an officer far too much to challenge their approach out loud; but he likes to keep his own records, conduct his own little experiments, and reach his own conclusions about guilt and innocence.

The back door of the inn swings open for a moment, and a woman empties some slops into the yard. She closes the door without seeing Samuel, but suddenly he feels awkward, crouching here in the gathering gloom alone, almost like a common criminal himself. He stands up and quietly slips out of the yard, thinking that he will return briefly to the Lambeth Street office before heading home. He would like to take one more look at that ladder, which is now stowed with other evidence of the crime in the large storeroom at the back of the magistrates' office.

As he leaves the courtyard and enters Rosemary Lane, Samuel feels a hand pull the tail of his jacket, and turns to see a haggard female face close to his left shoulder. He can smell the gin on her breath.

'On your own tonight, my dear?' murmurs the female, as Samuel pulls himself away from her grasp with a shudder, and lengthens his stride.

His head is still full of the burglary at the Two Brewers. The landlord insists that the gang of robbers included three brothers by the name of Watson, who were all regular patrons of the inn. He claims to have been alerted by the sound of breaking glass and the cries of a servant girl, and to have pursued the three miscreants down White's Yard. But when Samuel, who was the first officer on the scene, went to the Watsons' house, perhaps twenty minutes after the crime had been committed, he found the youngest of the Watson brothers in bed in his nightshirt, with his clothes folded neatly on a chair, a candle burning by his bedside, and old Mrs Watson insisting that her son had been in his bedroom all evening. She could, of course, be lying, but the order and calm of the bedroom gave substance to her story, and the candle by the bedside, as he noted, had burnt halfway down, which surely suggests that … Samuel's reveries are interrupted by the wails of a small, ragged child, standing on a doorstep on the corner of the Minories and weeping pitifully, while a group of four other urchins play in the gutter nearby. For a moment he wonders if he should stop and help the child, but he has more important things on his mind, so he hurries on to the magistrates' office, where the lamps are already lit by the doorway.

Early evening is usually a quiet moment in the office. Morning is a time of clamour and chaos, when the citizens of Whitechapel awaken to find their storehouses broken into, or a dead or unconscious body on the corner of their street. The hours around midnight, too, bring a steady stream of calls for help, as the prostitutes and pick-pockets make a handsome trade from the drunken crowds who spill out of the inn doors into the dark laneways north of the Commercial Road. Dusk is normally a lull in the day, but today, as Samuel Miller pushes open the door of the office, he is a little surprised to be confronted by his fellow officer, Moses Fortune.

'Ah, Sam,' cries Moses, 'I have been looking for you. There's a lady and gentleman here as would like to talk to you.'

He hates being called by the diminutive 'Sam.'

The 'lady and gentleman', he assumes, will be friends of the Watsons, eager to offer their alibis for the robbery at the Two Brewers. But as soon as he spots the oddly-assorted couple standing in a corner of the small office to one side of the empty courtroom, he realizes that he is mistaken. These two are altogether a different class of person from the patrons of the inn. The woman is about his own age, small and simply dressed, with a grey shawl wrapped around her shoulders, while the man – tall, dark haired, and of indeterminate age – has the air of a gentleman about him, though his jacket is worn at the elbows, and the toes of his boots are scuffed.

'Samuel Miller!' pronounces the woman, as he enters the room. Her tone instantly brings back to his mind the voice of Mrs Cobbly, the formidable teacher at the dame school he attended as a small boy, who always had the power to leave him quaking in his shoes, despite the fact that he had been one of the school's quieter and more diligent pupils.

'You may not remember me,' continues the woman, in the same decisive tone, 'but you knew my late husband, William Flint, who was Beadle and Headborough of the Liberty of Norton Folgate.'

'Indeed,' says Samuel in surprise, 'I knew him well. Such a sad loss. Allow me to offer my condolences, my very deepest condolences, Mrs Flint. He was a fine man, your late husband. A very fine man indeed. Much admired by all who knew him. So thorough in all his methods. I had occasion to call on his help myself – a matter of matching the shape of a crowbar with the marks on a length of stolen piping, as I recall. And to die at such a relatively young age—'

'And this,' interrupts the woman, 'Is Mr Raphael DaSilva. He … His uncle was the Liberty's Overseer.'

It seems an odd explanation for the gentleman's presence, but Samuel has no opportunity to question it, for Adah Flint continues, 'We are here about a crime which you and your fellow officers investigated some eight years ago. The kidnapping of the infant daughter of one Catherine Creamer. A woman named Sarah Stone was arrested and found guilty of the crime. I believe she was transported. You will surely remember the case.'

Remember? How could he forget? He has pushed the affair into the recesses of his mind so often, and yet it recurs, in the wakeful moments while his wife Jane lies sleeping on the far side of their shared bed, and the cries of the night-watchmen come and go in the street below their bedroom, and the mice scuttle to and fro behind the wainscot. There is surely nothing he could have done to change the outcome of the case. But still it lingers among his ghosts, alongside the look of terror on the face of William Golding, whom he prosecuted for burglary, as the fellow was led to the gallows, sobbing out his protestations of innocence every step of the way …

'Mrs Flint, Mr DaSilva, please take a seat over there. I will fetch a lamp,' says Samuel.

This distraction gives him a moment to consider how to respond.

He returns with the lighted lamp and places it on a side table, from where its fickle flame sends distorted shadows flickering across the wood-panelled walls with their row of dark portraits of solemn bewigged magistrates. In the centre of the row, a large portrait of the chief magistrate Sir Daniel Williams, seated before the silhouette of the Tower of London, looms over them. The uneven lamplight makes the portrait seem even bigger than it really is. Adah Flint, looking up at the portraits, encounters Sir Daniel's gaze – not so much a steely gaze, she thinks, but rather one overflowing with self-confidence. The small half-smile above the plump, dimpled chin gives the face of the chief magistrate an air of perfect serenity and self-approbation. This is the face of someone whose power is beyond challenge.

By contrast, the man who sits before her, his sallow, uneven features half in lamplight and half in shadow, looks the perfect picture of discomfort and uncertainty. Samuel Miller's head is cocked awkwardly to one side, and he avoids her gaze as he begins, 'That crime, as you say, occurred eight years ago. Or rather, a little less than eight years, if my memory serves me correctly. Perhaps seven years and eight or nine months, if we are to be precise. And it did indeed take place here in Whitechapel, close to the Commercial Road. Just *off* the Commercial Road, I should say. The child-stealer lived in Bishopsgate, on the opposite side from Norton Folgate. So if I may say so – if I may be so bold as to say this – it had no direct connection with your Liberty, that is, with the Liberty of Norton Folgate. So, that being the case, it puzzles me a little that the widow of the Liberty's Beadle – a most respected beadle though he certainly was, and most grateful though I am for the many kindnesses he showed me personally – it puzzles me somewhat that the beadle's widow and the nephew of Liberty's Overseer should be asking questions about this case now.'

'It may not have been a matter for the Liberty then, but it has become one since,' replies Adah, struggling to contain her impatience at the officer's exasperating indirectness. 'Another child of Catherine Creamer was found dead on wasteland within the boundaries of the Liberty, and this has made it necessary for us to look at the case again. I am not only the widow of William Flint, but also Searcher of the Liberty. It is in that capacity that I am here today.'

'Ah, a Searcher,' says Samuel, shifting uncomfortably on his chair, and tilting his head in the opposite direction. 'I would indeed be happy to help you if I can. Very happy. Particularly in the light of the kindness that your late husband showed me in relation to the matter of the crowbar. As it happened, his advice on the crowbar indeed provided the clue to solving that whole crime, and securing a conviction in a case that otherwise might have …' His voice tails off for a moment.

'But, Mrs Flint,' he resumes, 'you should be aware that I was not the officer in charge of the case of Sarah Stone. It is true that I was engaged in making some of the inquiries, alongside my fellow officers, but my part in the whole investigation was quite minor, one might indeed say, almost peripheral. The person who was in charge was, if my memory serves me rightly, Ebenezer Dalton.' He pauses again to reflect and then, before Adah can break in, continues. 'Yes, I believe that I can say with considerable certainty that it was Ebenezer Dalton, though our fellow officer Moses Fortune may also have had some part to play. But, you understand, only a peripheral part, like my own. And of course, all our inquiries were ultimately under the direction of Sir Daniel Williams, who prosecuted the case. You would surely be better to direct any inquiries you may have about this case to Mr Dalton. Or better still, should you not speak to Sir Daniel himself? Although he is a very busy gentleman, I am confident that he would find time to speak to you, given your position as Searcher of the Liberty of Norton Folgate, and given the fact that this gentleman, the nephew of the Liberty's overseer – or did I hear you say, the nephew of the Liberty's *former* overseer? – is also involved in this inquiry. Surely Sir Daniel is the person best able to answer any questions you may have.' And here he gives a little wave of his hand in the direction of the portrait, almost as though he expects Adah to direct her questions to the paint and canvas in their gilded frame.

Adah, who has been giving some thought to this interview, now leans forward in her chair and endeavours to look Samuel Miller in the eye.

'Mr Miller,' she says more gently. 'My husband William used to say how careful you are in your investigations. He had the greatest respect for your abilities. That is why we have chosen to come to you, and not to Sir Daniel. We believe that we can have confidence in the answers that you will give us. We are troubled by the evidence of some of the witnesses at the trial, which suggests that Sarah Stone may have been pregnant with a child of her own. May I ask you one question? The destinies of innocent people may hang on the truth of your answer. Were you really satisfied in your own mind at the time that Sarah Stone was guilty?'

'What can I say?' cries Samuel, gesticulating with distress. 'I was there on the deck of the East Indiaman moored in the Thames. We went out to the ship, you see. When Sarah Stone's landlady and her father informed us that their tenant had stolen a child, and was now on board ship with her husband – or, I should say, her common-law husband, for the landlady expressed her suspicions that the pair were not married, and those suspicions, as it eventuated, proved to be correct – when we learnt all this, we realized there was not a moment to lose, so we fetched Catherine Creamer and took her with us to the ship. The *Hugh Inglis*, it was, if I remember correctly. That was the name of the ship. An East Indiaman, moored out in the Thames. We had to take a carriage out to Gravesend and then board a small boat out into the river, and ascend the ship's ladder onto the deck, and it was a wild winter's day with the waves threatening to come over the side of our boat and the ladder swaying so much that I came over quite dizzy as we climbed it. I was there with Dalton at the moment when we took Mrs Creamer up the ladder onto the deck of the *Hugh Inglis*. She, I may say, never faltered, even though the ladder was swaying and bumping on the side of the ship in the wind. From the moment we set off on our journey, she had been so, what should I say? So much in a fever to see her infant again. Even as she reached the deck, we heard the cry of a child. To tell the truth, I myself was not quite sure at first whether it was a child or just the cry of some sea bird. But Mrs Creamer knew it at once. "My child!" she exclaimed, "My child!" Or perhaps it was "My Molly!" And when she saw Sarah Stone with the child in her arms,

Mrs Creamer instantly ran at her to snatch the child from her arms and hug it to her breast. I saw it all with my own eyes. She said, "This is my child.' How could we deny the evidence of the mother herself?'

Adah Flint looks at him intently for what seems like a very long moment. 'So you *did* have your doubts,' she says at last.

'What can I say, Mrs Flint?' pleads Samuel again, 'It was such a strange case. Unlike any other that I have encountered. And child-stealing, as perhaps you know, had only just been made a crime at the time when it occurred. I do believe that the law against child-stealing had been passed that very year, perhaps no more than five or six months before this crime occurred. This was such a famous case. Reported in all the newspapers, and cried out by the town-criers. Indeed, to tell the truth, in the weeks after we had the hand bills printed, we had any number of people coming forward to claim the reward, telling us that an infant had mysteriously appeared in their neighbour's house, or that they had seen a strange woman in an alleyway with a baby in her arms. All sheer mischief or fantasy, as it turned out. So when Sarah Stone's landlady came forward to tell her story and claim the reward, yes, I did indeed have my doubts that she was telling the truth. I had serious doubts. I spoke to Sir Daniel about them. But the date that the landlady gave us matched the date of the kidnapping perfectly, and Sir Daniel was so eager that we should solve this notorious crime. So we took Mrs Creamer out to the ship on the Thames where the landlady had told us we could find Sarah Stone and her sailor, with the baby that they claimed as their own, and when Mrs Creamer instantly recognized her child ... What else could we do? What else could we do but believe her?'

'And did you not wonder why Catherine Creamer had described the kidnapper as being about forty, while the woman you arrested was not much more than twenty? Did you not doubt the story told by Elizabeth Fisher, who at first gave her name as Mary Brown?'

'I was troubled by it, I must confess. But women of that class, you know, often give names that are not their own. And once Sir Daniel had interviewed her, she became so very insistent that her name was indeed Elizabeth Fisher.'

'And you did not question her neighbours? Or employ a Searcher to examine the person of Sarah Stone to see whether there were signs that she had borne a child?'

'But do you not see?' cries Samuel, rising from his chair and starting to pace about the room, wringing his hands. 'Do you not see? By then it was too late!'

'What do you mean, too late?'

Samuel does not answer for a moment. He walks to a table in the corner and fumbles randomly with objects on its surface, straightening a crooked pile of books, before turning back towards them and saying, 'It was too late, Mrs Flint, because – but surely your own investigations, your own very thorough investigations, must have revealed this to you already – it was too late because …' His voice drops to a mere whisper, which she fails to hear.

She raises her eyebrows questioningly, and Samuel Miller clears his throat and repeats, 'Because the child was dead. Because the child was already dead. We took the child from Sarah Stone's arms, and gave her to Catherine Creamer. Mrs Creamer seemed so certain that the infant was hers, and that Sarah Stone was the woman who had stolen it. We believed her. We were sure we would find proof that this was true. It all seemed so clear. But then, the more we investigated, the less the pieces fitted together. The woman in Rosemary Lane said that her name was Mary Brown, and then that it was Elizabeth Fisher. Sarah Stone's mother said her daughter had borne a child and fed it with her own milk, and then the young girl came forward to speak of having drawn Sarah Stone's milk. All the pieces began to fall apart. But then the child died. What were we to do? What were we to do, Mrs Flint? After all the ignominy to which the law was exposed after the blunders that were made with the case of the child-stealer Harriet Magnis, and after all the public interest in the case of Catherine Creamer's infant, how could we admit that there was doubt about Stone's guilt? How could we admit, after the death of the child, that we might, after all, have made a mistake?'

'But, Mr Miller,' says Adah Flint, her voice quiet, but her gaze unwavering. 'If you made a mistake, do you not see what you did? Not only did you blight the life of an innocent woman. If you made a mistake, there must have been a third child: Sarah Stone's own infant. Did it never occur to you to ask, if Sarah Stone gave birth, what happened to her child?'

'Ah, no,' says Raphael, speaking for the first time, 'surely we know now what happened to the infant daughter of Sarah Stone. She was taken from her mother's arms and given to Catherine Creamer, and within a month, she was dead. The true question is this: whatever really became of little Molly Creamer?'

But Adah Flint knows the answer to that question. With a horrible dawning certainty, as she rises from her seat to leave the room with only a brief nod to Samuel Miller, Adah realizes that she has known the answer to that question all along.

Magpie Alley

'Have you money for a cab?' she asks Raphael, as they run down Lambeth-Street towards the main thoroughfare. 'There's not a moment to lose, and it's too far to walk at this hour.'

'Where are you taking me?' cries Raphael, following in her wake.

But Adah does not want to put her thoughts into words. She needs first to confirm her fears with her own eyes.

'Spital Square,' she says.

The cab that stops for them is shabby. Its interior smells strongly of stale tobacco. Adah perches stiffly on the seat, looking down at her hands. The nail of her left thumb digs into the skin of her right thumb, just below the knuckle.

'Let it not be too late,' she says silently to herself, over and over again. 'Let it not be too late. If we are too late, after all this, how will I live with myself?'

Raphael watches her questioningly, but says nothing.

For seemingly interminable moments, their progress is blocked by a great, slow-moving cart, laden with sheep being brought in from the country to some London slaughterhouse. Adah tries to quell her rising frenzy of impatience. After so many months, what difference can a few minutes, or even a few hours, make? And yet the frantic words run like a prayer through her head. 'Let it not be too late. Let it not be too late.' The plaintive bleating of the sheep from the cart in front of them is a mocking echo of the fear in her heart.

It is already dark by the time they alight from the cab at the entrance to Spital Square.

'Can you fetch two lanterns?' says Adah. 'But don't light them yet.'

Without a word, Raphael disappears through the front door of his house and re-emerges a few moments later carrying a brass lantern in either hand and a tinder box tucked under his arm. Adah runs ahead of him down White Lion Street and into Blossom Street, looking up to see the wavering candle light behind the un-shuttered windows of her own house as they pass. Young Will promised to stay home with the other children this evening; she can only hope that he has kept his word.

Already gasping for breath, she reaches the laneway that leads off Magpie Alley, and begins to fumble with the twine that ties the gate shut. But the knots have been pulled too tight, and refuse to yield to her shaking fingers.

'Let me do that, Adah,' says Raphael. He sets the lanterns and tinder box on the ground and, to her surprise, produces a small, sharp sheath-knife from his coat pocket, and proceeds to cut the twine with a swift slashing motion. The flimsy gate collapses to one side, and Raphael stoops to light the lanterns, handing one to Adah. She leads the way along the dark path beyond.

The weak swaying flame of her lantern casts a wavering pattern of light on the rutted path and stray branches of hedge on either side. Her cloak catches on a bramble, and she feels the cloth tear as she pulls it loose. Damp clinging strands of cobweb brush against her cheek. Beyond, she can feel, rather than see, the wasteland open out before them.

'This is where Rosie Creamer's body was found,' she says over her shoulder to Raphael. 'Watch your step. Don't trip. There are boulders hidden in the grass.'

The area ahead is so dark that she can barely make out the jagged shape of the ruined stables, silhouetted against the fainter blackness of a hazy night sky, devoid of moon or stars. She moves cautiously, one step at a time. Grass and twigs crunch beneath her feet. Everything looks so different in the dark. She cannot recognize the spot where Rosie Creamer's body once lay: the grass has grown tall, and she is no longer sure of her bearings. The lamp light picks out a tangle of withered creeper, the skeleton of a dead thistle. Raphael says nothing, though she can hear his uneven breath behind her.

For an instant, her heart stops. A human form seems to be crouching in the corner by the stable wall. But as she moves closer, the patch of darkness changes shape, resolving itself into a harmless pile of logs. The evening air is still warm and slightly foggy, and the smell of soot hangs heavy over the city.

All is silent. Then a dog barks in the distance, and a sudden movement in the air startles her: a glimpse of shadowy wings as an owl launches itself into the night with a ghostly cry. Am I mad, she wonders, to think that there could still be life in the midst of this desolation.

As Adah approaches the entrance to stables, Raphael catches hold of her cloak and pulls her back.

'You're surely not going in there?' he says.

'But I must,' answers Adah. 'I should have known … I think she's in there.'

'Can we not wait until morning?'

'No, Raphael. No. I must find her.'

The void ahead is like the mouth of death itself. There is a musty smell of decay that was not here when she came here before in daylight. Just inside the stables, where the straw is piled by the entrance, something gleams for a moment in the reflected light of the lantern. She bends down, and finds two bottles lying on their sides, one empty, but the other half full of some pale liquid. Behind them is a small pile of shrivelled things that emit a faint, familiar odour. She squats amid the straw and touches them reluctantly. They are dry and fibrous. Apple cores. A pile of apple cores, chewed so thoroughly that little more than a few shrivelled pips and strands of woody stem remain.

She lifts her head. 'Molly,' she calls, helplessly. 'Molly. Are you there?'

The darkness within seems to swallow up her words.

'Have a care, Adah!' cries Raphael. 'For heaven's sake, don't drop the lantern.'

As if in reply, she stands and holds the lantern higher, hoping that it may cast some light on the obscurity within, but she can see and hear nothing. She stood in this very spot with Hetty Yandall, half a year ago now, sensing the presence of a living thing in the recesses of the stable. If only I had looked properly then. If only …

There is no sound from within except for a very faint fluttering and a momentary high-pitched squeak. Bats, somewhere in the skeletal rafters above. She steps forward across the creaking fragile wooden floor. The darkness embraces her like a shroud. The musty smell is growing stronger. One step after another, holding her breath. And then, as she looks down, she sees that she has almost trodden on the small bony human hand that extends from under a pile of straw and crumpled cloth.

'Oh no!' she cries.

Desperately holding the lantern high with one hand, she sweeps the straw away to reveal the shadowy shape of the child who lies on her side, knees drawn up towards her chest, one stick-like arm half covering her face. The child does not stir.

'Oh no!' cries Adah again, bending down to touch her. But as she does so, she realizes that the child's unmoving arm is warm. She grasps it, feeling the bone beneath the papery skin. Not warm but hot, burning up with fever.

'She's alive, Raphael. She's alive!'

She bends and tries to lift the child's head and shoulders from the floor. Long matted hair half obscures the little girl's face. The body feels startlingly light, but it is somehow tangled up in the ragged cloth that covers her. The child makes no sound. Though her mouth is half open, Adah cannot hear her breathing. But she is surely alive.

Raphael is at her side, already thrusting his lantern into Adah's hand.

'Hold this,' he says. 'I'll take her.'

He stoops down, sweeps the child into his arms and stumbles back towards the murky haze of the open air. Adah scrambles after him, trying to light his path, no longer thinking of the bats overhead or the uneven ground underfoot, but only of the burning heat of the human bundle that Raphael carries in his arms.

They run back down the dark pathway into the street, Raphael leading her now. As Adah flounders through the flickering darkness, her mind swirls with thoughts. They must find a bed for the child to lie in, but there are no spare beds in the Blossom Street tenement. Perhaps she could ask Richard and Will to sleep on the floor? But what if the child's fever is contagious, and her own children fall ill? As she reaches Blossom Street, her hands are already groping under her shawl for the key chain that hangs at the waist of her dress, but Raphael has not slackened his pace. With the dark bundle of the child clasped in his arms, he is running down the lane, past Adah's front door towards White Lion Street.

'Where are you going?' cries Adah, suddenly confused and afraid.

Raphael shouts something in reply, but she cannot make out his words. She follows him frantically over the slippery cobbles of Blossom Street. In White Lion Street, an old woman pushing a laden wheelbarrow looks up to stare with blank frightened eyes. What if we meet the officer of the watch? We must seem an alarming sight, thinks Adah – a tall man carrying the ragged, unconscious body of a child; herself pursuing him as fast as her legs will carry her. But luckily the night fog is thickening and the streets are almost deserted.

In Spital Square, Raphael finally slackens his pace, and stops to hammer at his own front door. Adah sees the widening crack of light, as Stevens answers the summons and exchanges a few words with his master before opening the door wide to admit him. Adah, following Raphael up the stone steps and through the hallway, finds herself being led into a room she has never seen before on the ground floor of Raphael's house.

It seems to have once been a small parlour or study, but is littered with an astonishing jumble of objects: broken painting easels; mountains of books and papers heaped on the floor, with an old iron kettle balanced precariously on the top of the tallest pile; framed paintings stacked on end in one corner. Against the far wall stands an aged-looking divan upholstered in faded red and green brocade, with the straw stuffing poking out through a hole at one end. Stevens pulls a crumpled and paint-stained sheet from behind a stack of paintings, and spreads it over the divan, and Raphael gently lays the child's supine form on top of the sheet, with a ragged velvet cushion under her head by way of a pillow.

'But,' exclaims Adah, catching her breath, 'she surely can't stay here! How can you take care of her?'

'We'll think of that later,' says Raphael simply. 'Stevens, we need warm water and a clean cloth. Oh yes, and fetch an old night shirt or the like from the linen cupboard. Never mind the size. Anything that we can use to cover her will do.'

Adah looks up at Stevens, expecting indignant remonstrations, but the old servant merely nods and shuffles away on his errand.

The child lies absolutely still on the divan, her dark lashes closed over her eyes, her mouth slightly open. She might be dead, but for the fractional rise and fall of her chest. In the lamplight, Adah can see that the child is dressed in the ragged remains of a frock and cloak. Her hair is long, dark, and so tangled that it looks like wool. Her hands and face are grimy, and the nails on her fingers have grown into curved claws. Her sunken, bony face is longer and thinner than her twin's, but still bears an unmistakable resemblance to the face of the dead child who lay on the bed in the Norton Folgate watch house some six months earlier.

'Molly,' whispers Adah. 'Molly Creamer. Where have you been all this time? What has happened to you?'

Once Stevens has brought the water and cloth and lit a fire in the hearth, Adah orders the two men out of room and takes over the task of tending to the child. She leaves the ragged, rank-smelling clothes in a pile on the floor, and wipes the child's face and body as gently as she can, noticing how quickly the water in the enamel pail turns murky with grime. As she works, she speaks softly. 'You poor dear. You poor lamb,' she says.

The child is completely unresisting, and her eyes remain closed. Her ribs protrude, her stomach is sunken and her little feet are scratched and calloused. Adah moistens the dry, cracked lips with water, and then finds her way to the kitchen and fetches another cloth soaked in cold water to lay across the child's feverish brow.

When the little girl has been washed and dressed in an old darned night-shirt many sizes too large for her, and covered with a frayed patchwork blanket, Adah leaves her lying on the divan and goes in search of Raphael, who is sitting before the fire in his study, deep in thought.

'Why did I not guess this earlier?' laments Adah. 'She must have been there all along. Last winter, when I went with Hetty Yandall to the place where Rosie Creamer's body was found, I thought I heard a noise of someone in the stables. And then again that very night, I thought I heard someone at the door of the courthouse, and when I opened the door I seemed to see the shape of a child in the dark street outside, but I felt I must have imagined it … I thought I was seeing ghosts … If only I had looked for her then! But how did this happen? Poor child. Poor child. Sleeping in that accursed stable all alone—'

'Don't reproach yourself, Adah,' interrupts Raphael. 'You are not to blame, though others are. The question is, what do we do now?'

'We should call a doctor to attend to her. I should report the story to Mr Beavis and the officers, but …'

Raphael nods quietly. 'But if we do, this will become an official matter, and the child will be taken to the foundling hospital or the poorhouse.'

'And then,' adds Adah bitterly, 'as sure as night follows day, she'll be dead within the fortnight.'

'As for a doctor,' says Raphael, 'I think I know a man who will help us, and ask no questions.'

'But she can't stay here, Raphael. How can you and Stevens care for her? And I must go home to my children soon. I should be home with them already.'

'Could your son William take care of the younger ones tonight?' asks Raphael. 'I can have Stevens make up a truckle bed for you here, so that you can stay with the child for this one night. In the morning, we'll decide what to do next. Perhaps she will be a little better by then.'

'Let me go back to Blossom Street and check my little ones first. If Will is there and all is well, I'll be back here within the hour,' replies Adah.

Her heart is heavy and her thoughts are in turmoil as she opens the front door of the Blossom Street house. She feels suddenly exhausted. Her head is starting to ache. The door creaks open, and she enters quietly, not wanting to wake the little ones if they are sleeping.

A figure is standing on the stairway that leads down to the entrance hall, one hand on the banister. A slightly built, female, unmistakable figure. Annie! With a cry of joy, Adah runs towards her daughter, arms opened wide.

'You're home! I wasn't expecting you.' But then a doubt strikes her, and she falters. 'Father…?' she says.

But Annie is smiling and shaking her head. 'Never fear. He's well. He's on the mend,' she responds, 'but he's a stubborn old man: up and about already, and insisting he can care for himself and work in the gardens again, though no doubt he'll welcome another visit in a few weeks' time. And that job at the big house came to nothing. They found another girl who had experience as a parlour maid already. I'm sorry, Ma. I meant to send a message before I came home, but there was no chance…' But the rest of her words are silenced by the smothering embrace of Adah's arms.

'Oh Annie, Annie! How glad I am to have you back! The most extraordinary thing has happened. How are the children? Is Will home? Are Sally and Amelia asleep already, and little Caro?'

'All's well, Ma. I put the little ones to bed myself. Richard's still awake. He seems better than when I last saw him, and Will's asleep in a chair by the fire.'

'Then come with me,' says Adah, 'and I'll tell you the story as we go.'

They hurry together through the thickening fog, Annie listening intently as Adah tells her the story of her visits to Rosemary Lane and the Lambeth-Street office, and the discovery of the half-starved child in the abandoned stables behind Magpie Alley.

'You may remember Mr DaSilva,' says Adah, choosing her words carefully. 'He was an acquaintance of your father's, and is a nephew of old Mr Franco the overseer. He's a good man, and has taken the child to sleep in his own house for tonight until we can find a way to care for her. I would have stayed there with her myself, for she's too ill with fever to be left on her own. But I don't like to leave our little ones in Will's care. Would you stay with the child for tonight? She'll need cooling cloths on her head to bring down the fever, and some thin gruel to drink as soon as she's awake and able to take sustenance. God grant she does wake. Mr DaSilva's manservant Stevens will help you. He's a crusty old soul, but he means no harm. I'll bring some garlic and honey in the morning, and Mr DaSilva has said that he will try to call a doctor tomorrow.'

When they reach the house in Spital Square, they find the child still lying on her back with her eyes closed and her mouth slightly open. She does not seem to have stirred since Adah left. Stevens has made up a small truckle bed before the fire.

Adah feels a sudden moment of awkwardness as Raphael enters the room and she introduces Annie to him, but the artist greets Annie with the same grave courtesy that she noticed when he first met Sally. Adah and Annie stand side by side for a moment next to the child's makeshift bed, staring down at the fragile, feverish form. Annie bends and strokes the child's bony claw-like hand. The open mouth emits a tiny sound like a sigh, then the child sinks back into silence again.

Adah kisses her daughter goodnight, and slips quietly out of the room. That night, lying in the bed that she shares with Sally, while Amelia and Caro sleep in the cot on the other side of the room, Adah dreams that she is running through the dark, across a vast grassy wasteland. She is carrying Sally in her arms, but Sally is just a new-born baby. As she runs, Adah is terrified that she will trip and fall upon the baby that she is carrying, but a deathly unknown terror urges her on. At the far side of the wasteland, she sees an open door, with bright lamplight shining through it, and a figure standing silhouetted in the doorway, waiting for her. She runs in desperation towards the door, but just as she approaches it, the door slams in her face and she hears a voice – she cannot tell whether it is the voice of a man or a woman – booming in her ear, 'That is *my* child!'

She starts awake. The bedroom door, which she had left open, has slammed shut in the wind that has picked up during the night. The fog has turned to ragged cloud and the moon is shining above the roof tops. In the cramped bedroom, her three young daughters sleep the deep sleep of childhood, their tousled hair spread like fronds of grass across their pillows.

SILENCE

In the morning, the child seems neither worse nor better. She lies as still as ever on the divan in Raphael DaSilva's spare parlour, her breathing shallow and her forehead burning with fever. Annie has been awake much of the night, sponging the child's head and moistening her lips with cooling water. Stevens has prepared some gruel, but until the child wakens, there is no way to feed her.

'I tried to help him make it,' says Annie with a rueful smile, 'but it seems that the kitchen is his domain. He doesn't like others intruding.'

Adah has brought an old nightdress of Annie's, which she has been keeping until Sally grows big enough to wear it. She and Annie remove the ungainly nightshirt from the child's emaciated body and dress her in this better fitting garment. Adah applies a couple of poultices of garlic and honey to the little girl's legs. Then they fetch a pair of scissors from Raphael's studio and manage to chop back the child's grimy hair close to her head. All the while, the little girl lies unresisting on the divan, allowing her body to be moved softly this way and that, without a murmur and without opening her eyes. When they throw the cut hair into the embers in the fireplace, it hisses and shrivels, filling the room with a slightly acrid smell.

Adah sends Annie off home to rest for a while, and takes her turn sitting by the child's bedside. The room is dimly lit by one small window, and by the faint glow from the fireplace. Beneath the linen nightdress, the child's narrow chest slowly rises and falls – in and out, in and out. Adah feels her eyelids drooping in sleep, and then starts awake. In and out, in and out, the child breathes. The sight of her first-born daughter, Sarah Ann, comes back to her. She remembers sitting by Sarah Ann's bedside, watching that infant's small body fight its losing battle with the fever, willing her child to take one breath after another, until the moment when Sarah Ann softly breathed out, and Adah waited and waited for her to breathe in again, and no breath came …

But this child's quiet breathing does not falter, and for a moment Adah sees the child's lashes flicker as though she might open her eyes, though instead she just rolls over onto one side and continues sleeping.

If she lives, what will we do with her? By rights, we should contact the Creamer family, for she is their daughter. But where are they? And how will they react if they learn that she is still alive, after all that has happened? If she lives, what will she be able to tell us? She will not remember the kidnapping itself, for she was only an infant then. But surely she has not been wandering the streets alone for all these years. She must have been living with someone – as like as not with her kidnapper, or someone connected to the crime. If she lives, what will she tell us about her abductors? And will she tell us how she came to be reunited with her twin, and how Rosie Creamer died?

The doctor comes in the early afternoon – a scraggy, weasel-faced man with thinning brown hair, who calls himself Doctor Smith.

'She's my niece,' say Raphael imperturbably, showing the doctor into the room where the child lies sleeping. 'Her parents are in Jamaica, and she was staying with a guardian, but she must have been unhappy there, for she ran away and has been wandering the streets these several weeks. Luckily we found her last night, and brought her back here, but as you can see, she seems half starved. We are very worried for the poor child.'

Adah marvels at the fluency with which he invents his story.

The doctor puts one hand on child's forehead, and runs his fingers along her arms. He feels her pulse, taps her chest and listens to her breathing. He lifts her nightdress and presses her stomach, but the child does not stir. Then he extracts a notebook from his leather bag and scribbles a series of letters and Latin abbreviations which he hands to Adah.

'Take this to the apothecary,' he says. 'She needs a tincture of Peruvian bark. Burwell's in Threadneedle Street is the best place. Not too much, mind. Just four drops in half a cup of water, two or three times a day.'

He shakes his head slowly as he writes out his bill and hands it to Raphael.

'There is very little I can do,' he says. 'She is very undernourished, and may have been drinking foul water. I'd apply the leeches if she weren't so young and so weak, but I'm afraid to weaken her further. Send your maidservant to have the medicine made up, and have it ready to give to the child the moment she is able to swallow.'

Raphael opens his mouth to correct the doctor's mistake, but then exchanges a glance with Adah and remains silent.

'She is gravely ill,' continues the doctor, still shaking his head discouragingly. 'With care, if she is strong, she may recover, but you should prepare yourselves for the worst. The parents should certainly be notified as soon as possible. But by then, of course, it may be too late.'

Old Mr Burwell the apothecary peers through his half-moon spectacles at the doctor's note, and then potters off into the back of his shop, muttering to himself all the while. Adah waits impatiently at the counter, running her palms over its worn and pitted surface. She surveys the great wooden medicine cases, which rise to the dark recesses of the vaulted ceiling. The shelves are lined with jars, bottles and vases of every conceivable size and shape. Tall ladders are propped in the corners to allow the apothecary's assistant to reach the vessels on the uppermost shelves. To Adah's right are rows upon rows of blue and white Dutch china jars, all neatly labelled with incomprehensible Latin words: *crocus sativus*, she reads on one; and *echium vulgare* on another. In front of her, behind the counter, are arrays of glass jars filled with coloured liquids and powders – amber, pale green, deep indigo blue. Strange roots and branches float within the liquids.

She listens to the rasping sound of the apothecary's pestle as the old man grinds and pounds the Peruvian bark, and she thinks of the child lying on the divan in Spital Square, suspended between life and death. The process of mixing the tincture seems interminable. The apothecary shuffles along the shelves, perusing the labels on the bottles, picks one up, consults the doctor's paper again, mumbling to himself as he returns the bottle to the shelf unopened, takes the neighbouring bottle instead, withdraws to the back of his shop to add a few drops of the liquid to his mixture, and then returns to the shelves to start the whole procedure over again.

But when, after more than an hour's absence, Adah returns carrying the precious bottle of tincture, she is astonished to find the child sitting propped up on a pile of cushions, with her eyes half open, and Annie cautiously spooning driblets of gruel into her mouth.

'She's awake,' says Annie wonderingly, 'though she hasn't spoken yet.'

Adah hastily mixes a few drops of the tincture to give to the child. When the liquid touches her tongue, the child grimaces a little, but she swallows the medicine without complaint. She turns her dark eyes towards Adah and Annie.

'Molly,' says Adah softly, 'little Molly. You're safe now. We'll take care of you. Don't be afraid.'

The child gives a small sigh, closes her eyes and falls asleep again.

The following day, she seems more alert. When Annie brings her a cup of warm milk, she grasps the cup in both hands, and gulps the liquid down so eagerly that Annie has to gently draw the cup away.

'Steady. Take it slowly. Careful you don't choke,' she says.

'How are you feeling, little Molly? Are you hungry?' asks Adah.

The child gazes at her with opaque dark eyes.

'They will have given her another name, the people she was with. She won't answer to the name of Molly,' says Annie. She takes the child's hand in her own. 'My name's Annie,' she says. 'What's your name? What do they call you?'

The child's eyes are alert and questioning. Dark brown, one iris slightly flecked with grey. She remains completely silent.

'Do you think she can hear us?' asks Adah. 'Perhaps she's deaf.'

By way of answer, Annie walks to the iron kettle, balanced on the pile of books behind the head of the divan, and strikes it sharply with a metal spoon. The child starts, and turns her head towards the echoing sound.

'She's not deaf,' say Annie. 'But think of all the troubles she's been through. And here she is, in a strange house, with strange faces around her. Let's just make her body strong. Then no doubt she'll start to speak again.'

Over the days that follow, the child slowly gains strength. The fever in her body subsides, and her forehead seems a little cooler. She allows Adah and Annie to feed and bathe her without complaint, and they are even able to ease her off the divan and, supporting her frail form on either side, guide her as far as the chipped china chamber pot which Stevens has placed in one corner of the room.

All the while, the child never speaks or makes a sound. She never cries, but she never smiles.

Raphael, when he visits the sick room, tries speaking to her gently in a foreign tongue – Adah is unsure whether it is

Spanish or Portuguese – for it has occurred to them that the child might have been stolen away by foreigners and brought up speaking another language. The child looks up with a puzzled expression as Raphael talks to her, but she makes absolutely no response.

On the afternoon of the fourth day, Adah comes to sit with the child while Annie rests. As she approaches the door of the child's sick room, she hears an unexpected sound: a human voice inside the room. A quiet humming. Very cautiously, she pushes open the door, and then pauses on the threshold, frozen motionless by astonishment. Stevens is seated beside the child's bed, singing a lullaby in his cracked old voice as his gently spoons gruel into the child's open mouth.

'What are we to do with her?' Adah asks Raphael, when the child has sunk into fitful sleep again, and Annie has gone home to rest for a while. 'She surely can't stay in your house forever.'

They are seated in his study, with the last of the summer evening light slanting through the windows, and the pigeons cooing in the eaves of the house. The light illuminates Raphael's face from one side, and Adah is suddenly aware how much he has aged since she first met him. The streak of white in his hair is becoming more pronounced, and the lines on his face tightening and hardening around the mouth and eyes.

'I have been thinking about this,' replies Raphael. 'Of course, we should try to send word to the child's family, but as long as their whereabouts are unknown, I think it best that she should be cared for here. And this relates to another matter that I have been thinking about of late. Stevens is growing old. He would never admit it, but the work about the house is becoming too much for him to manage on his own. If I were to employ a maid or housekeeper, this woman could help him with his tasks, and could also care for the child until we can find a permanent home for her.'

'Have you discussed this with Stevens?' asks Adah, raising her eyebrows. 'It's hard to imagine him accepting such an arrangement.'

Raphael smiles. 'I think you might be surprised, Adah,' he says. 'Of course Stevens will grumble and mutter and complain. But behind the sour looks, I suspect that he is happy at the presence of the child, and would even be grateful for the presence of a woman to help him with the housework. You know,' he adds, 'Stevens had a wife and child of his own once, long ago. They both died within days of each other, so I heard, of the smallpox. It must have been almost forty years ago, but I think not a day goes by when he does not grieve for them still.'

Adah is silent for a moment, absorbing this information, and picturing again the briefly glimpsed apparition of the crabbed old servant at the child's bedside, humming a lullaby that perhaps he had not sung for forty years.

'Do you know a good woman for the task?' she asks.

'Adah, I was wondering…' says Raphael, hesitantly, 'I was wondering if your daughter Annie might be willing … She is very young, of course, but seems so mature for her years, and so very gentle with the child. Only with your approval, of course. She could live with you and come to us during the day.' He pauses, and then adds, somewhat awkwardly, 'Stevens and I would treat her with the greatest respect, you know.'

Adah, completely taken by surprise, can only stammer, 'I … I really don't know. I'll have to think. I need to talk to Annie about this.' It would, of course, be a solution to some of their problems, but there are so many reasons why it might not be wise …

'But there's something else we must talk about, Raphael,' she continues. 'Someone else, I should say. Sarah Stone. What about Sarah Stone? We mustn't forget her. We have living evidence in our hands that she was innocent. She was convicted of a crime she didn't commit. Can you imagine? To bear a child, and then to have that child snatched from your arms by a stranger who claims that you are a child-stealer, and that your child is hers. And then for your infant to die within weeks of being taken from you. What more terrible thing could happen to a woman? It would be enough to drive anyone to madness. We must find Sarah Stone.'

'But how? In heaven's name …' exclaims Raphael. He leans forward in his seat, his face suddenly quite flushed and, to her surprise, almost angry. 'She was transported to the colonies years ago. How could we ever find her? And would it be wise even to look for her? This child I have sleeping in my house is not Sarah Stone's child, Adah. We cannot give Sarah Stone back the child she lost. For all we know, she may have made a new life, and want to put the tragedies of the past behind her.'

'Believe you me, Raphael,' retorts Adah heatedly. 'However much she may want to, she will not have put that past behind her. You tell me that not a day goes past without Stevens mourning his dead wife and child, and I believe you. But I will say to you with equal certainty: not a day goes by when Sarah Stone does not mourn for her lost child. True, we can't give her back her child. But if we can do nothing else, at least we can lift the burden of a guilty verdict from her shoulders. At least we can tell her that there are people who believe her to be innocent – no,' she corrects herself, 'we can tell her that there are people who *know* her to be innocent.'

'But how, and where, could we begin to look for her?' asks Raphael.

'You know, she may never have been transported at all. I remember William telling me that not half the people sentenced to transportation are ever sent to New South Wales or Van Dieman's Land, or wherever it is they send them these days. More than half languish in the hulks or in Newgate or in that great new prison they've built by the banks of the Thames …'

'Millbank,' says Raphael.

'Millbank, that's it. And if Sarah Stone was not transported, but was held in Millbank or in Newgate or some other prison in England, she may well be a free woman again by now. Her sentence was seven years. And more than seven years have passed since the trial.'

'But who would know which prison she was held in, let alone what happened to her afterwards? I fear it would be a fool's errand, Adah. We are busy enough caring for the child, and trying to think about her future, without taking on other impossible tasks.'

'It's a matter of justice, Raphael. It's a simple matter of justice.'

Raphael sighs, and rises from his seat to walk over to the window.

'I suppose there is one person who might know,' he says at length.

'Who?' asks Adah eagerly.

'If there's anyone who knows the whereabouts of women prisoners,' says Raphael, turning back towards her, his fingers toying with the fringe of the green velvet curtain, 'it would surely be Mrs Fry.'

'Mrs Fry?' echoes Adah blankly.

'Oh come now, Adah, surely you must know of her. The famous Mrs Elizabeth Fry, the lady prison reformer.'

'Ah yes, of course I have heard of her.' William, she recalls, always described Mrs Fry as 'that meddling busybody', more than once adding, 'she should stay at home and look after her own family, instead of making trouble for others.'

'But,' she continues aloud, 'how could we possibly seek the help of Mrs Fry? Such a prominent person. I heard she is even a confidante of the queen.'

'As it happens,' says Raphael pensively, 'I am quite well acquainted with Mrs Fry's brother-in-law, Fowell Buxton. I had some business dealings with him once, a few years back now. I haven't seen him for a couple of years – more, I suppose – but he always seemed a cordial and honest man. I could try to contact her through him. Of course, it might all be to no avail …'

'Please, Raphael,' says Adah. 'You may well be right. This may be a hopeless quest. But if I can at least feel that we have done all we can, I may be able to rest easy at night. And Raphael,' she adds more softly, 'thank you. Thank you for helping me and for caring for the child. And thank you for your offer to Annie. I will surely speak to her about it, and give you our answer very soon. You are a kind man.'

By the end of the next week, they have fallen into a daily rhythm. Annie rises at dawn every day and goes to Raphael DaSilva's house to light the fires and prepare breakfast for Raphael and Stevens, and to make a bowl of gruel or porridge for the child. She spends all day helping Stevens with tasks about the house and nursing the child, singing to her and telling her stories.

Adah takes her turn in caring for the child as often as she can, but other tasks distract her.

Amelia has a toothache, and Beadle Beavis needs assistance with a case that involves searching the persons and possessions of a group of girls arrested for picking pockets and selling stolen goods. The girls – the youngest of them just ten years old – seem to Adah to be some of the most hardened criminals she has ever met. They show neither remorse for their crimes nor fear of the officers who have arrested them, and when Adah strips them to search their persons, far from appearing embarrassed, they flaunt their naked bodies, lewdly waggling their hips and lifting their budding breasts in front of you. 'I'll wager you wish you had a pair like this, Grandma,' says one of the older ones. Adah clenches her fists tight to suppress the urge to give the girl a slap, and goes about her painstaking examination of their clothes, finding four stolen silver rings sewn into the hem of the young hussy's pinafore. What future can we hope for, she wonders, if girls barely out of childhood are already so practised in crime? Is it living in the midst of a great city like London that makes them so depraved?

It is a relief when she can find a moment away from her work and her family to sit quietly for a while at the child's bedside. The little girl's fever is gone, and her appetite has returned. The sunken sallow cheeks are beginning to fill out and even look faintly rosy. Her hair, which Adah and Annie have painstakingly washed with soda ash, is starting to grow back, thick and dark.

But she speaks not a word. She has a voice, for sometimes she sighs or sneezes, and once, when a half-empty bowl of gruel slips from her hands and falls to the floor, she gives a little cry of alarm. But neither Adah nor Annie can coax a word from her mouth. When Adah brings Sally along for a visit, hoping that the presence of the lively little five-year-old may evoke some response from the child, the two little girls stare at one another with unfeigned curiosity. The child takes hold of the rag doll which Sally has brought with her, examines it carefully, and then lays it gently by the side of her pillow, but she neither smiles nor speaks, and Sally quickly loses interest and wanders off in search of Raphael's broken mandolin.

Adah even tries a trick that always produced fits of giggles from her own children when they were young, screwing her face into a grimace and wiggling her ears up and down. The child stares at her with silent puzzlement, but without the ghost of a smile.

After all this searching, thinks Adah, I sit beside the person who knows the answer to all the mysteries I have tried to solve. She knows how she and her twin Rosie found each other again, how they came to be sleeping in the stables behind Magpie Alley. She probably knows the name of the person who snatched her from her mother's arms eight years ago; and she surely knows how little Rosie died. I sit here and look into her eyes, and all that I find there is silence. Poor child. Poor child. What has happened to you?

The child is well enough to stand now, and can walk, a little unsteadily, around her small makeshift bedroom, so Adah and Annie decide that it is time to take her out for fresh air.

'What shall we say if we meet anyone we know, and they ask about her?' says Annie anxiously.

'Let's just follow Raphael's story. We'll tell them that she is his niece who has been staying with him and has fallen ill, and that you've been hired to be her nursemaid.'

The following day, the rain falls heavily and incessantly, so they abandon the idea of an excursion. The bleak weather dampens Adah's spirits. It is St. Swithin's Day, and she worries that the bad weather portends another forty days of rain. But the folk prophecy proves false, for the morning after dawns clear and sunny. They dress the child in cast off clothes of Annie's, and a little pair of soft shoes that Adah found in an old clothes stall round the corner from Spitalfields Markets. With Adah and Annie holding her arms on either side, the child walks slowly and cautiously down the front steps of Raphael's house and into the open air.

At the foot of the steps, she pauses for a moment, gazing around as though trying to find her bearings. There is a pleasant clarity in the air after the previous day's rain. The child gazes up at the sky, which is patterned by a gentle speckling of cloud. Then she looks intently at the ground beneath her feet for a while, before allowing herself to be led slowly across Spital Square and down White Lion Street in the direction of Adah's house. The only familiar figure they pass on the way is the tall angular form of Hetty Yandall, who is busy sweeping up straw and horse manure on the far side of the street. Catching sight of the scavenger, Adah feels a fleeting moment of panic, for if there is anyone who might recognize the resemblance between their small companion and the dead Rosie Creamer, it is surely Mrs Yandall. But fortunately, Hetty Yandall is too far away and too intent on her tasks to do more than raise an arm in silent greeting.

At the Blossom Street tenement, Adah guides the child gently up the stairs to the bedroom, and seats her on the bed.

'Stay here a while, my love,' she says. 'We won't be a moment.'

While Annie puts soiled clothes in the wash tub, Adah goes to fetch a julep that she has mixed the previous day for the child to drink, only to find Amelia sitting on the kitchen floor in tears, a broken butter dish on the flagstones beside her, and whitish streaks of butter all over the hem of her dress.

'Lord have mercy!' cries Adah. 'Whatever have you been up to? That's enough butter to last us for the rest of the week, all gone to waste!'

At which Amelia's tears turn into wails of grief.

'Oh, never mind,' says Adah grudgingly. 'Let's clean you up. There's worse things happening in the world.'

She seizes a cloth and gives Amelia's dress a cursory wipe, scoops up the fragments of the butter dish and the spoilt butter from the floor, rinses her hands and pats Amelia on the head.

'Go and play with your sisters, now, and keep out of mischief. Heaven knows I've got enough to look after without any extra trouble from you.'

Adah has just started to climb the stairs with the tumbler of cool green liquid in her hands when she hears the sound of a voice – something like a small exclamation – from the bedroom above. Startled and fearful, she runs up the stairs as fast as she can, and finds the child standing, with her back turned, at the table in the corner of the room. Again Adah hears the same small sound, surely coming from the child.

'What is it?' she cries in alarm.

The child turns and look at her, and Adah sees the small solemn face transformed. The child's eyes are shining, and her lips are half parted in a radiant smile. Her face is no longer a blank mask. She is a living child again. Adah is suddenly, heart-wrenchingly, reminded of the sweet and innocent smile that used to illuminate young Will's face when he was just that age.

The child holds her hand out flat towards Adah. She takes a step forward. Some small thing is balanced in the centre of her palm. Something round and white. When she speaks, her voice is soft and a little hoarse, but perfectly clear.

'Button,' says the child. 'Captain's button.'

SEPTEMBER 1822

East Ham

As the wherry pulls away from the stairs and out into midstream, Adah loosens the ribbons around her neck and lets her bonnet drop back from her head so that the wind can ruffle her hair. The breeze is surprisingly mild for late September, and the sky is filled with autumn light. It is years since she last took a boat on the river. She feels like a wide-eyed child, gazing in sheer delight at the wonders around her. The river is a great highway thronged with traffic: barges laden with barrels of wine and mountains of gleaming black coal, coasters with their white sails rippled by the wind, little wherries like their own. Further downstream, she can see the masts of the tall ships rising from St. Katharine's Dock.

Raphael sits on the seat opposite her, legs stretched out before him, deep in thought. He has arranged this journey with care. She wonders how much it is costing, but knows better than to ask. The waterman's oar slices through the turbid water, from time to time sending a fine spray of droplets flying in their direction. The river's surface is slick as oil, its colour constantly changing from mud brown to ochre to pearly grey. The wind that blows in from the distant sea fails to dispel the pervasive smell of sludge and ordure and rotting fish, but even this cannot dampen the strange joy that fills Adah's heart as the boat skims eastward.

'Just look at that!' she says to Raphael, with a little laugh of amazement: the steam packet is pulling out from the wharf at Billingsgate, for all the world like a miniature factory adrift on the river, its tall chimney billowing a column of black smoke into the clear air, and its great mill wheel clanking as it slowly begins to churn the river into brownish foam.

If it were not for the distant but palpable shadow of Miriam in Jamaica, they might be a middle-aged couple enjoying a day out on the river. Or perhaps a respectable widow being courted by a suitable widower. Adah envisages Miriam as heavy-boned, dark and frowning. Raphael has never concealed his wife's existence, but never discussed it, except to say that Miriam's health is frail. She wouldn't be able to stand the rigours of an English winter, he says. There must, of course, be more to it than that. There is a sadness about the way Raphael speaks of her – an air of irreparable regret. It seems they married very young.

But, for today, Adah is content to pretend. She gazes at the multitude of coloured flags that flutter at the bows of the ships, trying to guess the countries they come from. She can imagine these ships, large and small, tracking their many shining courses across the oceans of the globe from every direction, all converging in this great lake: the Pool of London. To the south, the wind ruffles the river, seeming to push its flow back inland, but the water around the boat flows steadily seaward, carrying them towards their destination. They pass Limehouse, where the ancient sails of the windmills along the embankment turn ponderously, unhurried by the wind. The flotsam of the city drifts past the wherry: a crate of oranges, its bloated contents spilling out across the surface of the waters; the ragged remains of a fishing net; a dead dog. The dog floats on the surface with its paws extended on either side and its head lowered into the murky water as though in a gesture of surrender. Its long black fur spreads out like seaweed from its body.

Adah remembers the long dark strands of Catherine Creamer's hair extending from beneath the cloak that covered her. All she ever saw of Catherine Creamer were those few strands of hair and one white, mud-streaked arm; and yet how her life has become entangled with the life of this dead woman whom she never knew. And now with the woman's lost daughter …

They have left the child in the care of Stevens, contentedly arranging shells on the floor of Raphael's study. The child's speech is slowly returning, but only in single words, here and there. She loves to name colours, and sometimes surprises them with the range of her vocabulary – pointing, for example, to a tasselled velvet cap that appears in the corner of one of Raphael's paintings and pronouncing, with startling accuracy, 'vermillion.'

'How much do you think we should tell her?' asks Raphael suddenly, leaving Adah momentarily confused. But he is, of course, speaking of Mrs Fry.

Adah pauses, before replying hesitantly, 'We must tell her that we have firm evidence contradicting Sarah Stone's guilt. But perhaps it would be best not to say exactly what that evidence is …'

She has terrifying visions of armies of grey clad, soft spoken women descending upon them to bear the child away to some charitable institution. Logic tells her that this might be for the best – better, at least, than the ramshackle arrangements that she and Raphael have been making for her care. But the prospect of losing the child to the uncertain mercies of others, after all this, fills her with dread.

'What puzzles me still,' says Raphael, 'is how a mother could mistake the face of her own child. That Catherine Creamer might be mistaken about the identity of the child-stealer is one matter. But that she could mistake another woman's baby for her own? How can that be? Even if she imagined that the babe was sorely changed by neglect …'

'I think she was desperate to believe it was her child,' replies Adah softly. 'I am not quite sure why. But there was a strange thing that her neighbour Lizzie Murray said to me. I wish I could remember her exact words. Something that Catherine Creamer said when Rosie disappeared: that it was a punishment for her sins. Almost as though she felt guilty that Molly had been stolen. I have thought about it, but can't understand it. It was not as though the babe had been snatched while Catherine left it unattended. It is hard to see how she could have felt herself to be at fault, but somehow perhaps she did. Perhaps she felt that she should have protected her own child better, and that made her all the more frantic to find the infant she had lost.'

Adah had hoped that they would travel along the great loop of the river past Greenwich, so that she would be able see the grand buildings of the Royal Hospital there. She has heard that they are a splendid sight. But in fact they catch only a distant glimpse of the two tall towers of the Greenwich Hospital by the river's edge, before the waterman steers them towards the narrow canal that forms a shortcut across the north of the Isle of Dogs. A shortcut in terms of distance, but perhaps not in terms of time, thinks Adah, as they drift idly at the entrance to the canal, waiting patiently for the blue flag to rise and the lock gates to open.

Once inside the lock, as the water swirls and gurgles beneath the hull of the skiff, she stares in wonder at the great row of stone warehouses which lines the boundary of the West India Dock, and at the tall sailing vessels, their sails lowered as they are towed through the straight and narrow shining road of water ahead of them. As each ship passes their wherry, they look up and see the immensity of its wooden sides looming over them. One ship has a rather crudely carved figurehead of a mermaid on its bow, and another, ornate carvings of dolphins on its stern. As this second vessel passes them, the mahogany-brown faces of a group of seamen appear above the rail, and the men wave their caps in the air and shout cheerfully at the passers-by in a language that Adah does not understand.

'These docks are the place where I first arrived in London,' says Raphael suddenly. 'It seems like yesterday, though it must be … what – almost twenty-five years ago now. Hard to believe it. I can still feel the astonishment that I felt then as we sailed up the river, and I saw the city rising from the smoke and fog. Astonishment and fear,' he adds, 'and hope.'

He does not say whether the hope has been fulfilled.

Beyond the new canal they enter the immensity of the river again, with the great expanse of the Plaistow Levels stretching before them, a faint autumn mist rising from the marshlands. The taciturn waterman steers their wherry to a small wooden jetty just past the point where the River Lea flows into the Thames. On the shore nearby stands a fine new inn, with tables and benches set on a lawn looking out across the river.

The steps up to the jetty are wooden and slimy with weed, and Adah is grateful for Raphael's steadying hand as she climbs onto dry land. When she has stretched her cramped legs, they take a seat outside the inn and eat a light meal of bread and cheese, which Raphael washes down with ale, though Adah drinks only water, not wanting to arrive at the house of the famously pious Mrs Fry with her breath smelling of beer. Before embarking on the last stage of their journey, they wander for a few minutes in companionable silence along the sunlit water's edge, watching a couple of muddy-legged urchins fishing in the river with grubby strands of twine. The light gleams on the surface of the mud, which is patterned here and there with the footprints of seagulls.

How happy I am, thinks Adah absurdly.

Raphael has somehow managed to send ahead for a cabriolet, which is already waiting for them in the courtyard on the far side of the inn.

'Have you ever been to this part of Essex before?' he asks Adah, as their cab bowls along the dusty causeway across the marshes at an alarming speed.

Adah shakes her head. Compared to her companion, she has been to so very few places. Even the Essex marshlands seem exotic.

She watches the plump brown and white cows grazing on the rich grass of the higher ground that emerges here and there from the mire. One solitary crumbling farmhouse stands on a slight elevation in the marshes, the thatch of its roof rotting and sliding away in places, and a couple of willow trees by its doorway spilling their yellow leaves onto the still surface of the surrounding waters.

'Look, Raphael!' cries Adah softly, as three long legged birds – maybe herons – rise lazily from the marshes and vanish in the direction of the invisible sea.

The church bell in the squat stone tower at East Ham is just tolling two as they drive without halting down the main street, and on past a second cluster of cottages, grouped around a crossroads and a small village pond. From here, the country lane curves left through farm meadows to the grand stone-pillared gate of Plashet House.

Adah has been imagining something like the grounds of the big house in Fulham, but Plashet, as it turns out, is altogether on a grander scale. The long stone-paved driveway leads straight through an avenue of elms whose golden leaves lie in drifts on either side. Beyond, they can see wide lawns, smooth as velvet, dotted with flowerbeds which are past their summer best, but whose glory can still be imagined from glimpses of phlox and marigolds, and from ornamental archways adorned with the last few fading roses. The driveway ends at a circular space in front of a tall plain house built of sandstone, with mullioned windows. A woman, ascending the steps of the house with a basket of fruit over one arm, turns at the sound of the approaching carriage. Her grey dress and bonnet are so simple and severe that for a moment Adah is uncertain whether this is the mistress of the house or a rather superior servant, until the woman sets down the basket and comes forward to greet them.

'Mr DaSilva! Mrs Flint! Thank you for coming all this way to visit me.'

'Thank you for taking the time to see us, Mrs Fry,' responds Raphael.

Mrs Fry's open and friendly face, with its rather long nose but softly smiling mouth, is much as Adah expected, but she is startled to see the pronounced swelling of the belly beneath the grey gown. Although she must surely be about the same age as Adah, Elizabeth Fry is clearly soon to bear a child.

Catching Adah's glance, Mrs Fry smiles, her hand lightly touching her stomach.

'Yes, another gift from heaven on the way,' she says, 'due within the month, God willing. This is why I am unable to go to town at present. Have you many children yourself, Mrs Flint?'

'Six,' replies Adah, with a slightly rueful smile. 'The eldest are almost grown now, but Caroline, my youngest, is not yet three.'

'Ah, such a trial and such a delight to us, are they not, Mrs Flint? You have come on a glorious day,' continues Elizabeth Fry, 'I thought we might take tea in the garden, if the breeze is not too cold for you. But perhaps you would like to rest indoors a little first, after your journey?'

To the left of the house, at the end of a long ride of mossy grass, is a small bower with a roof of thatch resting on rustic pillars made from the trunks of trees. The stems of rambling roses wind themselves around the pillars. In the centre, a table has been spread with a spotless linen cloth and set for tea.

Mrs Fry leads them to the bower, speaking softly all the while to Raphael about her brother-in-law Fowell Buxton and his family and their 'recent tragedy', about which Adah knows nothing, and feels she should not enquire. While they talk, she looks out at the view that stretches before them, over the wide lawns and the ornamental pond where ducks are splashing in the sunlight, over the golden autumnal woods of East Ham and the marshes to the distant line of the river.

'You wish to ask for my help in finding a woman convict?' says Mrs Fry finally, when they have seated themselves around the table and she has poured the tea.

'Yes,' replies Raphael, for Adah has decided to let him tell the story. 'It is a very strange tale indeed, but one that I believe you may know of, concerning a woman named Sarah Stone, convicted some eight years back of stealing the infant of a pauper woman, Catherine Creamer. We believe that we have found clear evidence that Sarah Stone was wrongly convicted, though there are certain personal matters which make it difficult to divulge all the details of this evidence. We feel impelled to seek out Sarah Stone to give her a chance at least to clear her name. I know that your wonderful charitable work has brought you into contact with many of the female prisoners in London, and many of those awaiting transportation to the colonies. Sarah Stone was sentenced to seven years' transportation, though we don't know if this sentence was ever carried out. Is it possible that you may have met her during your visits to Newgate or the hulks, or that you may have heard news of her from other prisoners?'

But Mrs Fry, after a moment's thought, slowly shakes her head. 'No,' she says. 'No. I do recall hearing of the case, and am sure that I would remember if I had encountered the unhappy woman convicted of that notorious crime. But no, I am afraid I have no news of her. If she had remained long in Newgate, I would have met her, so we may be certain that she is not there now. The law, alas, is a blunt and sometimes a brutal instrument. It is sad enough to see the state of those poor unfortunate women who have been rightly convicted of crimes, but so much worse to meet those whose conviction seems unjust. The wealthy can afford to pay for experts to defend them in court, but the poor are so often at the mercy of ill-trained judges and biased jurors and mercenary officers of the law.' She pauses for a moment and then adds, with some embarrassment, 'I beg your pardon, Mrs Flint. I believe your late husband was a beadle, and am sure he was a most upright man, but alas, there are some that are careless or even corrupt.'

Adah smiles reassuringly. 'Indeed, Mrs Fry. Indeed. As I know only too well.'

'But this woman, Sarah Stone …' Elizabeth Fry continues. 'If my memory serves me correctly, the child she was convicted of stealing was one of a pair of twins?'

'That's correct,' responds Raphael. 'The victim, a poor woman by the name of Catherine Creamer, had twin babies, and other children besides. She was begging with her twins in her arms when the kidnapper lured her away with promises of money, and then snatched one of the twin girls from her.'

'But surely, then, this Mrs Creamer – was that the name you said? – Mrs Creamer must have recognized the kidnapper, and known her own child when it was found? Have you been able to speak to the victim about your doubts?'

'Alas no,' says Raphael. 'For she died not long ago.'

'And the child who was stolen? Is she dead too? I believe it was a baby girl?'

'Yes, there is the nub of the problem. The Lambeth-Street magistrates, who prosecuted the case, put out hand bills in an effort to find the culprit. We've spoken to one of the officers, who tells us that they received many responses to these bills. People from all over Lambeth and far beyond apparently came forward offering help and information, but most of it, he said, completely useless. There was one story, though, that the Lambeth-Street officers did believe: that story was given to them by the landlady of the house where Sarah Stone was living as the wife of a sailor. This landlady reported that Stone appeared to be big with child, and claimed to have given birth to a baby daughter on the very day when the Creamer child was stolen, but she mistrusted her tenant and suspected that the child was not Sarah Stone's own, and had been stolen.'

'Curious,' remarks Mrs Fry. 'Was any explanation given why Mrs Stone might have pretended to be with child, and then stolen another woman's infant?'

'None at all,' replies Raphael. 'And more curious still, both her common-law husband and her mother, who lived in the same house, were convinced that Sarah Stone was truly pregnant and that the child was her own. But the officers, it seems, were under great pressure to solve this notorious crime. The landlady and her father took their tale to the Lambeth-Street office, and informed the officers of Stone's whereabouts, for by then she had gone, taking the baby, to join her sailor husband on his ship on the Thames. As soon as they received this information, the officers took Catherine Creamer out to the ship to find the supposed kidnapper, and the moment she heard the cry of the baby, the victim claimed to recognize this sound as the voice of her own child. Yet, when she saw the infant, Mrs Creamer also said that the child was much changed – the infant's body was shrunken and wasted, and she seemed smaller than she had been when she was stolen six weeks earlier. A neighbour who gave evidence at the trial said exactly the same thing. They both seem to have assumed that this change had come about because Sarah Stone, having stolen the child, had no milk, and had failed to feed the infant properly.'

'You think, then,' says Mrs Fry, 'that the mother herself may have mistaken another's baby for her own?'

'Yes,' responds Raphael, leaning forward in his seat, 'yes indeed. Improbable though it sounds, that seems the only explanation that makes sense of the facts.'

'Improbable perhaps,' says Mrs Fry thoughtfully, 'though not, I think impossible. It puts me in mind of a true story I heard some years ago from Thomas Everett, who does such fine work for the Foundling Hospital. He told me once how a poor woman came to the hospital to leave her infant there, saying that her husband had abandoned her and she had no milk to feed the babe. Some weeks later, the same woman returned and asked to take the child home again. Her husband, she said, had come back with money in his pocket, and she was now confident that they could care for the child. But when the matron took her to see the child, they found it gone. It seems that just two days earlier, another, completely unrelated woman had come to the hospital to find and reclaim *her* child, and mistaking the infant's face, and had taken the wrong child away …'

Their attention is suddenly diverted by a small rotund figure speeding towards them down the grassy ride with a stick in one hand, shrieking, 'Mamma! Mamma!' with all the force of his diminutive lungs. He is pursued by a stout nursemaid whose waddling stride is no match for her nurseling's speed and energy.

'Sam, Sam!' cries Mrs Fry half laughing and half dismayed. 'What is this racket? Did I not tell you to be quiet while I talk to my visitors?'

'I'm so sorry for the interruption, madam,' gasps the nursemaid, as she seizes the little boy, who is attempting to bury his curly head in his mother's lap, and bears him away towards the house.

'So Sarah Stone was arrested on the spot?' asks Mrs Fry, when the wriggling and rebellious Sam has been removed, and calm is restored.

'Yes, and the child was taken from her. As soon as Catherine Creamer saw the child and claimed it as her own, the poor infant was at once given to her, and died soon after. But other witnesses gave credible evidence that Sarah Stone had her own milk. The evidence presented at the trial suggests that Stone had indeed been big with child, but no-one at the trial attempted to explain what might have happened to the child that Sarah Stone was carrying. And now we have strong evidence that the child who was stolen, Molly Creamer, is not dead, but is indeed alive to this very day, though both her mother and her twin have since died. All this is surely proof that Sarah Stone was not guilty, but was the victim of a terrible miscarriage of justice. This is why we feel we must try to find her.'

'When was Sarah Stone convicted?' asks Elizabeth Fry.

'Early in 1814,' replies Raphael.

'Then it is possible that she may have been sent to the new penitentiary at Millbank. The first women prisoners were sent, I think, around the middle of 1816. I have not yet had a chance to visit Millbank, though I hope to do so soon. At least, if she was sent there, she will have been spared the horrors of the convict ships, and if her sentence is complete, she may be free and living in England. If you would like to make inquiries at Millbank, I know of a young woman who will surely be able to assist you. Of course, if Sarah Stone has been transported, I can make inquiries of my contacts here and in New South Wales, but it might take many months to receive an answer.'

'That would be most kind. Perhaps we could start with the young woman in Millbank?' says Adah.

'Of course. I should be delighted to introduce you. One of our small success stories, I may say. A remarkable woman by the name of Day: a Miss Elizabeth Day. Born into a family of convicts, and in trouble with the law from childhood onward. Yet she has turned her life around, and become a devout Christian woman and an inspiration to her fellow unfortunates. Millbank has had its troubles – it was, unwisely, built on marshy ground, and the miasma from the river has caused much ill-health. But at least the prisoners there are spared the dreadful crowding and squalor of Newgate, the barbarities of the convict ships and the depravity of life in New South Wales. You see, Mrs Flint, little by little, our treatment of prisoners is improving. There is still such a long road to walk, so much to be done, and yet, year by year, the worst abuses are gradually mended.' Mrs Fry, as she speaks, gazes off into the distance, as though looking, not at the view spread out before them, but at some vision of a brighter future: a distant glimpse of Zion. Adah, following her gaze, notices how the clouds are gathering over the river, though the autumn sun still slants through them over the shining water meadows.

'In Millbank,' Elizabeth Fry continues, 'the prisoners receive an education and are taught a useful trade, rather than being left to boredom and vice, as they were in Newgate. Have you ever visited a prison, Mrs Flint?' And when Adah shakes her head, she adds with a gentle smile, 'Perhaps you should do so someday. I think it important for those involved with the law to see the places to which convicts are sent.

You have a kind and good face, if I may say so, and I truly believe that you might help us to bring a little light and joy to the women in Newgate if you were to join us on one of our visits.'

Adah looks down at her hands, nodding and smiling politely.

'And this Miss Day?' asks Raphael. 'How can we contact her?'

'Ah yes,' replies Elizabeth Fry. 'I will write you a note, and you can take it straight to her at the penitentiary at Millbank. She served out her sentence, and I first came to know her after her release, but such is her compassion and sympathy for her fellow prisoners that she chose to return, and was welcomed back by the prison officials, to work there. I believe she helps care for the patients in the infirmary.'

'That, to be sure, is a wonderful example of a life redeemed from crime,' remarks Raphael.

The wind is starting to rise from the river now, and Adah draws her shawl tighter around her shoulders as the sun disappears behind a cloud. Mrs Fry hurries them back towards the warmth of the house to write the note to Miss Day. As they cross the threshold into the marble tiled hallway of Plashet House, Adah hears the wrathful cries of a small voice yelling, 'I won't! I won't!' and the inaudible response of the nursemaid trying in vain to pacify a child's tantrum, and she smiles quietly to herself.

FATHER AMBROSE'S STORY

October 1822
Greenwich

Father Ambrose carries the taper into the darkness of the chapel and, moving slowly and deliberately from one side of the altar to the other, lights the candles, one by one. Gradually, the confined space of the little chapel begins to fill with a flickering glow. He performs the same ritual every morning before dawn. It is, he thinks, a symbol. Just as the flame passes from taper to candle, and the pools of light emerge from the darkness, so his chapel itself is a small flame, which may someday light others, little by little dispelling the darkness that has blanketed this country for so long.

He puts on his robes and, in the candlelight, mounts the steps to the altar again, carrying the covered chalice. He opens the big, leather-bound missal which rests on its oaken stand, and begins to recite the introit. There is no-one else in the chapel, but that is hardly surprising. It is rare for any of the small band of Greenwich faithful to put in an appearance at the weekday early morning mass. All the same, Father Ambrose loves this moment of quiet prayer at dawn. Above all, he loves the moment when Mass is over, and he steps out into the garden surrounding the chapel, where the pale early light of day catches the dewdrops on leaves and petals, and the first birds are starting to sing. The big white roses which are the glory of the garden in summer have fallen now, but the hollyhocks and asters are still in flower.

The hour after mass is the priest's time for walking and reflection. Most days, he enters the great park and climbs the hill towards the observatory, watching the fallow deer flee into the thickets at his approach. But today, for a change, he takes a different route, out along the winding country lane that leads to Westcombe. The narrow muddy track curves between deep gullies thickly overgrown with oaks and elms whose leaves are just beginning to turn red and golden. Where the hillslope is less broken, the land opens up into farm meadows. Here and there, he glimpses a wreath of blue smoke rising from the chimney of a cottage. A milkmaid, carrying a yoke with two wooden pails over her shoulder, comes running down through the long grass, whistling to a herd of dappled cows clustered in a corner of the field.

At the summit of the lane, the priest pauses for a moment to catch his breath, perching himself on a fallen tree trunk and gazing out at the landscape that stretches below. This is his favourite spot. From here he can see the daylight gathering over the twin turrets of the Royal Hospital, and, beyond the river, the marshes and the misty outlines of the vast city. Every time he stops here, he is reminded of the scene in the Bible where Satan leads Christ up into a high place and shows him all the kingdoms of the world: "All these will I give to thee, if thou wilt fall down and worship me." But it is surely the people in the great smoky city below who have taken to worshipping Mammon, if not Satan himself. So much sin and disbelief; so much to be done; and Father Ambrose has reached the age now where he knows that there is little he can do to change these things.

With a sigh, he rises to his feet and starts to head down the hillside. He passes the imposing wrought iron gate of

Woodlands House, and then, a little further down the track, the mellow brick wall with its small green doorway which surrounds the Farrells' old place. The paint on the doorway is cracked, and some of the bricks have fallen from the archway above. Through the gap in the wall, he can glimpse the tall grass of the garden within. Fluffy tendrils of old man's beard are entwined amongst the ivy that grows thickly over the wall. Less than a year after poor Mrs Farrell's death, the place is already going to wrack and ruin.

'Good morning to you, Father!' cries a sharp familiar voice.

He turns to see a plump figure bustling down the lane towards him, a covered wicker basket over one arm.

'And a good morning to you too, Mrs Corcoran. That was a fine array of flowers you made for the chapel at Michaelmas. You did us credit again.'

'It was a pleasure, Father, a pleasure. And look what I have here,' says Mrs Corcoran conspiratorially, sidling up to him and lifting the cover from her basket to reveal a mound of fleshy, pale brown mushrooms within. 'Picked from the woods first thing, with the dew still on them, when they taste their best.'

'A fine harvest indeed, Mrs Corcoran,' responds the priest with a twinkle in his eye. 'But mind you don't have any poisoned ones in there now!'

'Good gracious, Father! I've been picking mushrooms in these woods for twenty years or more, and never picked a bad one yet.' She pauses. 'Though I sometimes wonder if there's others in these parts who may have been picking poisoned mushrooms, for motives of their own,' she adds slyly.

'Whatever do you mean, Mrs Corcoran?'

'Her in there,' she whispers, jerking her head towards the Farrells' house. 'There's rumours, you know. Not that I'm one to speak bad of another soul. But you must admit, it's odd. Her mistress, dying so sudden, and leaving all her wealth to the housekeeper. And what about the little girl? Mrs Farrell had a little daughter, I heard, though I can't say

I ever saw the child myself. By rights, she should have left everything to her daughter, but they say that no-one's seen the child since the day her mother died. There's them as thinks that housekeeper Bridie O'Sullivan had a hand in one death, if not two.'

'Oh come now, Mrs Corcoran,' replies the priest sternly. 'You mustn't go spreading these tales. As it happens, I was at Mrs Farrell's bedside when she died, and the doctor right there beside me. There was nothing strange about her death. Nothing strange at all. Very sad, of course, her dying so young, but nothing unnatural. It was the lung fever, so the doctor said. And as for the little girl, Mrs Farrell told me with her own lips that the child had been sent away to stay with relatives. So you see, there's no mystery about it at all. You can tell that to the people who told you this gossip. Bridie O'Sullivan's a good churchgoing Catholic. It doesn't do to spread stories about your fellow parishioners.'

'But you must admit,' persists Mrs Corcoran, unrepentantly, 'there's something very odd about that woman. Still living there all alone in that great crumbling house. Hardly ever shows her face out of doors, and when she does she's still all veiled in black, and will barely give you the time of day. There's some are saying that house is haunted.'

Father Ambrose suppresses a sigh. 'You must excuse me, Mrs Corcoran,' he says. 'I'd like to stop and talk, but I have pensioners to visit at the hospital this morning. I'll see you at Mass on Sunday. Good day to you.'

But as he heads down the lane, back towards Greenwich, he finds that the calm of the morning has been unsettled. Mrs Corcoran's words have brought back the scene at Francesca Farrell's bedside, when he went to give her the last sacraments. He spoke to her in Italian, which she seemed to find comforting. She was calm, even smiling, as she said to him, 'Little Grazia will be happy. She has gone to be with her family.' It seemed an odd choice of words to him then, and still seems so now. But by then Mrs Farrell's mind was beginning to wander, and he could ask no more. Her last words, he recalls, were something about the King of Hungary. But perhaps he misunderstood them.

There is a certain atmosphere in Greenwich that reminds him of his years in Rome. Maybe it is the contrast between the porticos, colonnades and wide paved expanses of the Royal Hospital and the huddled, pulsing poverty of King Street and Fishers' Alley: like Rome, with its intermingled grandeur and squalor. He misses the warm Mediterranean sunshine, of course, and choirs of sacred voices soaring into the dome of St. Peter's. He misses the olives and the good red wine. But here in Greenwich, more than anywhere else in England, he feels almost at home.

On Saturday afternoons, he goes to take the sacraments to poor Billy Boland who lost his legs at Lake Champlain, and to Bento Joaquim, who is crippled by arthritis these days. He likes to sit with these men for a while in their 'cabins' in the Royal Hospital: tiny rooms crammed to the ceilings with the flotsam and jetsam of long lives on the high seas.

'Did I ever show you this, Father?' asks Billy Boland, after Father Ambrose has heard the old sailor's confession, and they've said their prayers together.

His conversations always begin that way: 'Did I ever show you this?' And the old man will then swing himself up on his two wooden legs and hobble with surprising agility over to one or other of the shelves that line the room, to retrieve some memento of his long and colourful life, and then recite a yarn to go with the object in his hand: a tale which may or may not be true. Father Ambrose has learnt not to be too literal minded in his dealings with these men.

Today it is the battered remnants of a wooden crucifix, which seems to have once been ornately carved and decorated with silver. Billy Boland sits with the crucifix grasped in his left hand, while his right hand holds the long-stemmed pipe on which he puffs intermittently as he tells his tale. His rheumy blue eyes peer out from under bushy eyebrows as he speaks, gazing at some distant spot behind the priest's head.

'It was at the Siege of Cattaro, in the days when I still had me own two pegs,' he begins. 'The sea calm as the water in a well, and twice as deep. Bottle green all the way down. Our Captain was a bit of a tartar, that he was. Ordered us to set up ropes and tackle on the slopes above the city, and haul a great 18-pounder right up to the mountain top to bombard the French. I'll tell you, I may have had two whole legs, but I was none too young even then, and I've never strained and sweated as I did over that accursed gun.'

As Billy Boland tells his intricate tale of crafty Frenchmen and the valiant troops of Bishop Petar, and of a woman warrior who gave him the crucifix in return for the gift of a loaded blunderbuss with which she planned to shoot her husband, Father Ambrose gazes through the coils of blue pipe smoke at the wonders that line the shelves of Billy's cabin, his mind wandering. There is a battered tin box which (as he knows from earlier visits) is filled with coins from every corner of the globe, a huge speckled object which Billy Boland insists is a dodo's egg, and an ornate Indian painting of an elephant, which suddenly reminds the priest of the picture that used to stand on the lacquered cabinet in Mrs Farrell's parlour, amongst all the other trinkets that her seafaring husband had brought back from the Orient …

'So I turn around, and the next moment she's unwinding this crucifix from around her neck, and is pushing it into my hand,' Billy Boland is saying. 'I'll never know to this day if it was just a thank you present, or if she meant something else by it, but I can tell you I ran down the mountain away from that cottage as fast as my legs would carry me. Never did see that woman again, but I've always kept the crucifix by me. Not that it brought me much luck at Lake Champlain, though… Which reminds me, Father, did I ever show you this…?'

The sky is darkening by the time Father Ambrose escapes from Billy Boland's stuffy little cabin and crosses the great courtyard in the middle of the Royal Hospital. To the east, the evening light is still clear, but a great bank of dark cloud obscures the setting sun. He should be back in the chapel already by now, hearing the Saturday confessions. The blue-coated pensioners who have been out and about, strolling in the grounds with family and friends, are hurrying back to the refectory for supper, and the lights are starting to glitter behind the tall windows.

Father Ambrose strides up Back Lane to the chapel, lights the candles, and seats himself in the little confessional in one corner, composing his mind in prayer, and waiting to see if any of his parishioners have sins that are troubling their consciences. In a place like Greenwich, you never quite know what to expect. As often as not, it's some elderly woman whose worst peccadillo is forgetting her morning prayers or over-indulging in molasses on her porridge, but he's also had retired pirates repenting of long past murders, and once a seaman who felt impelled to confess that he'd eaten the flesh of his dead companion when they'd been marooned for two months on an island in the Bay of Bengal.

This time, Father Ambrose sits in the silent and empty confessional for almost an hour, quietly searching his conscience for his own sins. It's the sins of omission that trouble him as much as anything. All the things he'd planned to do and hasn't done. When he came back to England, he was so fired with hope and energy, believing that he was part of a new wave that was bringing the Holy Faith back to his homeland. But in the end, what has he achieved? Baptised some babies, said a few thousand masses, heard a few thousand confessions. And now somehow he feels so tired. The knees ache of an evening, and he is finding it harder to catch his breath when he climbs the hill to the Observatory …

He hears the door creak open. A penitent comes into the silent chapel and kneels down at a pew to pray. The priest waits patiently for the invisible person to approach the confessional. The slow minutes pass. Perhaps this is a parishioner, or even a stranger, who has simply come to sit in the quiet of the chapel, inhaling its odour of candles and incense, as some do. The hour for confession is almost over, and the priest wonders how much longer he should wait.

Then the hesitant footsteps approach – a woman's footsteps, Father Ambrose notices – and the silhouette of a face appears in the half-darkness beyond the lattice window of the confessional.

'Bless me, Father, for I have sinned,' says a familiar voice, with a slight Wicklow lilt. 'It is one year since my last confession.'

Indeed. He has been wondering when Bridie O'Sullivan, who is such a regular churchgoer, would make her next appearance in the confessional. He hasn't seen her there since her mistress Mrs Farrell died.

He waits for her to speak, but there is a long silence. Then, quite abruptly and yet with oddly little emotion, she says, 'God will never forgive me for what I've done.'

'Hush, hush, my daughter. Never say such things,' murmurs the priest in alarm. 'God in His infinite mercy always forgives the repentant sinner, no matter what the sin. Only repent sincerely, and you will be forgiven.'

His heart is beating faster. Surely not, he thinks. Surely that dreadful tittle-tattle Mrs Corcoran has been spreading can't be the truth? Surely it cannot be that this pious, stern-faced, taciturn woman killed her mistress for her money; or, worse still, killed that poor little child too.

But it seems that the sin Bridie O'Sullivan wants to confess to is something different, more complicated, for she begins, very quietly, 'I meant only good at the start of it. She was so heartbroken, you see, the poor signora. I could not bear to see her so sad. It seemed as though she might go out of her mind with grief after the Captain was lost at sea. They had been such a devoted couple, you know. I never knew two people so in love with one another. A sight to see, indeed it was. After the news came that the Captain was gone, I believe there was only one thing stopping her from throwing herself in the river to be with him, and that was that fact that she was carrying his child. That child was her hope. "If it's a boy we'll call him Frederick after his father," she'd say. She was sure it would be a boy, you see. But when the child was born, it was not to be. It was a little girl baby, the dearest wee thing you ever saw, Father. If the signora was sorry it wasn't a boy, she never said a word about it. I can still remember the lovely smile on her face as she held that baby in her arms by the window. "We'll call her Frederica," she said. But in less than a week she was gone. That baby's little life had just slipped clear away. Such a tiny thing she'd been. Too beautiful to live, it seemed. We buried her in the churchyard, near the monument the signora had put up for her Captain – for they'd never brought his body home, of course. And then, once we'd laid that little body in the ground, I was truly afraid.

'For a whole week, the signora would eat nothing. Barely took a sip of water. Lay on her bed like a corpse, not wanting to speak. I tried everything. Tempted her with her favourite morsels. Prayed at her bedside. Begged her to live. "What for, Bridie?" was all she'd say. "What for? What have I left to live for?" It was then I bethought me of a story I'd heard from a woman in the fish market some weeks back – about a man and wife who couldn't bear a child of their own, but bought one instead from a poor woman who had more children than she could care for. "The good Lord gave you your life for a reason," I said to the signora. "It's not yours to throw away. The Lord may have called your poor babe to be with Him in heaven, but there's plenty more on earth that has no-one to care for them. Why, I know a poor babe just a few weeks old whose mother's a pauper, not enough food to feed her children. And here's you with your big house and your empty arms, just longing for a child. It's a cruel fate that's robbed you of your little one, but perhaps it's a kind fate for that other child."'

Father Ambrose, listening with curiosity to this circuitous tale, is startled by a sudden rumble of thunder and the patter of rain beginning to fall on the roof of the chapel. He leans his ear nearer to the confessional grill to catch Bridie O'Sullivan's next words.

'Well, that was where my sins began,' she continues, 'for I knew of no such child. But I was sure that somewhere in the great city there were poor babies who needed a mother, and I truly believed I could find one and bring it to her. I was desperate, do you see? Desperate to see a smile back on that beautiful sad face. And sure enough, after I spoke those words, something began to change in the signora's heart. Not all at once, but over the next few days. She drank a little soup and even left her bed to walk to the window and look out over the garden, and then, perhaps it was four or five days after I'd told that tale about the poor child, she said to me, "Bridie, you know you spoke of a poor babe whose mother cannot care for her? Could you bring me that babe so I could see her face?" Well of course, I couldn't say no. I thought, if it's the last thing I do in this life, I'll bring the signora a little pauper babe, and see the smile on her face as she cares for it.'

She pauses for a moment, seeming to listen as the drumming of the rain grows louder outside. Father Ambrose belatedly recalls there are a couple of the linen altar cloths hung in the garden to dry, that should have been brought in before the rain began.

'I told the signora that the child lived in the city, and I had to travel to London to fetch her. I said I'd spend a night or two with my cousin who lives near Blackfriars. The signora seemed so grateful, and gave me ten pounds for my trouble. To tell the truth, I was loath to leave her even then, looking so thin and wan and sad, but she seemed to be on the mend, and I thought I would take the chance. It was only as I sat on the boat to Wapping that I saw what a thing I had done. In my despair I had invented a story, and now I had to make that story come true. But where to find a mother so poor that she would willingly give her child to a stranger, even in return for money? The moment I was in London, I began to walk the streets, hunting for a likely child. Oh how I walked! So many miles. So many children's faces everywhere. Clean faces, grimy faces. Plump healthy faces, pale sickly faces. Tiny infants too. But I was never going to be a child-stealer. I needed to find a woman who might let me take her child.'

Now at last Father Ambrose begins to see where this story is going.

'It was in St. Paul's churchyard I saw her,' says Bridie O'Sullivan. 'A poor haggard woman, reduced to begging, with twin babies, one in each arm, and another ragged little daughter playing in the gutter as the mother begged for a few coins. Well, here's the answer to my prayers, I thought. If ever there's a woman with one mouth too many to feed, it's her. But I took it cautiously, of course. Little by little. I could hardly come right out and say, would you let me take a child off you, could I now? So I gave her a penny, and started to talk to her about my mistress, and how she loved children and lived all alone in a great house. I had an idea to take the mother and her children all the way to Westcombe, and let her see the signora in that beautiful big house, and understand what a chance it would be for one of her little twins to grow up there. You may say I was mad, of course. Perhaps I was. I think so now. Mad with worry over my dear signora. But the woman – Creamer, she told me her name was – she seemed to listen to me at first. She agreed to walk with me towards Ratcliffe Cross, where I thought I might persuade her to board a boat at the stairs. When we'd gone some way, she even let me carry one of her twins. I remember the warmth of that babe in my arms to this day. It was a long walk, and as we went along, I thought to sit down in an inn along the way and explain more clearly what I planned. But by now – whether the mother had understood me clearly from the start or not I don't know – she seemed to become warier and more shrewd, and kept asking me again and again how much money my mistress was going to pay to see her baby, and how much money she might pay to have a child stay in her house for a while. I'd tried to explain things to her gradually, d'you see? I said my mistress loved children, but didn't have any of her own, and that she would just love to see a child's face in her house every day.'

Bridie O'Sullivan is silent for a moment, as though remembering, and then continues haltingly.

'When I look back at it now, I almost think she might have sold her child, if I'd only kept my nerve. Maybe the sum of money I mentioned wasn't enough, or maybe we'd been talking at cross purposes all along, for she started glancing at me suspiciously, and saying, "How do I know I can trust you? Where are you taking me?" We passed an officer of the watch in the Commercial Road, and the mother stared at him, as though she might be about to call out and tell him what I had been saying, and suddenly I became so afraid. The woman turned away for a moment to attend to her other daughter, and in that moment – may God forgive me – I fled. I ran down an alleyway with that babe still in my arms, and didn't stop running until I reached a road – I can't remember which one now – and hailed a passing cab to take me to Wapping Stairs and found a boatman willing to go to Greenwich.'

She gives a deep sigh, and pauses for a moment in her tale.

'In my heart I knew I'd done wrong, but at first it all seemed to be for the best. The change that came over the signora's face when she saw that babe was a sight to behold! I told her the mother had given the child up willingly, because she couldn't care for her. Worse, Father, I told the signora that I had given the ten pounds to the mother to help her care for her other children. I'd done no such thing, of course, but I put the money away in the chest in my room, thinking that I would somehow use it to make things right. The money kept preying on my mind. Apart from that, in those first days, everything seemed perfect. The babe was such a delightful little thing, plump and healthy. The signora still had her milk, and fed the child at her breast, almost as if she had forgotten that it was not her own child. But that money kept troubling me, so one day, perhaps a month or so after I'd brought the child to Westcombe, I went in search of the mother. She'd told me that she lived in a court off Cowheel Alley in Golden Lane. I was too afraid to face the woman again, of course, after what I'd done, but I had some idea I might put the money under her door, or in some other place where she could find it, and that might ease my conscience. But when I got to Cowheel Alley, I asked an old dame if she knew where Mrs Creamer lived, and she replied, "Oh, you must be looking for that woman whose child was kidnapped. She lives in the corner of Swan Court. We've had so many people asking after her. A terrible case. The officers all over the city are giving out hand bills to try catch the child-stealer." Well, then I truly knew what a thing I'd done, and I was so afraid I just fled the scene and came straight back to Greenwich. I put the money back in my trunk, and promised myself I'd keep it for little Grace – that is what we'd named the babe, but you'll know that, of course, since you baptised her. I thought I'd keep the money for little Grace when she was bigger.

'Such a dear child she was. No-one asked questions, because the signora and I, we lived very quietly, and people knew that the signora had been big with the Captain's child. She was a very quiet little child. Always happy, it seemed. Well, you saw her yourself, Father, so you'll know. She learnt to speak, and seemed to love some words. Would say them to herself over and over. Or sometimes make up her own little nonsense words. But she didn't speak much, and very rarely cried. Seemed to be away in her own little dream world much of the time. It's an odd thing, Father. She was always such a quiet little thing, and yet, now she's gone, the house seems so empty without her. Well, we were happy together, the three of us. All might have been well, but then the signora fell ill, and I was at my wits' end what to do. It was the signora who said, "You must find little Grazia's mother. If I were to die, she is the one who must decide what is to happen to the child." She never knew the truth, you see, the signora. She thought the mother had willingly given me her infant in return for ten pounds. To the end, she believed that Mrs Creamer knew our names and where we lived, and she wondered aloud sometimes why the mother never sent to ask after her own child.'

So this, thinks Father Ambrose, explains the strange words that Francesca Farrell spoke, about the child having gone to be with her family.

‘Well, I was at such a loss to know what to do, Father. I didn’t know how I would care for the child by myself if the signora died. So when it seemed as though the end might be near, I took little Grace with me and went to Golden Lane. All the way there I was wracking my brains to think what to do when we arrived. I didn’t have the courage to seek out the mother and speak to her frankly, you see. I thought perhaps I might leave the child standing on their doorstep, and watch to see what happened, to see if the family would recognize their own lost child. God help me! What was I thinking of? Anyway, it was years since I’d been to that place, and when I saw it again, it was so dirty and poor and rat-infested, I thought, how can I leave our little Grace to live here?

‘My head was whirling with fear and confusion. I thought I’d check first to see whether the family was still living in that place off Cowheel Alley, for if they’d gone, I could return to the signora and say in all honesty that I’d looked for the mother and failed to find her. I left the child by the entrance to the alleyway for a few moments, and found the house where the Creamer woman lived, and looked through the windows to see if they were still there. Well, there was someone living there, to be sure, though I couldn’t tell who. There seemed to be no-one at home, for the fire was not lit in the grate, but there were plates and dishes on the table. Then I went back to the spot where I’d left the child. But, Father, she had gone! Vanished into thin air! There’d been children playing nearby, but they’d gone too. Now I was in panic and terror. I ran down the street, calling her name. I peered in the alleyways. I asked passersby if they’d seen a little girl wandering lost in the street. Then a couple of costermongers told me they’d seen two little girls running down the street together, hand in hand – two little girls who looked just like each other, but one with longer hair than the other. When I described our Grace, they nodded and said, “That must be one of them.” Glory be, I thought, she’s found her twin! I fooled myself, of course. I thought it was all for the best. She’s found her twin, and the twin will take her back to her own family. That's what I wanted to believe, and by then I was in such a fever to get back to the poor sick signora and be at her bedside… I told her the child was safely back with her own family, and she believed me and was glad. You saw for yourself how that dear lady died, with a sweet smile on her face. You never saw a more blessed end.'

The priest's mind goes back to the scene at Mrs Farrell's bedside. The sound of her ragged breathing, and the wind rattling the windows as he anointed her forehead with consecrated oil. He thinks for a moment that Bridie O'Sullivan is at the end of her story, but then the woman continues.

'Well, after her death I was busy for a while with the funeral and all. I thought about little Grace every day, of course. I missed her sorely. But I believed it was all for the best. Such a fool I am! But then the signora's will was read, and I couldn't believe my ears. I knew she had family in Italy, though she'd rarely had contact with them, and of course I believed she would leave all her money to them. But no. She had left it all to me. Every penny! And the house as well. But with a note in the will that said, *I bequeath this to my companion Mrs Bridget O'Sullivan, knowing that she will take care of the ones we love*. Well, of course I knew what that meant at once. She wanted me to provide for little Grace. So two months or more after she'd died, I went back to Golden Lane with twenty pounds in sovereigns in my purse. I was a coward to the last. I didn't dare to face the mother even then, but thought I might leave the money with a note in a spot where she would find it. But when I found that house in Swan Court, it was empty and boarded up. I went to the house next door to ask after Mrs Creamer and her family, and the woman who lived there said …'

Here her voice falters, and when she speaks again the soft, steady tone has dissolved into gasps of sobbing.

'She said they'd gone, and the mother was dead … "And what of the little twin girls?" I ask … And she says … she says …'

The priest waits patiently.

'She says they're both dead too,' gasps Bridie O'Sullivan. 'God have mercy! What did I do? I couldn't bring myself to ask how they'd all died. I just fled that accursed alleyway, and every day since then, when I wake or when I try to pray, only four words come into my head. What have I done? What have I done? Sometimes I think I should go to the law and confess my crime, and be hanged for the murderess that I am … But I am a coward. I am a coward still. I cannot bring myself to do it.'

There is a long silence, broken only by the gasping breaths of the penitent. The rain seems to have stopped now, and the retreating thunder rumbles distantly somewhere beyond the horizon. The priest closes his eyes, until little by little words come to him.

'My daughter,' he says, 'you have indeed committed a grave sin. Not the crime of murder, for you were not responsible for those deaths. Nor even a sin born of greed or malice, but one born of foolishness and fear. Your sin is grave, but however great your sin, if you truly repent, our Saviour will surely redeem you. For your penance, you are to attend Mass every day for a year to pray for the soul of your dead mistress, and for the souls of that poor mother and her dead children.

'Sometimes in life we do wrongs that can never be righted. The sin you have committed is one of those. You say that you think of going to the law and confessing to stealing that child. But what good would that do now? The victim and her children are dead. You might be punished, but that would not bring them back to life, or undo the wrongs that you have done. But, although you can never right this wrong, you *can* make good come from evil.'

Here he puts as much conviction into his voice as he can. 'Take the money your mistress left to you,' he says. 'Sell the house. Go back to your hometown, and spend every pound you can to care for poor children there. There are certainly many hundreds of waifs and orphans in Wicklow who are in need of care. It is too late to save Mrs Creamer and her children. But it is not too late to save many others.'

He ponders for a moment, for the secrets of the confessional always weigh on his heart.

'Whether you ever tell your story to another is a matter for you alone to decide. But even if your sin remains a secret between yourself and God, He is compassionate, and will forgive you if you perform your penance. You can yet save many children who are in desperate need of care. If you do that, if you devote all the days that are left to you to that task, then God in his boundless mercy will surely forgive you.'

And he raises his hand in blessing and says the words of absolution, 'Deinde, ego te absolvo a peccatis tuis in nomine Patris, et Filii, et Spiritus Sancti. Amen.'

'Amen,' echoes Bridie O'Sullivan. 'Amen, and thank you, Father.'

She rises to leave the confessional, but as she does, she turns back to him and speaks in a low but distinct voice. 'I am a coward, Father,' she says, 'I do not believe I will ever have the courage to tell this story again. I will perform my penance, and I pray that God in his infinite mercy may indeed forgive me. But, Father,' he can barely hear her parting words, 'Father, I shall *never* forgive myself.'

ADAH'S STORY

October 1822
The Cabbage Patch

'Do you never get lost in this place?' asks Adah.

'Yes, often enough,' replies Miss Day. 'But if you keep on going for long enough, you always come back to the point where you started.'

They are standing in the narrow, dimly-lit antechamber of the Millbank penitentiary. Adah has glimpsed the prison from afar several times before, on each occasion being reminded of a childhood fairy-tale her father used to tell her about an ogre who built his castle on the banks of a river so that he could swallow up ships which sailed too close. But this is the first time that she has approached the building closely enough to comprehend its full enormity.

Although Raphael has written in advance to arrange their visit, they are kept waiting for half an hour or more outside the grill window in the prison wall, and then, after being admitted to the antechamber through a small side door, kept standing for many more minutes while one official goes in search of Miss Day, and another sits with his back ostentatiously turned towards them, scribbling energetically in a large leather-bound book.

'Ah, there you are, Eliza. There's gentry to see you,' remarks the scribe, without looking up, when a door on the far side of the antechamber finally opens to admit the startling figure of a woman.

Adah was expecting a demure, smiling person in a lace cap – a younger version of Elizabeth Fry, perhaps. But Eliza Day is severe and rather masculine, and almost as tall as Raphael himself. Her dark hair is cut straight across her forehead, and although she is now a free woman, she wears a grey gown which looks very much like prison uniform.

When they hand her the letter of introduction from Mrs Fry, Eliza Day opens it slowly and stares at it in silence for a while. Adah wonders how well this woman is able to read.

'As Mrs Fry writes,' she says gently, 'we are here in search of a woman named Sarah Stone, who was convicted of child-stealing some eight years ago. She was sentenced to transportation, but we think it possible that she may have been sent here to Millbank.'

Her quest has been so long and arduous that Adah is fully expecting more blank stares and shaken heads, and is almost taken aback when Eliza Day replies simply, 'Yes. Sarah Stone was sent here. We came here together.'

'But perhaps she has been released by now? If so, do you know her whereabouts?'

Eliza Day looks at them rather oddly.

'Oh no,' she says. 'Sarah Stone was not released. Sarah is still here.'

'Can you take us to her then?' asks Adah eagerly.

The woman stares at her again for a moment. 'What is your business with Sarah Stone?' she asks.

'We have found evidence which leads us to believe that she may have been the victim of a miscarriage of justice, and we would like to share this evidence with her.'

Eliza stands in silence for a moment again, as though deep in thought, until Adah begins to wonder whether this woman is perhaps a little weak-minded.

But then she says sharply, 'Follow me', and leads them at a brisk stride across a courtyard which separates the antechamber from the main body of the prison. They walk in an awkward silence which Raphael tries to break by saying, 'Mrs Fry has told us about the fine charitable work that you do in the penitentiary.'

Eliza Day responds without turning her head. 'It's not *charity*,' she says, giving the word a slightly scornful emphasis. And then, dispelling Adah's doubts about her intelligence, she adds severely, 'It's atonement.'

Although she is a former inmate, Eliza Day seems to have the trust of the prison officials, for she carries a large bunch of keys chained to a belt, from which she selects a particularly large one to open the heavy wooden door that leads into the prison beyond.

They find themselves in a very long, stone-flagged, vaulted corridor, with rows of small closed doors on either side. Each door is fitted with a metal grill, through which Adah can see cell-like stone rooms within, all of them apparently empty. At the end of the corridor is another locked door, which Eliza Day opens to admit them to a spiral staircase, and at the top of the staircase they enter another corridor exactly like the first.

They walk single file, without speaking, Adah following Miss Day, and Raphael bringing up the rear. There is an oppressive, monastic silence about this place. Talking aloud would seem as sacrilegious as laughing in church. The walls and floor are a uniform yellowish grey. Even the sound of their own footsteps seems muffled. When they reach the fourth long corridor, they find that one side opens up into a balcony with a stone balustrade, from which they can look down upon a large room below, where rows of benches are set facing one another along either wall. On each row of benches sit a dozen or more women, all dressed in the same reddish-brown uniforms, each with her head bent, silently intent on her sewing.

Beyond, they descend another staircase which brings them to a small brown-painted door in an outer wall of the building. Eliza Day extracts a key from the bundle on her belt and opens the door, and, to Adah's surprise, they step out into what appears to be a huge kitchen garden, surrounded by a very high wall built of yellowish brown stone. The wall is surmounted by fearsome looking iron spikes, but the garden itself is a picture of order and fertility. Row upon row of slightly raised beds are planted with vegetables: most of them cabbages, some now starting to go to seed, but to one side Adah also sees beds of potatoes and onions. There is a strange atmosphere about this garden. Unlike the building they have just left, it is not silent. Adah can hear the chatter of starlings, and, from somewhere beyond the high wall, the sound of hammering. And yet there is an odd stillness in the place, as though the silence of the penitentiary were leaking out into the open air from under the locked door behind them. The unmistakable smell of river mud fills the air.

At the very furthest side of the great garden, Adah can see the figures of two women.

Eliza Day has halted just beyond the door through which they have passed, but Adah hurries eagerly ahead of her towards the women, wondering which of them is Sarah Stone. One is leaning on a shovel with which she has been digging the earth, while the other is bent over, apparently pulling up weeds. The shadow of the wall falls over their figures, making it difficult to see their faces at first, but as Adah approaches, the woman with the shovel turns towards her.

Adah's stride falters. The woman facing her is surely too old. Her hair is as white as snow, and her wrinkled face is that of an old crone. But the other woman, Adah can now see, is barely a woman at all – seemingly little more than a child of thirteen or fourteen.

She turns in confusion to Eliza Day, who has silently come up behind her.

'Surely neither of these women can be Sarah Stone?' she says.

'Oh no,' replies Eliza in her slightly hoarse, mannish voice, 'they are not Sarah Stone.'

'Then where…?' asks Adah.

Eliza gives a shrug, and extends her arms on either side towards the vast expanse of the cabbage garden.

'Here …' she says, 'here she is.'

Adah looks around her again, seeing what she had failed to see before. Row upon row of raised beds: ten or twelve rows, each containing a dozen or more small mounds of earth. Hundreds of them. Each mound exactly the same size. Each about six feet long and two feet wide, or perhaps a little less, marked not with stones or crosses, but with tidy rows of cabbages and onions …

'They would not tell me which one is Sarah,' says Eliza Day. 'Perhaps they do not know themselves. If they had told me, I would have put flowers there every day.'

They are both silent as Adah absorbs these words, and then Eliza Day continues. 'I knew she was innocent all along, of course. They all knew, or would have done, if they had used their eyes. She had the marks of childbirth on her belly. Anyone could see she had borne a child.'

'But why? How? How could this happen?' cries Adah, aghast.

Eliza Day shrugs again. 'Typhus, dysentery, lung fever, poor food, or too little food, neglect, despair,' she replies, and then adds, 'killing the body might not be so bad, if they had not first killed the spirit.'

'But how can this be?' exclaims Adah again, still reeling from the shock of Eliza's words. 'Surely, if people knew what is happening here … I have heard that mistakes were made in this prison in the early days, but surely they are being rectified now. Good people like Mrs Fry are working so hard for prison reform. She told us herself how things are slowly improving. Too slowly, for sure. But we are a civilized nation. For heaven's sake. Poor Sarah. How can such things happen? How can they be allowed to happen?'

She looks around to find Raphael, and sees him standing some distance away – too far, she thinks, for him to have heard Eliza Day's words. Yet he seems to have understood without the need for explanation, for he is gazing with an expression of deep sadness at one row of particularly small mounds of earth in a far corner of the cabbage patch.

'I have much respect for the work of Mrs Fry,' says Eliza Day, her face turned away so that Adah cannot read her expression, 'but as for civilization and improvement, I do not believe that men are so easily improved and made civil. I have been in Newgate and I have been a prisoner here, Mrs Flint. The difference between them is that here the cruelty is more distant and more refined, so that those who inflict it can keep their fingers cleaner.'

And as Adah struggles to think of a response, she adds harshly, 'You mark my words, Mrs Flint, in a hundred years' time, in two hundred years, they will still be locking up the innocent as well as the guilty in places as inhuman as this. They may find ever more civil and clever ways to do it, and they may keep their fingers ever cleaner. But the innocent will still be locked up in places as inhuman as this. And they will still be calling it justice and mercy.'

And Eliza Day bends down to tug at a stubborn weed with all the angry strength in her large calloused hands.

Evening is starting to fall as Adah and Raphael walk home together. This is surely the end of the search. Adah's heart aches at the thought of Sarah Stone. How must it feel to go to such a forlorn grave, knowing that you are innocent, but believing that all world has judged you guilty? All the world, that is, except for that strange young woman Eliza Day. If only, she thinks, if only we had reached her in time. Now so much remains unknown, and will forever be unknowable. The solution to the child theft, which seemed for a moment so close, has dissipated again into the swirling crowds and fogs of the city, vanished into voids of silence and random words. But we have done what we could do. All that remains is the uncertain fate of the one survivor: the small child who still occupies the untidy back room on the ground floor of Raphael's house. What will become of her?

They walk through the London streets for a long time in silence, until at last Raphael touches Adah lightly on the arm and says, 'It has been a long day, and a dispiriting one. Will you not come to my house for a little, Adah, and take a glass of wine? I have a fine bottle of madeira that my uncle gave me just last week.'

She thinks for a moment, imagining the fire burning brightly in Raphael's study, and Stevens bringing a cut glass decanter, and the two of them raising their glasses to one another in the circle of the flickering firelight … But then she hears the mournful cascade of church bells in the distance shakes her head.

'No, thank you kindly, Raphael,' she replies. 'As you say, it has been a long day, and I am rather tired. Another time, maybe. Today I had best go home to my children.'

THE CHILD'S STORY

March 1823

When spring comes, they go out to plant parsley in the herb garden of the big house. The woman she calls Annie holds her hand and leads her down the brick path. After long months shut up in the house in London, she likes to take three big breaths as she walks along the path, drawing in the smell of earth and cut grass. There are thin lines of greenish-brown moss in the cracks between the bricks. The old man whom Annie calls Grandpa walks behind them, carrying the tools.

In the herb garden, the old man helps her make small holes in the earth for the parsley plants.

'Just little holes, Lily. Not too deep.'

They call her Lily, but she doesn't mind, although it is not her real name. She knows her real name, and could speak it if she wished. But if she made that sound, it would open a window through which the past might flood like a black river into the present. So she was happy when the old man said, 'Let's call her Lily. A new name for a new life.' She even says the name herself. She likes the feel of it on her tongue. Lily.

The soil is rich and dark. Fresh grass and dandelion leaves are pushing up through its surface.

'Not too close together, mind. Space them out nicely,' says Annie.

On the back of a dock leaf she finds a strange grey creature, elaborately furrowed and coiled, with black spots and a sharp yellow nose: a miniature monster.

'What have you found there, Lily?' asks Annie, bending down to see what she is looking at. 'Why, it's a chrysalis. Do you know what's inside it?'

The child shakes her head.

'A butterfly. A cabbage white, I should think. Any day now it will come out and stretch its wings and fly away.'

'Chrysalis,' says the child. She reaches out her hand towards its crusty grey surface, but she doesn't quite like to touch it.

They go together into the greenhouse with its warm smell of fertile decay. The old man carries out the tray of parsley seedlings to plant in the holes they have dug. The knuckles on his hands are gnarled like the roots of trees where they stick out from the ground.

Once they have planted the seedlings, they push back the earth around them, being very careful not to bury any of the ants and small beetles that are crawling on the surface.

'Now I have an important task for you, Lily,' says the old man. 'Are you ready?'

They leave the herb garden and cross the wide lawn, under the cypress tree, along the edge of the flowerbed. As they pass it, the child reaches out her hand to touch the flowers, as she always does, speaking the name of each – 'Daffodil, hellebore, crocus, Solomon's seal.'

The old man laughs and pats her on the head with his loamy hand. 'My clever little Lily. We'll make a botanist of you yet.'

At the far side of the lawn is a deep hole which he and Annie have dug already, with a bucket of water beside it.

'Do you want to put the water in?' asks Annie. 'Pour a bit into the hole. Just enough to fill it half full.'

Some of the water slops onto the child's shoes, soaking through to her toes.

A small sapling, bare of leaves, stands in a pottery tub on the grass. The old man gently tips the sapling out of the pot, and places its roots in the child's cupped hands. The soil feels slightly warm, and tiny filaments of root dangle between her fingers. Very carefully, the child places the roots into the cold pool of water in the hole. Then they shovel earth back around the roots, and the old man pats it down.

'It's a copper beech,' he says. 'Look over there.'

He points towards the big house, where a vast tree stands, spreading its lattice of branches high into the pale spring sky. Small buds are just starting to appear on the ends of the branches.

'When you reach my age,' says the old man, 'this little sapling will look just like that great tree.'

She looks closely at his crooked pointing finger. Someday my hand will be like that – weathered brown, seamed with crevasses, with deep black cracks on the fingertips and knuckles like tree roots. The old man seizes hold of her hand and gives it a small squeeze.

The child runs across the lawn to the tree and presses her face against the great copper beech's trunk. The bark is covered with powdery green lichen which has a sharp, bitter smell. Her arms barely reach a quarter of the way around the trunk. She looks up into the heart of the copper beech tree, which is an entire world in itself. A spider creeps up the tree trunk, and chaffinches flutter in the lower branches. It seems impossible that the fragile sapling they have just planted could ever become a world like this. The child closes her eyes, and rests her cheek against the smooth bark. She stays like that, quite still, until Annie comes to fetch her.

'Come on, Lily,' says Annie, 'we'd better wash your hands before lunch.'

She leads the child to the pump behind the cottage. The child stands on the slippery green flagstones, watching how the light leaps and sparkles in the water as she plunges her fingers into its stream while Annie plies the creaking black iron handle of the pump. Then they walk in silence together, through the open cottage door and into the kitchen, where they can hear the kettle singing quietly to itself on the hob, and smell the bread that is almost ready to be taken out of the oven.

EPILOGUE

Norton Folgate
July 2015

THE RAIN IS STARTING to fall – softly, tentatively – as I get off the bus at Liverpool Street Station and make my way through the back-streets in the direction of Spitalfields Market. The brick terraces that line the narrow streets have changed little in the past century, but behind them soar towering cliffs of glass and steel: objects from some other inhuman world, reflecting grey London skies.

Spitalfields Market: Discover the Authentic London says a sign at the entrance to the great covered emporium. The skylights above are suspended on webs of metal girders, and children rollerblade and practice cartwheels along the broad walkway within. In the echoing clamour of the market, I catch snatches of French, Chinese, Korean, Italian, English with a multitude of accents. An African woman – Ethiopian, maybe? – smiles rather sadly at her customers as she serves them pancakes from under a multi-coloured umbrella. An elderly man gazes in fascination at the array of dress-maker's dummies, each with a top hat perched on her head. Beyond the market, as the rain is falling harder now, I take refuge in a neo-Japanese restaurant offering 'detoxifying drinks'. I have come from the other side of the world by a circuitous route, and feel in need of detoxification.

In Folgate Street – once known as White Lion Street – many of the windows are adorned with little posters saying SAVE NORTON FOLGATE. Some of the eighteenth century houses that once lined the street are still standing, though the Norton Folgate courthouse has long since been pulled down and replaced by a twentieth century edifice of particularly impressive ugliness, itself evidently scheduled for demolition. It was on this spot that my great-great-great-grandmother Adah Flint, who became a Searcher of the Liberty of Norton Folgate following her husband William's sudden death, lived and raised her children.

Would Adah Flint forgive me, I wonder? I have taken the bare bones of her life, and turned them into something she would barely recognize. Would she be outraged at my fictions, or might she be just a little pleased that I have brought her long-forgotten existence back into the light of memory, or at least of imagination? Of course, I have not rescued her from the tides of oblivion, because my words too are just as much at the mercy of those tides. All I have done is to shine one more fleeting moment of memory into the unimaginably vast expanse of forgetting.

I once read an essay in which an expert on issues of identity remarked that the one thing we can never invent is our own grandparents. But we do, of course. We invent our parents, our grandparents and all who came before them, reimagining and creating their lives and emotions in our own likenesses.

To the left lies Blossom Street, where Adah Flint moved her family when, after a prolonged battle with the trustees of Norton Folgate, they were evicted from their home above the courthouse. Its pavement is cobbled, and even today there is a dank feel about it which makes it easy to imagine the crowded tenements that once lined either side.

It is the unreachable reality of these lives that tantalizes and disturbs. Adah must have walked this street hundreds of times. Her children played here. What has become of the universe of their days and nights, their hopes and fears? With all our scientific wonders, we are not one step nearer to knowing the answer to that question.

Back in Folgate Street, I join a group of tourists walking in utter silence around number eighteen, the Georgian building beautifully preserved and recreated by the late American novelist and collector Dennis Severs. We begin in the basement kitchen, down a dark flight of wooden stairs, where the air is heavy with the smell of woodsmoke from the iron stove, baskets around the walls are filled with vegetables, and a yellowing cone of sugar sits amongst the tea cups on the kitchen table. From there we move gradually upwards through the house, hearing the clamour of church bells and the clop of horses' hooves on the pavement outside, and seeing the clothes hung up to dry and the papers still spread on the parlour table, waiting to be signed. This is, of course, as much a fiction as my story – an act of imagination. We move from one century to another as we climb the stairs. But I find myself drawn into Dennis Severs's illusion, my fiction mingling with his. Might Adah Flint have listened to these sounds and smelled these smells? *My canvas is your imagination*, wrote Dennis Severs.

Just a few minutes' walk away, in Sun Street, the new London has engulfed the old. Fluorescent lights gleam in the vast expanse of open plan offices where some small corner of the world's financial fate is being determined. Red plastic bollards fence off the area next to Starbucks, where the next retail, residential and office development is about to take shape. It was to this street, on 14 October 1814, that a woman named Sarah Stone returned, carrying in her arms the baby to whom she claimed to have given birth in a room off Rosemary Lane. Six weeks later, on a ship in the Thames, she was arrested for kidnapping by officers from the Lambeth-Street Magistrates Office, who removed the infant girl from Sarah's arms and gave her to Catherine Creamer.

The kidnapping was a sensation in London. There had been moral outrage over an earlier crime, which had led to the recent passing of the first law to criminalize child-stealing. One of Catherine Creamer's baby twins had certainly been stolen on 14 October 1814, and Catherine was sure that the child in Sarah's arms was hers. In January 1815, Sarah Stone was found guilty of child theft at the Old Bailey, and was sentenced to seven years' transportation. By this time, the child at the centre of the case was already dead. Sarah Stone became one of the first convicts to be confined in the newly constructed Millbank Penitentiary. There is no record of what happened to her after that.

Did the lives of the real Adah Flint and the real Sarah Stone ever intersect? Probably not, though they might have done. Adah Flint would surely have heard something about the famous kidnapping, alleged to have occurred so close to the place where she lived. At this distance in time, it is impossible to be say for certain whether Sarah Stone was innocent or guilty. But reading the multiple records of her trial, it seems extraordinary that she should ever have been convicted on the basis of the contradictory chaos of rumour, innuendo and omission presented to the court.

The prosecution, it is recorded, had been funded by public subscription, but Sarah Stone had no legal assistance. She could not have afforded it. It would probably never even have occurred to her to seek it. The man with whom she lived and the mother who shared the house with them were both convinced that she had been pregnant, and that the child she bore was her own. No-one challenged the evidence of twelve-year-old Martha Cadwell, who testified that she had been paid to draw Sarah's excess milk; no-one questioned the story of the woman who called herself Elizabeth Fisher, although, when first approached by the officers, she had answered to the name of Brown. A sharp-eyed neighbour testified at the trial that Sarah Stone had appeared to be pregnant 'for ten months': a remark that provoked guffaws of laughter in the crowd of onlookers who thronged the court. But the same witness admitted that she had never spoken to Sarah personally, and Sarah, it seems, had only been living in Sun Street for three months or less. No-one paid attention to these contradictions.

Surely no present day trial would convict the accused on such weak and inconsistent evidence. Surely not – but then again, can we be sure?

And what if she was innocent? If she was innocent, the child who died in Catherine Creamer's arms was Sarah Stone's infant daughter. And what happened then to the child who was kidnapped – the child who did not die? Are her descendants too still walking the streets of this city?

The next day I am back again at Liverpool Street Station, catching a taxi to Tower Hamlets Local History Library, housed in a fine Victorian building on the campus of Queen Mary University of London. The route to the library cuts through the heart of Whitechapel, past the betting shops and the clothing manufacturers' and the billboards saying *Double your Donation this Ramadan*. The weather has cleared, and in the library, the sunlight streams through the tall arched windows and illuminates the ornate stucco ceiling.

The librarian provides me with clean white gloves and brings two great leather-bound tomes, one fastened shut with brass clasps – the minute books of the Norton Folgate Trust. Inside is an amazing profusion of every day detail, written out in a meticulous hand. Here is an order from 1783 that William's father, Richard Flint, newly appointed Beadle of the Liberty, should receive the coat and hat passed down from his recently deceased predecessor; and here is the resolution allowing Richard Flint and his family to live above the courthouse, rent free. Richard somehow secures the appointment of his son William to the position of Beadle (though the post is not meant to be hereditary). William Flint receives his pay, makes his rounds and is exhorted to attend particularly to the indecent behaviour and language of *the various disorderly persons who assemble in the High Street on the Sabbath day, offensive to the inhabitants and disgraceful to the*

Liberty. Other pages record the payments made to Mr Ruffy the lamplighter and to Mrs Yandall the scavenger, and detail debates on the installation of the new gaslights in the Liberty.

Then suddenly and without explanation, William Flint is dead, at the age of 45. A new beadle, Benjamin Beavis, is hastily elected, and William's widow Adah is appointed a Searcher of the Liberty of Norton Folgate. A few pages later, there is even an inventory of Adah's furniture, made when (with one dissenting voice) the trustees of the Liberty vote to expel her and her children from the courthouse so that it can be occupied by the new beadle.

After that, Adah Flint fades from the scene, except for one small entry. On 6 June 1826, a committee was established on the order of the Trustees of the Liberty of Norton Folgate to investigate the truth or falsehood of *the Rumours in circulation, concerning Mrs Flint's Daughter*. Some weeks later, when the investigation was complete, Adah Flint's salary as Searcher was halved, though she was not dismissed from her position.

What were the rumours? I turn the thick pages of the minute book again and again, scanning their curling brown-ink script for the answer. But there is only silence. The story has not been recorded. Or rather, it must surely have been recorded somewhere, but the record has been lost forever.

THE END

Thank you for reading this book. If you enjoyed it please leave feedback on Amazon, and if there is anything we missed or you have a question about then please get in touch. The author and publishing team appreciate your feedback and time reading this book.

Please join our mailing list for free kindle crime thriller, detective, mystery, and romance books and new releases. http://www.joffebooks.com/contact/

Our email is office@joffebooks.com

http://joffebooks.com

We hate typos but sometimes they slip through.
Please send any errors you find to
corrections@joffebooks.com

We'll get them fixed ASAP. We're very grateful to eagle-eyed readers who take the time to contact us.

Printed in Great Britain
by Amazon

45361917R00149